A BODY TO SPARE

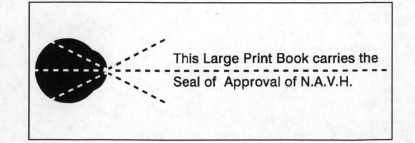

This Large Print Book carries the
Seal of Approval of N.A.V.H.

AN ODELIA GREY MYSTERY

A Body to Spare

Sue Ann Jaffarian

THORNDIKE PRESS
A part of Gale, Cengage Learning

GALE
CENGAGE Learning®

Farmington Hills, Mich • San Francisco • New York • Waterville, Maine
Meriden, Conn • Mason, Ohio • Chicago

GALE
CENGAGE Learning®

LIBRARY OF CONGRESS CATALOGING-IN-PUBLICATION DATA

Names: Jaffarian, Sue Ann, 1952–
Title: A body to spare : an Odelia Grey mystery / by Sue Ann Jaffarian.
Description: Large print edition. | Waterville, Maine : Thorndike Press, 2016. | ©
   2015 | Series: Thorndike Press large print mystery
Identifiers: LCCN 2015041975| ISBN 9781410486493 (hardcover) | ISBN 1410486494
   (hardcover)
Subjects: LCSH: Grey, Odelia (Fictitious character)—Fiction. | Overweight
   women—Fiction. | Legal assistants—Fiction. | Large type books. | GSAFD:
   Mystery fiction.
Classification: LCC PS3610.A359 B63 2016 | DDC 813/.6—dc23
LC record available at http://lccn.loc.gov/2015041975

Published in 2016 by arrangement with Midnight Ink, an imprint of
Llewellyn Publications, Woodbury, MN 55125-2989 USA

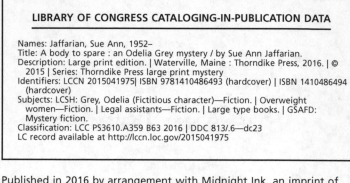

Printed in Mexico
1 2 3 4 5 6 7 20 19 18 17 16

For all the librarians of my past, my present, and my future.

I'm of a fearsome mind to throw my arms around every living librarian who crosses my path, on behalf of the souls they never knew they saved.
— *Barbara Kingsolver*

ONE

Found me! That's all the note said. Written in careful block capital letters in black ink across common lined notebook paper, the two words mocked me. They might as well have had *neener, neener, neener* written after them. But written or not, I heard the taunt.

A finger tapped the note. Actually, it was a copy of the note, the original long since packed in an evidence bag for protection and off being analyzed somewhere. "What can you tell us about this, Odelia?" The finger belonged to Andrea Fehring, a Long Beach homicide detective I'd come across a couple of times in the past. Even though Fehring had been a guest in my home on occasion, it was difficult to say whether or not I considered her a friend in the traditional sense of the word. She was a colleague and friend of my friend Devon Frye, a homicide detective who worked for the

Newport Beach Police Department.

I stared down at the note, willing it to say more. To tell me where it had come from and how it had gotten — well, where it was found. People wanted to know more, and they were looking to me for the answers. I closed my eyes, as I had done just a couple hours before, but when I opened them I was in a police station interrogation room, not sitting in the California sunshine as I had been when this nightmare started.

The warmth of the sun had been welcome after the two straight weeks of cold and rain that had blasted Southern California with both surprise and ferocity, causing flooding and mudslides up and down the coast. February can be cool, and we often get rain during the month, but this February had been brutal after last February's unseasonable sunshine and dryness. My friends that live elsewhere in the country laugh whenever I mention "cold" temperatures being in the forties and fifties, but we're simply not used to it for long stretches of time. After a few days, it gets on our nerves and makes us as disagreeable as soggy nachos. Next to me on the bench was my mother. She was enjoying the sun and spending the time pecking away on her iPad.

"I'm blogging about how you Californians are wussies when it comes to a little rain and cold," she told me, not looking up. Mom, who'd moved back to California from New England nearly two years ago, maintained a blog called An Old Broad's Perspective. The blog was surprisingly popular — and not just with the AARP crowd.

My wussie-assed meditation on California living was interrupted by my cell phone. It was the ringtone set for my husband, Greg Stevens.

"Hi, honey," I said upon answering.

"Where are you, sweetheart?" Greg asked. "I came home hoping to surprise you and take you out for lunch."

"I'm in Long Beach. I had an errand to run. Now I'm at the car wash. My car was pretty disgusting."

"I need to get the van washed too," my hubs said. "Are you going to be long or should I grab something from the fridge and head back to work?"

I looked out across the parking lot of Twinkle Clean. Men wearing matching Twinkle Clean tee shirts and clutching drying cloths were crawling over lines of wet cars like beetles over dung. The place was packed, and vehicles were pulling into the lot at a fast pace. I wasn't the only one tak-

9

ing advantage of the break in the weather to get my car cleaned with the half-off price offered every Wednesday. I only work part-time, so whenever I can, I like to grab the Wednesday deal. I spotted my sedan in the front line of cars being dried.

"My car's being dried off now," I said into the phone. "So we should be out of here in about ten minutes or less."

"We?" my husband asked.

"Mom's with me." I lowered my voice and turned away from Mom. "Should I dump her at home first?" If my mother overheard my question, she was choosing to ignore it.

"Bring her along," said Greg with a laugh. Easy for him to say. He got along with her better than I did. "Why don't you two meet me at the Gull? I'm craving one of their lamb burgers."

"Hey, Mom," I said to my mother. She looked up from her iPad. "Do you want to go to lunch with me and Greg after we leave here?"

"Sure," she answered with a shrug. "Why not? Got nothing else to do but wait for death to find me." It was a typical Grace Littlejohn response.

A woman came out of the Twinkle Clean office and looked around for a place to sit while waiting for her car. I shifted on the bench, moving closer to my mother to make room for her to sit down next to me. I smiled at her, and she returned it and mouthed a silent thanks. In her hand was an iced coffee from the fast food restaurant next door to the car wash. It looked refreshing. Then I remembered that the Gull also had great coffee drinks.

"Sounds good, honey," I told Greg, judging the time it would take me to get to the restaurant from the car wash. "We'll see you there soon. Why don't you order me a large iced mocha latte to start." I turned to my mother again. "Mom, would you like an iced coffee drink? Greg will order them for us so they're waiting when we get there. They're super good at this place."

"Nah," she said, her head of white hair still bent over her iPad. "They give me gas. I'll stick to plain coffee."

When the call ended, I dug into my purse and retrieved the claim slip for my car and a few dollars for a tip. I glanced at my car to estimate its progress. The man drying it had finished the front and sides and was about to start on the back. Another was cleaning the dashboard and inside windows. I closed my eyes and went back to sunbathing for a few minutes.

My relaxation and visions of cold, creamy

chocolate and coffee were interrupted by a loud, piercing cry. I wasn't sure if it was coming from a man or from a woman with a three-pack-a-day habit, but it was close enough to send chills up my spine. My eyes popped open to find several Twinkle Clean workers dashing toward the front line of cars being dried — specifically, they were crowding around *my* car.

My first thought was that someone must have hurt themselves. Did my car mysteriously kick into neutral and roll over someone's foot? Did one of my windows break and a worker was bleeding all over my upholstery? Was it my insurance or Twinkle Clean's insurance that covered such things?

I scrambled to my feet and quickly made my way across the wet pavement, nearly slipping. Putting a hand out, I placed it on a freshly washed Beemer and steadied myself as I threaded through the line of cars toward my own. Mom trailed behind me several steps, her thick rubber-soled shoes squeaking in the shallow puddles. A man stepped forward and stopped me from getting closer. His name tag identified him as Xavier and the manager of the car wash.

"Just step back, please," Xavier told me. "We have this under control."

"My name's Odelia Grey." I tried to look

around his bulky presence to see what was causing the commotion. "That's my car." I pointed to it just so he knew which one I meant, though with all the hubbub surrounding it, I didn't think he'd be confused.

Xavier looked at me funny but didn't move aside. Instead, he latched a large hand onto my upper arm, holding it in a firm grip. "Stay here, please."

"What's going on?" Mom asked.

"I don't know, Mom." I turned to Xavier and parroted the question. "What's going on?"

Ignoring me, he turned and said something to one of the other workers in Spanish. The only word I recognized was *policia* — police. The other man pulled a cell phone out of his pocket and made a call.

"Stay here," I said to my mother. With some effort, I yanked myself free from Xavier's grasp and sprinted the final few feet to my car. Well, sprint is a strong word and not entirely accurate when you're in your late fifties and weigh around two hundred twenty pounds. It was more of a wog — half jog, half waddle. Either way, I made it to my car in spite of efforts to stop me.

My trunk was wide open, like a surprised gaping mouth. Several men had gathered around it, gabbing away excitedly in Spanish. I elbowed my way through and stared into the butt end of my car.

I screamed.

Other patrons had left the waiting area and were coming forward. My mother had caught up with me and I felt her grab the tail of my sweater in a death grip. My teeth vibrated with more screams and cries. These were new ones and not coming from me but from the people starting to crowd behind me with curiosity.

Tucked inside my trunk was a naked man with long blond hair. He was in the fetal position, with duct tape on his wrists and ankles and patched over his mouth. He was wedged neatly between the case of water I'd bought two days ago and a couple bags of old clothing I kept meaning to drop off at Goodwill. It took several double takes for me to believe my eyes.

A dead man was stored in my trunk as snuggly as a second spare tire.

My legs gave out. I slipped to the pavement and into a puddle, nearly taking my aged mother with me. Next to me, a man with a dog on a leash snapped photos of the body with his cell phone. The woman with the iced coffee was puking it up on the clean tires of the car next to mine. Several patrons were making excited calls. Around me people parted, giving me room, but no one reached out to help or to ask questions — not even my own mother.

People stared at me open mouthed like I was a freak or carried a highly contagious disease. I knew how it would play out at dinner tables across the city tonight. "There was this fat lady at the car wash today," they'd say, "and she had a real live dead body in her trunk." The thing is, no one would correct the contradiction of the comment. There is no such thing as a real live dead body. Trust me, I know. I've seen more than my share. After all, I was the Corpse Magnet — the woman who stumbled over dead bodies as often as most people stumbled over uneven pavement. What can I say? It's a gift — an ugly, inappropriate gift — like a hideous red candle of a naked woman with fruit on her head that you can't wait to re-gift at the next office secret Santa exchange.

I felt the cold water beneath me penetrate my jeans and soak my panties. I struggled to get on my feet, still receiving no help from anyone around me. Xavier stood next to me, looking ready to make a grab should I try to bolt. My mother was on her cell phone speaking with excitement to someone. Once I was stable on my feet, she held the phone out to me. "It's Greg," she said. "I called him."

With trembling hands, I took the phone from Mom. "Greg, it's me."

"What in the hell is going on?" Greg asked, his voice going up, as it often did when he was stressed. "Did Grace just say something about a dead guy?"

In answer, I aimed the phone at the body and took a photo of it. A second later, the photo was hurtling towards Greg in a text message. I didn't send a message, just the photo.

"Check the text I just sent from Mom's phone," I said into the phone after returning to the call.

In the distance, sirens could be heard. Closer . . . getting closer . . . coming for me. Another body. Another endless barrage of questions that I couldn't answer.

Just a few seconds passed before my husband shouted through the phone, "Dammit, Odelia! Just walk away. Don't you dare get involved with that."

"Too late, Greg," I told him as a police car screeched to a halt in the street, blocking all cars from leaving Twinkle Clean. "That's my car. That's my trunk."

TWO

"Where's my mother?" I asked Fehring.

"She's being questioned," Fehring answered. Since I'd last seen Andrea Fehring, she'd let her hair grow long enough to be pulled back away from her face. She was a trim woman somewhere in her forties with great posture and a no-nonsense demeanor. She was dressed in a black pantsuit and blue blouse — her usual working uniform. She was good at her job and I respected that, even if at the moment I wasn't pleased to be the object of her scrutiny.

"Did you cuff Mom too?" I asked, rubbing the red mark around my wrists. Shortly after the police had arrived at Twinkle Clean, I was read my Miranda rights, then cuffed and stuffed into a patrol car and driven to the station.

"Of course not," Fehring said with a slight smile she tried to suppress. "Greg showed up and brought her to the station. They're

17

both here now."

"Am I officially under arrest?" I asked. "I'm a little foggy on that point."

"Should you be?" Fehring asked.

Before I could answer, a tall, trim African-American man entered the room. "Her husband called their attorney," he announced to Fehring. "The guy should be here soon. The mother's not saying another word until he gets here."

"My attorney?" I asked with surprise. I knew I hadn't asked for one, but the fact that Greg had already called someone told me he'd felt it necessary. That also meant I should follow Mom's lead and shut my mouth for the time being, but for me that's more difficult than it sounds.

"To answer your question, Andrea," I said, using the detective's given name, hoping it would give a chummy feel to the awkward atmosphere, "no, I should not be arrested. I haven't done anything wrong. I have no idea what this note is about or who the dead guy in the trunk is."

"Guilty people usually say stuff like that," said the guy.

I turned to him. "And you are . . . ?"

"Forgive my bad manners, Odelia," Fehring said with heavy sarcasm. "This is Special Agent Shipman."

"Special Agent?" I asked, the question squeaked out as if half strangled.

"Federal Special Agent Gregory Shipman," the man clarified. "I'm with the FBI."

"Gregory," I repeated, choosing for my sanity's sake to ignore the rest of his title until I could wrap my head around it. "Like my husband. And Shipman would mean you two have the same initials: G. S. Your middle name isn't William by any chance, is it?" I was babbling — something I do when nervous.

"No," Special Agent Shipman answered. His face was stern, except for his eyes. They danced with cautious amusement. "It's Winston."

"Huh," I said. "The same initials for sure — G. W. S. Hopefully that's an auspicious sign."

The amusement in his eyes dimmed. "I've heard all about you, Odelia Grey," he said. "You're the famous Corpse Magnet." He pulled out a chair across from me and folded his long, lean body into it. Fehring remained standing. "You're a legend. A seemingly ordinary woman with a nose for dead bodies and friends in low, dark places."

"You like Garth Brooks, too?" I asked. I was being glib, but under the table my right leg was vibrating in a nervous seizure.

Special Agent Shipman studied me. "One of these days, you might be responsible for one of the bodies you stumble across. Maybe this is that time?"

I fixed Shipman with a weepy look and spoke through trembling lips. "I've already crossed killing a human being off my bucket list, Special Agent. It happened several years ago. Or didn't you do your homework beyond listening to gossip?" I didn't have to fake the weepiness. Every time I recalled the horror of pulling the trigger of a gun and ending someone's life, the waterworks started. It was something I knew I'd never get over.

I wiped the back of one hand across my eyes, not caring if I smudged my makeup, and turned my attention back to Fehring. "Can I speak to Greg while I wait for my attorney?" My gaze bounced off Shipman. "*My* Greg," I clarified.

"At the moment," answered Fehring, "*your* Greg is with Mrs. Littlejohn, helping her through her statement."

I was glad for that. Mom's a tough old bird, but who knew what she would say. She thinks my finding the odd body and getting embroiled in danger is cool — and fodder for her blog. I couldn't trust her not to embellish once she got on a roll. Greg would keep her grounded.

"It's probably best he help her," I said.

Shipman got up. "Would you like a soft drink or maybe some coffee, Ms. Grey?"

"Oh hell, *Greg,*" I said with false bravado, "call me Odelia. All the other cops do."

He leaned forward. His narrow face was so close to mine I could smell toothpaste. Like Fehring, he was probably in his forties but closer to fifty than to forty. "And you can call me Special Agent Shipman." He straightened up and started for the door. "What's it to be?"

I thought about the iced mocha I'd been craving earlier. "You don't happen to have an iced mocha anywhere on the premises, do you?"

"Did you see *Starbucks* posted anywhere on the front of this building, Odelia?" Shipman asked. The sarcasm was heavy, and this time there was no amusement in his look or tone.

I was pressing my luck. "A black coffee with no sugar would be nice, Special Agent Shipman. Thank you."

Once he left, Fehring took the chair he'd abandoned. "I see you're just as adept at making friends as always, Odelia."

"Never hurts to ask," I answered with a shrug. "Who knows, you might have one of

21

those pod coffee machines around. They make lattes."

Fehring chuckled. "With our budget, we're lucky we don't have to reuse the coffee grounds a couple of times."

She leaned back in her chair. "So who's coming? Seth Washington or Mike Steele? Or have you finally put a criminal attorney on retainer?"

"Probably Seth. Steele's on his honeymoon."

"His honeymoon?" Fehring sounded surprised. "He never struck me as the marrying kind."

"He finally found someone who could handle him. And he didn't have to chloroform her to get her down the aisle either." Fehring and I shared a laugh. Mike Steele was my boss, an arrogant attorney and royal pain in the ass. "She's a doctor," I continued. "A pediatrician. Her name is Michelle Jeselnik. She's super nice and down to earth, and he's head over heels for her. They're currently skiing in Switzerland."

"Nice," Fehring said with a nod of approval. "Speaking of friends taking life-changing plunges, what do you think about Dev Frye's retirement announcement?"

"Dev's *retiring*?" I looked at her with saucer eyes.

Fehring looked like she'd just let an angry cat out of the bag and was trying to figure out a way to stuff it back in. "I'm sorry. I thought he would have told you since you're such tight friends. I heard about it last night from another Newport Beach detective. It was just announced."

"Dev did invite Greg and me to dinner tomorrow night," I told her. "Maybe he was going to tell us then." It made sense, especially since Dev specifically said he had some news to tell us, but I didn't like being out of the loop so late in the news crawl.

"I'm sure that's it," Fehring said, making a quick save. "He probably wanted to make it a special announcement."

I glanced at the closed door and leaned forward like Fehring and I were girlfriends sharing a secret. "So what's up with Mr. FBI?" I asked.

A half smile crept partway across Fehring's face before coming to a halt and changing its mind. "You've hit the jackpot this time, Odelia. You've stumbled into a federal investigation."

"What?" I asked, nearly coming out of my chair. "That dead guy is wanted by the feds?"

Before Fehring could say anything more, a uniformed officer brought in my coffee with Shipman and Seth Washington on his heels. The two men were about the same height, but Seth had a wider and more solid build that he carried with expert posture. Seth and his wife Zenobia, better known as Zee, are our best friends. Zee's been my bestie for more than twenty years. Seth had obviously come from his office and was dressed in a snappy gray suit. He nodded to Detective Fehring, having met her on several occasions. "I'd like a few minutes with my client," Seth told Fehring and Shipman.

Client? I didn't like one of my dearest friends calling me his client. Nope. Not one bit. But at the moment I'd have to swallow it like a bitter pill. Seth isn't a criminal attorney, but he'd be able to guide me through the questioning and determine whether or not I would need more expert representation. It had been Seth who'd tagged me with the nickname *Corpse Magnet* many years ago. The obnoxious moniker had obviously stuck, having spread to the Long Beach Police Department and even the feds.

When the detectives left us alone, Seth placed his briefcase on the table and got down to business. "What in the hell is going on, Odelia? Greg said you have a dead body in the trunk of your car."

"Had," I corrected. "I'm sure they've

24

removed it by now."

"This isn't a time for your flippancy, girl." Seth unbuttoned his suit jacket and sat down in a chair next to me. A very handsome African-American man in his late fifties, Seth had a deep baritone voice. Jacob — his and Zee's college-age son — was the spitting image of him. His close-cropped hair, once jet black, was now salt and pepper. It looked great on him.

"I have no idea how that body got into my trunk, Seth. Really, I don't."

He pulled a pen and a legal yellow pad out of his briefcase and started jotting down notes. "When was the last time you opened the trunk of your car?"

I gave the question some thought before answering. "It was Monday afternoon — President's Day." I told him. He jotted it down. "I'd done some grocery shopping and bought two cases of water. Greg and I always keep a case of water in each of our vehicles for emergencies and sporting events, and it was on sale. I pulled one case out and moved it to Greg's van shortly after he got home from work that night."

"Wasn't his office closed for the holiday?"

"Yes, but Greg went in for a few hours to catch up on some paperwork. He got home sometime between three and four, I think. I know it was before supper time. And that's when I transferred one of the cases to his van."

"And there was no body in your trunk at that time?" Seth asked.

I looked at Seth as if his brain had skipped a beat. "Don't you think I would have noticed a little thing like that?"

"One would hope, Odelia," he said, his eyes on the pad as he jotted down the information. "How about the name Zach Finch?"

"Who's Zach Finch?" I took a sip of my coffee. It was the temperature of pee and of a similar taste — not that I've actually tasted pee.

Seth looked at me. "The dead guy in the trunk. At least that's the story his prints are telling. That's all Shipman told me just now. They didn't mention his name to you?"

I shook my head. "But I'm sure they would have gotten around to it."

"For some reason," Seth said slowly as he poked the end of his pen at the pad, making an abstract figure of tiny dots, "the name sounds familiar to me, but I can't place from where or why." He looked up from his art project. "Does the name ring a bell with you?"

I closed my eyes and quickly ran the name

through my personal data bank, whirring it around like laundry on the spin cycle. I shook my head. "Nothing comes to mind."

"Then why would he be in your trunk with a note pinned to him saying 'found me'? Were you looking for anyone?" Seth held the pen over the pad and waited for any answer.

"These are the same questions the police have been asking me," I complained.

Seth continued to hold the pen aloft over the paper. "And now I need to ask them if I'm going to help you."

"First off," I began, trying not to let my exhaustion amp up my already considerable crankiness, "the note was not pinned to him. He was naked; there was nothing to pin anything to. The note, I believe, was taped to him with silver duct tape — the same tape that bound him. At least that's what the police told me."

After writing down that the note had been taped to the body, Seth looked at me expectantly for the rest of my explanation.

"As for looking for the guy," I said, "I have no idea who he is . . . or was . . . so how could I be looking for him?"

"So you're not helping out one of your oddball acquaintances or friends with a little amateur sleuthing on the side?" he asked, then tacked on for good measure, "It's not like you haven't been involved with stuff like this in the past, Odelia."

"Let me remind you, Seth, that I count you and your family among my oddball friends." I put down my pee-temperature coffee hard enough to make it slosh onto the table. "And whose side are you on, anyway?"

"Your side, Odelia." Seth put down his pen. "But I need to know everything. We have to figure out why this guy and why your car? It's only natural, given your past, that this might have something to do with your penchant for stumbling into trouble. If we can't find a link to something or someone else, you're going to go to the head of the suspect list. Do you want that?"

"Oh, please," I said, trying to be indignant when really I was ready to have a major stroke. "If I killed that guy, do you think I'd casually forget and drive my car, with the body in the trunk, to Twinkle Clean?" I gave Seth a one-eyed stare. "With my mother in the car, no less?" I paused, then asked. "And how did he even die? The police didn't tell me that." I took a short breath and continued my rant. "And do I look like I'd be able to hoist a grown man's body into the trunk of a car? Even though that guy — that

Simon Fletcher or whatever his name was . . ."

"Zach Finch," Seth corrected.

"Zach Finch," I repeated. "Even though Mr. Finch was trussed and folded like a turkey in a roasting pan, he looked pretty strong and fit to me. And young. I can barely lift the kettlebells at the gym more than a few times."

"You could have had help," Seth suggested.

"Right. Mom helped me. Together we're quite the killing machine." I started doodling in the puddle of coffee to calm myself down.

Seth leaned toward me. "Odelia, did the police ask you about Willie Proctor or Elaine Powers?"

My heart stopped. My mouth went dry. I stopped playing in the spilled coffee and took a gulp of what was left in my coffee cup, draining it. Years ago William Proctor had embezzled millions from an investment company that he had created and headed, leaving thousands of people bereft of their nest eggs. He went on the run and has been in hiding since to avoid prosecution, even though a few years back he returned every penny. Our paths crossed when I started snooping into the murder of one of the

29

clients of the law firm I worked at then. Over the years, Willie has become a special friend to both Greg and me, and not too long ago my half brother Clark, a retired cop, went to work for a company that is believed to be owned by Willie, though nothing can prove that.

Elaine Powers is a killer — an older woman scarred for life to the point of no return. Her street name is Mother, and she heads a very scary organization of women who specialize in hits for hire. We've crossed paths a few times, and even though she's saved my bacon and assisted me in the past, I'd hardly call her a friend, as I would Willie. Just thinking about Elaine makes me want to hide in a closet. Both Willie and Elaine have magical powers when it comes to ferreting out information about people, especially people who live and operate in the darkness of illegality.

"No," I answered. "They haven't mentioned either of them yet, although Special Agent Shipman did allude to my having friends in low places. By the way, did Shipman introduce himself to you before bringing you into this room?" Before Seth could answer, I added, "He's with the FBI. Is that why he's here? Because they think this might be related to Willie or Elaine?"

"Yes, Special Agent Shipman introduced himself to me." Seth scratched something on his legal pad. "And I'm sure it's a connection they're thinking about. I don't know about Elaine Powers, but Willie is definitely a federal matter."

"Do you really think Willie or Elaine would willingly put me in jeopardy? Both of them operate in the shadows. This is the sort of bold statement neither of them would make — not to mention, Willie is *not* a killer."

"Since I've never met either personally, I'll have to reserve my opinion." Seth looked directly at me. "Odelia, someone killed Finch and put his body in the trunk of your car. That on its own is crazy enough, but adding that note was a message. It's a challenge, perhaps a taunt, to either you or someone you know who might be looking for Finch. Otherwise why would they choose your car out of the millions of cars in Southern California?"

What Seth said made sense, but as much as I squeezed my gray matter, nothing came out. It was like trying to get juice from a shoe. "I need to somehow ask Willie and Elaine about it," I finally said. "But how can I do that with the police watching? Not to mention, I don't even know how to

31

contact them." I actually knew I could probably reach Willie through Clark, but when it came to reaching Elaine I was clueless, and for the most part glad of it.

"It's not just the police," Seth said. "If the note was aimed at one of them, it could be a ploy to get you to flush them out into the open."

"So I don't try to contact them and hope that justice will prevail and my big behind isn't put in jail? What if whoever did this set me up to take the fall by planting that body?"

He shrugged. An attorney who shrugs makes me nervous. If they're clueless, how in the hell am I supposed to feel confident in justice prevailing?

"Yes, that's another thought," Seth said when he was through shrugging. "One of the other creeps you've tangled with in the past could be trying to even the score. That's one of the things we're going to suggest to the police. Maybe they can go back and check on the whereabouts of the people you've helped put behind bars. Maybe they're not behind bars any longer. Maybe they have friends on the outside trying to even the score. Wasn't there one situation several years back involving a federal matter?"

I put my brain through a series of tricks again. "I think so." It was my turn to shrug, after which I dropped my head into my hands and uttered a moan that sounded like a wounded animal. "And maybe I should just accept a murder rap and save everyone the trouble."

THREE

"Would you quit griping about your car, Odelia?" my usually sunny husband said when we finally made it home, Mom in tow. "It's evidence in a murder investigation. Who knows when or even if we'll ever get it back? We'll lease one for you in the meantime."

I shivered as the image of that man's naked dead body in the trunk of my car flooded my brain. It almost felt like I'd found him in my home. "I'm not sure I want it back," I said as I deposited the Chinese takeout we'd bought on the way home on the counter along with my purse. I knelt down on the floor and gave Wainwright, our golden retriever, a hug. He was very happy to see us, but I could tell the animal was a bit put out. Normally, he goes everywhere with Greg, but as soon as Greg realized he had to hit the road for Long Beach for an indefinite amount of time, he'd swung back to the house and deposited his canine companion at home. Fortunately, we'd caught him before he'd gone very far on his way to the Gull. Muffin, our tiny gray cat, came up for her own greeting. I hugged, kissed, and petted them both, enjoying the simplicity of it after an afternoon of interrogation.

"If you don't want the car back, Odelia," Greg said as he propelled his wheelchair over to where I was receiving furry love, "then we'll buy you another and sell that one when we get it back. I'll call the insurance company tomorrow and see what they say. Who knows? Maybe there's an odd clause about stuff like this."

"I'll bet you could sell the car on eBay," Mom said. She put her purse on the coffee table and sat down on the sofa with a tired plop. She looked like she'd been dragged behind our van all the way home. "I'll bet you'd get a bundle for it if you advertise that a dead body was found in it. You could call it the Murder Mobile." Greg and I turned to her like synchronized swimmers. She was dead serious. Tired or not, she hadn't lost her gift for the bizarre.

Greg's cell phone rang. Looking at the display, he announced, "It's Clark." Again, both of us turned our heads toward Mom.

"You called Clark, didn't you?" I accused my mother.

"No, I did not," she answered, her pointed, straight nose tilted upward in defiance. "I *texted* him and sent him the photo of the dead man in your trunk."

"Oh, no," I said, lowering my butt onto the floor with a thud. Falling backwards, I lay there on the hard wood with my eyes shut, just imagining what my brother was going to say about this. Both Wainwright and Muffin thought I was playing. Muffin crawled all over me while the dog gave my face an enthusiastic bath.

"Hi, Clark," Greg said, finally answering. "By the way, I have you on speaker."

"I've been calling you, Odelia, and Mom for hours now," Clark yelled into the phone. "I was thinking the worst after seeing that pic Mom sent."

"We had to have our phones off while at the police station. I just turned mine on," Greg explained.

I rolled over, got to my knees, then to my feet, and staggered to where I'd left my purse. Grabbing my phone, I looked at the display. Sure enough, there were six messages, all from Clark — four texts and two hysterical voice mails. I turned my ringer back on, glad it was off before. The thing

36

must have been vibrating in my purse like a runaway sex toy while I was talking to Seth and the police.

"Was that body really in Odelia's car?" Clark asked, finally checking the volume on his voice.

"Yes, it was," called out Mom. "I told you that in my text."

"Just confirming, Mom," Clark said.

"What? You don't believe me?" Mom said, getting all huffy. "It happened at the car wash today. The dead man was tucked into her trunk as nice as you please, except that he was naked."

"Yes," Greg confirmed before a family phone brawl broke out, "there was a dead body in the trunk of Odelia's car. We have no idea how it got there. And yes, he was naked."

"Who was he?" Clark asked. "Some guy who made fun of Odelia's obsession with Thin Mints?"

"Really, Clark?" I snapped as I moved closer to the phone.

"Sorry, sis," Clark swiftly apologized. "It just sort of slipped out. As macabre as the situation is, it's also pretty funny. A new low for you. Or should that be a new high?"

"We're not laughing here, Clark," Greg said, his own voice getting edgy.

"Have you been drinking, Clark?" Mom asked, her brows scrunched with worry. Both she and Clark were recovering alcoholics, and both take their longtime sobriety seriously.

"No, Mom, I haven't been drinking," Clark assured her. "It's just that this is the sort of stuff that winds up on TV, and I'm not talking about the news." He paused. "So what are the details? Did the cops ID him yet?"

"Yes," Greg answered. I was glad he was fielding the questions because I'd answered more than my share already today. "His name is Zach Finch. He's around twenty-three years old and from a small town in Illinois outside of Chicago. Sound familiar to you?"

There was silence while Clark gave it some thought. "It does sound familiar," he finally said, "but I can't place from where right now."

That was when I decided it was time to get involved. I indicated for Greg to give me the phone, which he did. I switched it off speaker. "Hi, Clark," I said into it. "It's just me on the line now." I started moving toward our bedroom for some privacy. Just before I closed the door shutting the master suite off from the rest of the house, I heard

Greg say, "I'm going to unpack the food and get ready to eat. I'm starved."

"Clark," I said to my brother, "attached to the body was a note that said 'found me.' The cops are wondering if it has anything to do with some of my past run-ins with criminals, including Willie and Elaine Powers — you know, the mother of hitmen, or should I say hit*persons.*"

"The police asked you directly about Willie?" Clark asked with concern.

"Not right away," I explained. "At first they danced around my connections to known criminals, but after I lawyered up they asked about them by name. They're wondering if whoever left the body was trying to get to one of them through me — at least that's one of their theories. Another is that it's payback for someone I messed with along the way."

Clark was silent again on the other end of the phone, putting his cop training to work. "But 'found me' sounds like you've been looking for this guy, or at least someone has. Are you sure you're not sticking your nose where it doesn't belong?"

"My nose is clean and is minding its own business, thank you very much."

"At least for the past few months." Clark snorted. "I'm proud of you, sis. You made it through Thanksgiving, Christmas, and New Years without a corpse, although you were damn close to Thanksgiving with that last one. Too bad you couldn't have made it to Easter."

"Not funny, Clark. You and everyone else seem to think I do this for laughs or out of boredom. Well, I don't."

There was a short silence from Clark's end, except for the occasional huffs and puffs and grumbles. Clark is in his early sixties and can come off grumpy and snappish, but he's solid as granite. He lives outside of Phoenix, Arizona, in a swanky fifty-five-plus community and oversees security for the company everyone believes is linked up the food chain to Willie.

"Tell you what, sis," Clark finally said. "Let me check around on my end and see if the name rings any bells with either of your underground friends."

"You know how to get in touch with Elaine?" I asked, my mouth falling open.

"Not really, but I might be able to find people who know people who do. One thing I'm pretty sure of, though: I doubt she did this. It's too flamboyant. Hitmen work behind the scenes, in the shadows. They don't wave flags to get attention."

"That's what I told Seth."

"Is Seth Washington representing you?" Clark asked with surprise. "He's not a criminal attorney, is he?"

"No, but I don't think I'll need one. He helped me through the questioning. He's done that before."

"Well, if things heat up, don't hesitate to get yourself a good criminal attorney," Clark advised. "I think the world of Seth and Mike Steele. Both of them are top-notch guys and attorneys who would go to the ends of the earth to protect you, but neither have the expertise to help you if this gets messier and deeper on your end."

"Seth already said that," I told my brother. "He already has someone lined up, should we need him."

"Good," Clark said with relief. "In the meantime, keep Mom out of it. I've already told her in a text that she's not to post anything about this on her blog or on Facebook or Twitter. Damn social networking," he groused. "Why can't she just knit or watch talk shows like most women her age? Having this splashed across the net just might be what the perps are hoping will happen."

Clark had been right earlier. In spite of the situation's gravity, there was an underlying current of the ridiculous to it — a gallows humor that hung over it like a noose shown via shadow puppets on the wall. "Don't worry," I told him. "Seth gave her a very kind but forceful lecture on the subject before we left the police station. And if that doesn't work, I'll beat it into her."

He laughed. "I'll be out there tomorrow. We can beat her together."

"You're coming to California tomorrow?" With great speed, I searched my memory but couldn't remember Clark telling us about this trip. "I hope you're not coming here because of this. We have it under control, Clark."

"Nope, it's a last-minute trip," he explained. "Dev asked if I'd come out and go to dinner with him and you guys tomorrow night. At first I wasn't sure I could make it, but today my calendar cleared up a bit so I'm driving over bright and early. I'll be in town for a couple of days unless something crops up at work."

"Are you staying with us or with Mom?"

"Frankly, I'd prefer staying with you and Greg, but Mom would be hurt if I do that. Besides, if I stay with her I can keep an eye on her shenanigans until her interest in this latest corpse dies out."

"Why don't you take her back to Arizona with you like you did before?" I suggested.

"Just until this blows over."

"She'd never fall for that ploy again, Odelia. She's too sharp to be bamboozled twice." He hesitated, then added, "And so am I."

It was my turn to be quiet for a few seconds. "Clark," I ventured, "do you know why Dev is gathering us up for dinner tomorrow night?"

The hemming and hawing on the other end of the phone was more than sound — it was solid and touchable.

"He's retiring from police work, isn't he?" I added when the stall continued.

"Yes," Clark admitted. "He is. It's something he's been discussing with me on and off for a few months. He wanted another cop's perspective on life after the badge, but he asked me not to say anything. He wants to retire and enjoy life. He's only sixty, but he's been on the job for close to forty years. He got into it right out of school. How did you find out?"

"Andrea Fehring told me today at the Long Beach police station. Apparently Dev just announced it at work, and the news traveled fast among other cops." I smiled to myself. Dev worked hard and was one of the best people I'd ever met. He deserved to retire and enjoy his life. "Do you know

43

yet what he's going to do with his time?"

"I'll let him tell you that at dinner," Clark said. He took a deep breath. "Okay, sis, I'm going to run and pack for my trip. I want to be on the road before dawn. Will you be at work tomorrow or is it one of your days off?"

"I'll be going in for a bit. Steele's off on his honeymoon and wants me to keep a lid on things in his absence, although Jill's perfectly capable of that herself."

"That's right," Clark said with a chuckle. "Mike Steele got married this past weekend. How was it?"

"Lovely, just like his bride. The ceremony and reception were tasteful, elegant, and intimate — and, like Steele, not a hair or rose petal out of place." I laughed. "I can't wait to see you tomorrow, Clark. Call me as soon as you get into town."

"Will do, sis. And you keep your corpse count down to just this one, okay? At least until I get there."

FOUR

Before leaving the bedroom, I changed out of my still-damp jeans and panties into dry, comfy yoga pants. The food was already on the table, along with plates and utensils. Greg was pouring iced tea for us while he brewed Mom a cup of decaf coffee. Mom was still on the sofa poring over her iPad.

"Clark will be here tomorrow," I told Greg. "He's going to dinner with us and Dev."

"Yeah, your mother just told me he was coming," Greg said, putting down the iced tea pitcher.

"He sent me a text while we were at the police station," Mom called from the sofa. "He asked if I wanted to go to dinner with you all, but I declined. I have plans tomorrow night."

Greg and I exchanged glances. My mother seemed to have a very busy social life, but we were only privy to part of it. Sometimes she did things with Greg's parents and sometimes with friends from her retirement community. For all we knew, the rest of the time she was a CIA operative. "What's up tomorrow night, Mom?" I asked.

"Me and a few of the girls are going to one of those Indian casinos tomorrow," she explained, not looking up from her tablet. "We're even staying overnight. It's one of those bus trips for old people designed to rob us of our social security money. They're running a special for a two-day, one-night trip. Should be fun."

I looked at Greg and shook my head. He just grinned. "Fun to be robbed or fun to spend time with friends?" I asked her.

"I'm not much of a gambler," my mother said, still keeping most of her focus on what she was doing, "and sometimes those old biddies get on my nerves, but I love to people watch at the casino. And there's always some great food and entertainment. I've been on these trips before."

"You have?" I asked. This was news to me.

"Sure," she answered. "They're usually on Tuesdays or Wednesdays, when the casinos aren't as busy, but this one was for Thursday since Monday was a holiday."

"Did you tell Clark you'll be gone?" I asked, walking into the living room from the dining area. Except for the bedrooms and bathrooms, our home has a huge open floor plan, with the living room, dining room, and kitchen flowing one into the other. Greg designed it, buying a duplex and turning it into one very large easy-care home. "He said he was staying with you while he's here."

"He's a big boy, Odelia. He can stay by himself a day or two. And he has a key to my place." She looked up at me. "But I guess I should tell him, shouldn't I?"

"Ya think?" I scowled at her. Grace Little-john had never been mother of the year, and she wasn't about to start now. She'd had three kids by three different fathers. Clark had been fathered by Leland Little-john. I was conceived with Horten Grey, whom my mother had married after taking off and leaving Clark with his father. When I was sixteen and my parents were already divorced, Mom left me and ran off with some guy who impregnated her with our half brother Grady. She returned to Leland after Grady's father abandoned her, and Leland adopted Grady and gave him his name. And that's where she was when I finally caught up to her several years ago. Both my father and Clark's are now de-ceased, and so is Grady.

For better or for worse, that leaves me with just two blood family members. Clark and I have become quite close; we are a lot alike and even resemble each other a bit. And both of us have this love-hate relationship with our mother, which has improved over the past few years. I have friends who complain that their aging parents have no life outside of that of their children, but Clark and I worry about the life Mom has away from our watchful eyes. What's worse, she seems absorbed in my occasional trips to murderland and sees us as a sort of mother-daughter PI team. I can't tell you how many times Greg has told me how thankful he is that his parents are normal. They are, and I love them for it.

Mom looked up at me through her glasses, the thick lenses enlarging her eyes. She looked like a startled lemur. "But maybe I shouldn't go."

"I'm sure Clark won't mind, Grace," Greg told her. "And you're only going to be gone one night."

"I'm not worried about him," Mom told him. "I'm worried about that dead body. Odelia might need me to help figure out where it came from."

I had to nip this line of thinking right in the bud, and pronto. "The police are handling it, Mom," I told her firmly. "Tomorrow I'm going to work, then later to dinner with Dev, Clark, and Greg. That's it."

"I'm sure you're going to do all that, Odelia, but I'm not stupid. Your brother, Dev Frye, and even you and Greg are going to be looking into this, and I want to help. In fact, I already have."

I moved closer until I was right in front of her, staring into her lemur eyes. "What do you mean, Mom?"

In answer, she turned her iPad around. "I've been online looking up whatever I can on that Finch guy."

I was annoyed. Not because she looked up the dead man online, but because she had done it before I did. It was something I had been planning to do later. "And?" I asked, putting aside my pettiness in favor of information.

"And if this is the right guy," Mom said, pointing at the tablet, "the top just got popped off a whole different can of worms."

I sat down on the sofa next to Mom and picked up the iPad to study it closer. As I read, my eyes widened and my heart nearly stopped. I checked the date of the old news article Mom had unearthed. It could be the same Zach Finch, or Zachery Finch. The age of the person in the article about

49

matched up with the age of the guy in my trunk, given the time lapsed. There was even a photograph, taken years ago, and I could see similarities. I hadn't gotten a good look at the man's face while he was in the trunk, but the police had shown me and Seth photos of him taken after the tape across his mouth had been removed. He'd had a high forehead and small eyes, between which was a long nose with a bump on the bridge, like it had been broken a long time ago. In the photo, his thin lips were gray and waxy. It was too early to be definitive, but the initial cause of death was thought to be suffocation, and the time of death was estimated as sometime late Tuesday night or in the wee hours of Wednesday morning.

"Honey," I said to Greg, "you need to see this."

"The food's getting cold," Greg complained as he rolled into our living room. In his hand was Mom's coffee.

"I'll take that," Mom said to him, holding out her hand. Greg handed her the coffee mug. Mom wrapped her hands around it and brought it close to her thin chest like it was a teddy bear.

"We can nuke the food if we need to," I told Greg. "This is important." I handed him the tablet. "Read that."

Greg pulled his reading glasses from a pouch on the side of his wheelchair where he kept things he needed quick access to and slipped them on. I watched as he scanned the page, then moved to the next, then back to the first one. Behind his glasses, his eyes swelled in surprise like inflated party balloons. "Do you think this is our guy?"

"The article says that Zach Finch was from Illinois, and the age in the article would come close," I pointed out. "The cops told me the guy in my trunk was from Illinois, but that's all they said besides his name." I looked at Greg while my mind wrapped around the information in an effort to contain it. "The cops had to know about this, right?"

"If he's the same guy in this article, I'm betting they did." He tapped the screen of the tablet. "Kidnapping is a federal crime. No wonder Special Agent Shipman was there. It's also why they didn't say much to you. They'll be playing it close to the chest until they get more information. At least I would if I were them." He looked up at me. "Are you hearing me, Odelia?" he said, changing to his lecture voice. "The *feds.*" He said the word as if invoking the power of God himself. "If Shipman's presence

51

wasn't enough to put you on alert, this sure should be."

"Are you saying to forget about it?" I asked.

He hesitated. "I'm saying we need to be very, very careful with this or we're going to get our asses in a sling and possibly a few of our friends' asses too." I knew immediately that he was talking about Willie. Although Elaine had done me a solid in the past, I didn't think Greg cared about protecting a killer.

He put the iPad down on the coffee table. "Nice work, Grace." Next to me my mother beamed and took a sip of her coffee. Greg started back to the kitchen. "Zach is dead, and I'm not. Let's discuss this further over dinner." He stopped and spun his chair around. Looking straight at my mother, he said, again using his lecturing voice, "Grace, you cannot put this up on your blog or anywhere else. Do you understand?"

"Clark already said the same thing," Mom snapped back, "and so did Seth Washington. But none of you are the boss of me. Got that, hot wheels?"

"Grace," Greg said, rolling back closer to her. "You're my mother-in-law and I love and respect you, but don't think for a minute I won't lock you in our guest room if that's what it would take to keep you safe."

Holy crap. I watched the scene play out, wisely keeping my nose out of it. My mother could be a cantankerous and willful battle-ax at times, but my husband took his duty as head of the household and its protector very seriously; in that respect he was very old-fashioned. I didn't doubt for a minute that he would find a way to take Mom out of commission if he had to. Being in a wheelchair wouldn't slow him down for a second. It seldom did.

Mom twitched her nose, a habit we shared, and took a drink from her mug. For the time being, she seemed to surrender. "How about sending the link to that page to Clark," I said to her. "He's going to do some checking for us. He can add that to the list." She put down her coffee and got right on it. She was really quite good at this kind of stuff, which was both surprising and worrisome.

I got up but didn't head for the table. Instead, I retrieved my phone and dialed Clark. "Hi, it's me," I said when he answered. I went back into our bedroom to talk to him.

"So the display says, sis. What's up?"

"Mom is going to send you a link to a website in a minute. It's something she

53

found about a Zach Finch. We think it's the same Zach Finch that was found in the trunk of my car today."

"So is he some wanted criminal or something?" Clark asked. "His name is really setting off bells in my head."

"More of a something," I answered, "if it's the same Zach Finch." I paused and closed my eyes, knowing this was not going to be a simple matter. No dead body was, but this had the potential of blowing up into an epic problem. "His father is some big mucky-muck. When he was fifteen, Zach was kidnapped and held for ransom. According to the article, the ransom was paid but neither Zach nor his abductors were ever found."

"Geez," Clark said and was silent for a very long time. Then he added, "That's why the name sounded familiar. I remember when that all happened."

"Me too now, sort of. It was in the news back then, wasn't it?"

"Yeah. As I recall now, it was kept quiet until after the ransom disappeared and Zach wasn't recovered," Clark explained. "Then it was in the news constantly. So what does this have to do with you or anyone you know?"

"That's the fifty-million-dollar question,

Clark. This kid's been missing for more than eight years. And this doesn't sound like anything connected to either Willie or Elaine, does it?"

"No, it doesn't," he agreed, "but you never know. Was Elaine ever involved in kidnapping for cash?"

I didn't have to scratch my memory very deep to answer. "She kidnapped Mike Steele a few years back for someone. That's how we met." I let that tidbit of information sink into Clark's skull for a moment. It had happened before I'd found Mom and met Clark. "Still," I added, "as strange as it sounds, Elaine does have a moral code. It's not the same as ours, but she does have one. I don't think she'd involve me in one of her jobs like this."

Clark took a deep breath. "I'll do some snooping and hopefully will have something to tell you tomorrow. In the meantime, keep your head down, you hear? This is going to involve the feds, and that's way out of your league. They won't be as accommodating as your local cops."

"Um, the feds are already involved," I told Clark. I held my breath for a heartbeat before continuing. "There was an FBI agent questioning us along with Andrea Fehring."

"Then they already know who this guy

55

is," Clark said. "The local cops probably called the feds after they ran his prints. Like I said, you're out of your league, but at least you have some sense of what's appropriate." Clark groaned. "Mom's another story. I don't like the idea of her running wild on the Internet with this information. It could bring the bad guys out of hiding sooner than later."

"Don't worry," I assured my brother. "Several of us have already told Mom to keep all this to herself. Greg even threatened to lock her up if she blogged about it."

Clark laughed. "I've always liked your husband, sis. From day one I liked him. He would have made a damn fine cop."

"By the way, Mom is leaving tomorrow for some old geezer bus trip to one of the Indian casinos. She'll be gone for two days. She forgot to tell you."

"She just did," Clark told me. "I just received the email with the link about Finch. It included the news that she's going out of town. Pretty convenient timing." He paused. "Just make sure she gets her skinny ass on that tour bus tomorrow."

FIVE

"Was that your car on the news last night?" Jill Bernelli asked as she offered up a cute basket full of her outstanding cranberry scones. Jill's a secretary at Templin and Tobin, the law firm where I work as a corporate paralegal. We're in the Orange County office, a satellite office of the mothership based in Los Angeles. Mike Steele is the managing partner of the OC office. Jill is also the wife of Sally Kipman, one of my high-school classmates. Together for many years, Jill and Sally got married this past New Year's Day in a small ceremony that Greg and I attended. Feeling magnanimous and in love himself, Steele paid for their honeymoon in Hawaii, but not before extracting the promise from Jill that she would be back in the office bright and early the day after she returned.

"My car was on the news?" I asked, feigning surprise.

"Don't play dumb with me, Grey," Jill said, addressing me by my last name as Steele did. She only did that when she wanted to cut through the bull — or rather my bull. "I saw you pull into the parking garage this morning in a different car, and even though they blocked out the license plate, the vehicle on the news looked just like your car, right down to the *I BRAKE FOR BEN AND JERRY'S* bumper sticker."

"Got me," I said and took a big bite of scone. Jill should be working for the FBI instead of Gregory Shipman.

"So what's the story?" she asked. "I promised Sally I'd worm it out of you and call her."

"Good grief," I said after taking a slurp of coffee. "Is that why you brought the scones? Did you think you could bribe the information out of me?"

"Yep," she answered honestly. "Both you and Steele are putty in my baker's hands, although he's a tougher customer. With him I usually have to throw in a chocolate bundt cake or blueberry muffins on the side to get what I want."

"Nice to know I'm such a pushover." I wiped my mouth with one of my good linen napkins — a piece torn from the paper towel roll I kept in my office.

"So what's the story?" Jill pressed. "Sally's waiting for my call, and she has a busy day."

"Well, pardon me if I hold up her schedule," I snapped.

Jill smiled at my sarcasm. She could roll with it like a pro. After all, Sally was the queen of snark, and Steele was no slouch in that department either. I was the featherweight of the group. "According to the news last night," Jill said, not missing a beat, "a body was found in the trunk of a car at a Long Beach car wash yesterday — Twinkle Clean. Isn't that where you go?"

"A lot of people go to Twinkle Clean." I took another bite of scone and took my time chewing and swallowing. Across from my desk, Jill sat in front of me with the serenity and patience of a Tibetan monk. Over the years, she and Sally had become very important in my life, and not just at the office. Even though Sally and I were frenemies in high school, we've now become close; I consider them both like sisters, as I do Zee. I trusted and loved them. Sally had been a bridesmaid at my wedding.

"Yeah, that was my car," I finally admitted after swallowing the bite I'd masticated into pulp. "And yes, a dead body was in the trunk."

"Did you know the dead guy?" she asked,

picking at a corner of one of the scones in the basket, which was now sitting on my desk.

I shook my head. "I didn't have a clue who he was or how he got there." Which was true. I hadn't known who he was when he was found. I wasn't ready to tell Jill what we'd discovered since. I still needed to sort that information out for myself.

"Yes!" Jill cried. No longer calm and collected, she pumped a victory fist into the air. Her head bobbed with excitement, each thrust causing her cropped brown hair to shimmer like short fringe on a suede jacket.

"I beg your pardon?" I looked at her with surprise.

"Sal and I had a bet," she explained. "She bet you knew the corpse; I bet you didn't. I just got out of doing all housework for two weeks. Thanks, Odelia." She grinned at me.

"That's what this is about?" I asked, narrowing my eyes at her. "A stupid bet? Don't you care about who and why that body was there?"

"Sure I do, and so does Sal," she answered, trying to slap a serious look on her face. I gave her a C+ for the effort. "But it's not often," she continued, "that I win a bet with Sal. You find bodies all the time."

"I didn't find this one," I explained. "The

car wash people did when they opened my trunk. I had no idea it was there."

"Wow." Jill leaned forward, now paying close attention to the details. "If you hadn't gone to the car wash, you might not have found it for several days — at least not until it started to stink."

It was the same possibility Greg had voiced when we were in bed last night watching the news account of the story. The news report had not disclosed my name, just the name of the car wash and the information that a body had been found in the trunk of a car there. They also didn't disclose the victim's name. Maybe the police hadn't given it to them. There was footage of the car wash and my car, with the license plate blurred as Jill had said, but the Ben and Jerry's bumper sticker was plain as day. Anyone watching who knew me well would know that was my car. More to the point, anyone watching would know that was me.

Greg and I had watched in horror as the news showed a video clip taken by someone's cell phone. The person had obviously been waiting with us at the car wash and had whipped out their phone as soon as all of the excitement started. On the clip you could see me from behind standing with the

61

Twinkle Clean people in front of my open trunk. It was definitely not my best side. You could hear shouts and screaming while I slipped to the ground in a big wet puddle. Next to me wobbled my mother. It cut there while the reporter on location, a perky blond named Gloria Connors, stood with Twinkle Clean in the background and explained that the police were questioning the owner of the car containing the body but that no arrests had been made. She also reported that the police were withholding the victim's name pending notification of family. When the reporter was finished, one of the anchors made a joke about checking his trunk before going to the car wash next time.

Yuk. Yuk.

Greg hadn't helped my mood when he commented, "Talk about great advertising for Twinkle Clean."

Yuk. Yuk. Times two.

What if I hadn't gone to the car wash? How long would it have been before I realized something was amiss in my car that no amount of air freshener would remove? I shuddered at the thought. That car, which I really liked and which wasn't that old, was lost to me either way, as I honestly didn't think I could ever get over the idea that a dead body had been stored in its trunk.

Getting up, I went to my door to close it. Just as I did, Jolene McHugh, an attorney, walked up to Jill's vacant desk. "Hey, Odelia," Jolene said, "have you seen Jill? I need to give her something." Before I could say anything, she glanced at me and added, "Did you know that there was a car on the news last night that looked just like yours? Someone found a dead guy in the trunk. Sure sounds like something that would happen to you."

Instead of answering, I waved Jolene by the arm into my office, closing the door behind us both.

"You wanted Jill," I said to her. "Here she is." I moved to sit back behind my desk. "And while you're here, Jolene, have a seat."

Jolene, Jill, and I had all followed Steele over to Templin and Tobin from Wallace, Boer, Brown, and Yates, our last firm, although I came a bit later after a whole lot of drama and Steele coming to my rescue. The three of us knew each other well.

"Are you leaving the firm?" Jolene asked me in a panic. "You know Steele will go apecrazy if you do."

"No, he won't," I told her. "At least not as long as he has Jill here. But no, I'm not leaving the firm."

Jolene rubbed her tummy in relief. She'd had a baby a few months before, and even though she was back in her skinny clothes she hadn't lost the habit of unconsciously rubbing her stomach. I guess it was like rubbing a buddha belly for good luck.

"This is about my car," I told her. "As I was just telling Jill here, that *was* my car on TV last night. Couldn't you tell by the video of me on my butt on the ground?"

"There was video of you?" Jill asked with disappointment. "They didn't show it on my station."

"OMG," said Jolene, slowly saying each letter with individual emphasis.

"Come on, Jolene," Jill said to her with a chuckle. "It's not like Odelia's never been involved with a corpse before."

"But in your car?" Jolene was clearly more horrified than either Jill or I. Jill was finding it amusing. I was finding it a huge pain in my behind. "Ewwww," Jolene said with a curl of her lip. "Why would you hide something like that there?"

"I didn't. Someone else did," I explained, "and we don't know why. Both the police and the FBI are looking into it."

"OMG!" Jolene said again, her pale freckled face turning pastier, which made her red hair look like a lit match. "The FBI?" If she rubbed her belly any harder, the fabric of her skirt was going to catch fire and match her head. "Why are they involved?"

I looked from Jolene to Jill. "What I tell you cannot leave this room. Do you both understand?"

"I have to tell Sally," Jill said.

"Okay, you can tell Sally," I told her.

"If she gets to tell Sally, then I get to tell my husband," sniffed Jolene. "And who's going to tell Steele?" She looked at Jill. "Has he even called in yet?"

"No, he hasn't," Jill answered. "It's a first. He's usually on the phone to mc at least once a day when he's on vacation, so he must really be in love."

"Or Michelle threatened to push him off the side of a mountain if he called," Jolene said. The two of them broke into giggles.

I stared at them with the wide eyes of someone about to jump the sanity track until they got the hint and shut up. "No one is to tell Steele if he calls. Got it?" I ordered. They both clamped their mouths shut and nodded. "Like I said, the feds and the Long Beach police are looking into why that body ended up in my trunk. Who knows, they might even come sniffing around here asking questions about me. If they do, be polite and tell them the truth. I

65

have nothing to hide."

"Just a dead body in your trunk," Jill pointed out. The two of them giggled again like they were a bit tipsy.

I wrapped a knuckle on my desk. "Do you guys want to know about this or not?"

Both of them sat up straight and zipped their lips. Jolene pantomimed toward the basket of scones. I tore off a couple paper towels. "Knock yourself out," I told her as I handed her the towels.

While they nibbled on cranberry scones, I told them about finding the body and being hauled into the police station. I told them about the questioning and about Zach Finch and how I didn't have a clue who he was outside of being a teen kidnapped many years ago. I left out the part about Willie and Elaine being long shots. I didn't know if either knew about them from my past experiences, but just in case I certainly wasn't going to parade my underground criminal connections in front of Jolene and Jill. The less they knew, the safer they would be.

"So what are you going to do now?" Jolene ventured, once she was sure I was finished with my story.

"I'm sure the police, especially the feds, are going to play this close to the chest," I said, "so my brother is looking into any possible tie-in to me on his own. He's a retired cop, you know, and still has a lot of connections." Yeah, connections I can't talk about.

"Can't Dev Frye help?" offered Jill. "He's been a big help to you in the past."

"Clark is coming into town today, and we're meeting Dev for dinner tonight. Not for this purpose," I quickly explained, "but I'm sure it will come up."

The phone on my desk chirped. It was the front desk. I answered it by punching the speaker button. "Yes, Mandy."

"At least I reached one of you," our receptionist said. "I've been paging Jolene and Jill. Do you know where they are?"

"Right here with me." I looked over at my two companions, who were listening with interest while licking crumbs from their fingers. "We can't hear the paging system with my office door closed."

"Do you need me, Mandy?" asked Jolene first.

"Actually, I need all three of you," Mandy said. "Steele's on the line. He asked for Jill first, then you, Jolene. Now Odelia."

The three of us looked at each other and shook our heads. Steele couldn't even make it through his honeymoon without calling the office. "Put him through," I told Mandy, then to the others I said, "Not a word, do you understand?" They nodded.

Once the call was transferred, I answered it. "Hey, Steele."

"Hey, Grey." He sounded relaxed and not at all annoyed at having to wait while we were rounded up.

"Jolene, Jill, and I are all in my office. So you've got a threefer." I steeled myself for a smart-ass remark about us not working while he was gone, but it didn't come.

"Great," he responded again with enthusiasm. "One-stop shopping. I just wanted to check in and make sure the place was still standing. Everything going okay?"

"Everything's peachy," I told him.

"Yep, boss," added Jill. "Did you get the emails I've sent you?"

He laughed. "To tell you the truth, I haven't checked my emails even once since I've been gone."

The three of us looked at each other in disbelief. "Don't they have an Internet connection at the hotel?" Jolene asked.

"Sure they do, McHugh," Steele said with another laugh. "But I've been sort of busy." He paused so we could read between the lines. Jill sneered. I rolled my eyes. Jolene blushed. "Anything I should know now or can it wait until I return next week?"

"It can all wait," Jill told him. "I've given Jolene anything that couldn't."

"Yes, a couple of things came up yesterday on the Maxwell deal, but they've all been handled," Jolene reported.

"Perfect," said our boss. "And are you staying out of trouble, Grey?"

I shot my two office pals a warning look. "Trouble? Me?" I answered and thought — not for the first time — that he had my office bugged. "I filed those two incorporations you wanted on Tuesday, and the drafts of the organizational documents are on your desk. Other than that, it has been pretty quiet on my end." Across from me, Jill smirked and elbowed Jolene.

"Outstanding," Steele said, not in his usual snarky tone but with pleased enthusiasm. Again Jill, Jolene, and I stared at each other in confusion and surprise.

"Well, I'm off," Steele announced. "Michelle and I have reservations at this great little bistro tonight. You guys be good and stay out of trouble, at least until I get back next Wednesday." He paused. "That's an order." Then he laughed and was gone.

I picked up my mug and took a drink. My coffee was now cold, but I didn't care. In all the years I've worked with Mike Steele,

I've never heard him so chipper and, well, happy.

"Do you think he fell while skiing and bumped his head?" Jolene asked.

"He's getting bumped, all right," Jill said with another smirk, "but it's not on the ski slopes."

Our little coffee klatch was disbanding when my phone rang again. "Maybe Steele came to his senses," Jolene said, "and remembered that he forgot to abuse us."

I looked at the display on my phone. "Nope, it's Zee Washington. Could you guys shut my door when you leave? I need to take this."

"Didn't you say her husband represented you yesterday?" asked Jolene.

"Yes," I answered, offering nothing more.

As soon as they were gone and my door was securely shut, I answered the phone. "Hi," I said to my best friend. "I'm surprised you waited this long to call." It was true. I had expected Zee, upset with my latest body find, to be on the phone to me last night.

"Seth ordered me to give you some time before I called," Zee told me. "Frankly, I'm surprised you didn't call me first." I could tell she was a bit hurt.

"I just couldn't talk about it anymore yesterday, Zee. I figured Seth would fill you

70

in. In fact, it was Greg who called Seth last night with our latest finding." It was true. After dinner, Greg had called Seth and told him about the missing Zach Finch. Seth had agreed with our theory that the cops probably already knew about it and that it was why the feds were involved.

"Seth didn't tell me much, Odelia," Zee said, her voice running out of patience. "In fact, he didn't tell me anything about meeting you at the police station yesterday until I saw the news with you and your car on it. There you were, plain as day, on your butt in the water in front of a body." Zee and Seth must have watched the same newscast we did. "Then," she continued, still miffed, "he reluctantly explained that he represented you in the questioning yesterday. He claimed attorney-client privilege."

"He's right about that," I said with caution. Steele might have had a change of cranky personality, but I wasn't banking on Zee doing the same. I knew her too well. She was mad that she was in the dark about what was going on, hurt that I didn't tell her myself, and worried about my safety. It was a trifecta of emotions that would be parlayed into an outpouring of motherly lecturing and loving hostility.

"But it's about *you,* Odelia," she complained. "Since when do we have secrets?"

"Since never, Zee," I assured her. "But it wasn't Seth's place to tell you since he was involved with my representation. It was mine, and I just hadn't gotten to it yet. I was going to call you this morning after getting to work, but I was waylaid by Jill and Jolene, who had both seen the news and recognized my car." I paused. "So now that I have you on the phone, let's talk about it." I told her everything I'd just told Jill and Jolene, thinking I should have called Zee and conferenced her in to save time. The only difference in my narrative was that I did tell Zee about the police's suspicion about Willie and Elaine.

"The police have been crawling all over our garage and carport," I told her. "They're looking for evidence that points to the body being put in the trunk at the house — maybe in the middle of the night. They've also gone all through the house this morning looking for evidence that Zach was ever in our place. Nothing like having your home torn apart by cops to start your day. Thankfully, Cruz is there today putting everything back together, because I was about to lose my mind." Cruz Valenz is our housekeeper — a woman in her sixties who brought order to our house on a weekly basis. She also worked for Steele and occasionally for my mother. Before I left for work, I'd slipped a little extra cash into Cruz's weekly pay. Just thinking about the police and my encounter with them yesterday and this morning made me want to dive face-first into the basket of scones like I was in a county fair's pie-eating contest.

"But wouldn't Wainwright have heard the creeps if they put the body in the trunk at night?" Zee asked.

"You'd think," I said, "but the dog is getting old. He's pushing fifteen. According to the vet, Wainwright is in his eighties in people years. Greg and I have both noticed Wainwright's hearing isn't the best anymore; nor is his eyesight. If the people who stashed the body were very quiet, they wouldn't have roused Wainwright if he was in the house and asleep in our room." I paused to catch my breath — not that talking was wearing me out, but the idea of Wainwright getting old and dying was crushing the air out of me. We'd lost our cat Seamus just over a year ago. He was also old and had suffered a stroke. Losing Wainwright would kill Greg, just as losing Seamus had nearly done me in. After the last vet visit, Greg and I talked about the inevitability of losing Wainwright and whether or not Greg should get a replacement dog now, knowing the length of time it would take to train one properly. Wainwright was more than a pet and Greg's constant companion; he was also a service dog trained to protect Greg in sketchy situations. For now the animal was in good shape for his age, but he definitely was slowing down.

"So what are you going to do now?" Zee asked. "With the FBI involved, this is a whole different kettle of fish. I hope you know that?"

I shrugged as if she could see me. "I do, Zee. Trust me."

"Knowing the danger and seriousness has never stopped you before, Odelia." Zee was being a normal worried mother while my own mother wanted to play Sherlock Holmes, regardless of the danger.

"Clark is looking into a few things for me," I told her, "and I'm sure Dev will have some choice words of caution tonight. We're having dinner with him." I paused, wondering if I should spill the beans about Dev, then decided what was the harm. It seemed everyone was finding out one way or another through the grapevine. "Dev is retiring from the police force."

"Seth did tell me that much," Zee said, still sounding a bit peeved about being the last in the information chain. I'd forgotten I'd told Seth while we were at the Long Beach police station. "Do you know what his plans are for retirement?"

"Not yet," I answered, "but I'm sure he'll tell us tonight."

Through the phone I heard Zee's throaty, rich laugh. After her grumpiness, it was like music played in a tunnel lined with mahogany. "Maybe he could become a PI and work just for you," she suggested. "You could keep him busy."

"Cute, but I already have Clark working that end." It was meant as a joke but had a definite ring of truth to it. "I'll let you know what his plans are if he decides to tell us."

"Hmm," hummed Zee on the other end. It was one of the things she did when thinking out loud. "I'm wondering if he'll finally join Beverly. Didn't she move to Seattle?"

Zee was referring to Dev's old girlfriend. Just over a year ago she'd gotten a new job in Seattle and moved there. She'd asked Dev to go with her but he'd declined, citing his job and not wanting to leave his daughter and her family. They had broken up. "I don't know," I answered. "I think that's over, and it would mean leaving his grandchildren."

"I know how that is," noted Zee with sadness. "Ever since Hannah and Rob announced at Christmas that they were pregnant, all I can think about is that baby being in New York while I'm here."

I chuckled. Much to Zee's grief, her son-in-law's work took them around the country. Recently they'd landed on Long Island when Rob's company sent him to their office in New York City. "Something tells me you'll be racking up frequent flyer miles this year."

"That's exactly what Seth said." Zee chuckled. "But you know it's going to kill me. With Jacob gone off to college and his sister in New York, I'm lost. I'm not cut out to be an empty nester, Odelia."

I knew it well enough since Zee poured a lot of her maternal energy out on her friends now, including me — especially me. "You'll be fine, Zee," I assured her. "You can travel more and do the things you've always wanted to do."

"Hmm," she said again, but this time it wasn't her thinking hum but her skeptical grunt — another tune I was familiar with up close and personal. Being put out to pasture was not going to be easy for this supermom.

"In the meantime," I told her, returning to the topic of the dead body, which seemed an easier problem at the moment, "Greg and I are squeezing every inch of our brains trying to remember anything and anyone we've crossed paths with who might have a connection to this, but so far nothing."

"Are you sure it's not one of Elaine's . . . um . . . projects?" Zee asked.

"She's smarter than that," I said, meaning it. "Elaine knows the cops are aware that we have a connection. Leaving that body in my trunk would immediately put the spotlight on her, and that's the last thing she and her business would want. If there's one thing the police, Clark, and Greg and I all agree on, it's this." I paused. "It would be more likely that someone is trying to flush out either her or Willie with this action, but even that isn't a good fit to my thinking. But either way, we're looking into all angles."

"Can you get in touch with Willie to ask him?" Zee asked. Zee didn't know about Clark's connection to Willie's legitimate business, and neither did Seth — at least that we knew of. They just knew that Clark headed up security for a company in Arizona, and Greg and I agreed on keeping them in the dark about it. It was one lie, or careful omission, I didn't feel guilty about.

"We're trying, but that's pretty hit or miss," I said. "Especially with the cops watching me so closely now."

"Good," Zee said with such bluntness that I knew without seeing it that a determined jerk of her chin went along with the statement. "Maybe with the police keeping such a tight rein on you, you'll stay out of trouble this time."

I groaned with frustration. "I didn't ask for this, Zee. Trouble came to me, packed nice and neat in the trunk of my car along with a calling card."

"And it's an invitation you don't need to accept, Odelia."

I wasn't going to win this battle. I could argue with Zee all day long about how, in spite of her warnings, she liked to tag along on some of my fact-finding missions, but I knew it would only net me more argument. I could dispute and manipulate facts and situations with the best of them, but Zee was at the top of the class. It was one of her supermom talents. She would have made a great litigator. So instead of responding, I stuffed my mouth with a big bite of scone and mumbled something about having to get back to work.

Six

"I'm guessing you folks have already heard the news," Dev said after our drink order was taken by our waiter. "I know you've had another run-in with Andrea Fehring." He was sitting across the table from me and looked directly into my eyes when he said the last bit. His face showed no emotion — not sad, amused, angry, or even concerned. It was a craggy, blank canvas.

"Just to clarify, Dev, it was not a run-in." I stared right back at him as I spoke. "I was simply brought in for questioning in a matter."

This time Dev's face didn't remain expressionless. It broke into cracks and crevices as he tilted his head back and laughed. The people at the next table glanced over at the noise. On either side of me, Clark and Greg were also chuckling. I'm sure glad they found my situation so funny, because I sure didn't.

"Boy, I'm sure gonna miss you guys," Dev said as he wiped a tear from his left eye. The tear, I'm sure, came from his laughter, not my predicament or his pending news. "You've certainly made these last several years interesting." He stopped laughing, and his face fell back into place and returned to somber. "Seriously, Odelia, and you too, Greg, even though there were times I came close to locking you both up and have lost sleep over your escapades more than once or twice, I have treasured every day of our friendship."

"You make it sound like you're dying, not retiring, Dev," Greg said. "Just because you won't be a cop doesn't mean we won't need or want you in our lives."

"Yeah, about that," Dev began just as the waiter returned with our drinks — beer for both Dev and Greg, a glass of wine for me, and club soda for Clark. The waiter served us our drinks and asked if we were ready to order. Dev waved him off, asking if we could have a few minutes. When the waiter retreated, Dev said, "As you know, I'm retiring. It's happening at the end of this month."

"What are you going to do, Dev?" Greg asked.

Instead of answering, Dev glanced at

Clark. "You didn't tell them?"

"Had to leave something for you to do, didn't I?" answered Clark with a half grin.

Dev took a long pull from his beer, then said, "I'm moving to Seattle to be with Bev. We're getting back together."

I shifted in my seat as the news hit me like an unexpected spray of cold water. I liked Bev a lot, and she and Dev seemed good together, but I didn't want to lose Dev to the northwest. Bev had relocated because of a great job offer. She and I sometimes emailed each other, and I could tell from our spotty correspondence that she was in love with both her new position and the area. Wanting Dev to stay was selfish of me. "What about your daughter and your grand-children?" I asked.

"My daughter's on board with the plan, even if she's not thrilled by it," Dev answered honestly. I knew how his daughter felt because I was in the same camp. "It's just a short plane ride away," he continued by way of offering assurance. "It's not like I'm moving to Siberia. And I think a change of scenery would do me good."

"What about your house?" Clark asked.

"With the market still soft, I've decided to rent it out for the time being. My daughter will keep watch on it for me. We found someone — a friend of hers who got transferred by his company and needs a place for his family by the end of the month. My stuff's almost packed up, and most will go into storage. I'll stay with my daughter until I leave, which will be the day after my last day on the job."

"It's all happening so fast," I complained.

"Yeah," Dev answered as if surprised himself. "As soon as I made the decision, everything fell into place. Guess that's a good sign." He didn't sound one hundred percent sure to me, but again it could just be selfishness on my part making me see what I wanted to see. "I also didn't want a big deal made of it." He looked right at me when he spoke.

"Well," added Greg, "if Seattle doesn't work out for some reason, you'll still have your house to come back to."

"That's what my daughter said." Dev looked away, lost momentarily in his thoughts.

"So you're going to be a man of leisure?" I asked. "That doesn't sound like you." Glancing again at my two sidekicks, I could see that they agreed with me.

Dev shrugged. "Guess I'm tired of chasing bad guys." He jerked a thumb at Clark. "He knows what I'm talking about."

"I do, Dev," Clark confirmed with a knowing nod of his head. "But after a month you're going to start getting antsy. Why do you think I went back to work?"

"Well, maybe I'll find a sweet part-time gig in Seattle," Dev said, but from the set of his jaw, I knew he wasn't convinced himself.

"You mean like a security guard or a mall cop?" I asked, my voice filled with disbelief. "I can't see you doing that for a minute. It would be a waste of talent."

"Maybe I'll become a Walmart greeter, Odelia," Dev said with a half smile. "Who knows, I might look kind of spiffy in one of those vests." Everyone laughed.

"I think you should be a PI," Greg said, chiming in. He took a drink of his beer. "I could see that easily."

Again Dev looked at Clark. "Does Willie Proctor have any legit businesses near Seattle? If he does, maybe you can put in a word for me."

The table chat fell away as silence replaced it. Three pairs of eyes darted around the table while the fourth set watched with amusement. It was like we'd farted and Clark, Greg, and I were trying to figure out who should take the blame; no sense in all three of us being embarrassed. When the pinball of eyeballs stopped, everyone was looking at me. Guess I'm the stinkpot.

"How did you find out?" I asked Dev as I tapped the fingers of my right hand on my menu. A waiter went by balancing a huge tray of food trailing yummy smells. While I waited for Dev's answer, I watched the waiter expertly thread his way through the busy restaurant with his burden, confident in his course. I would have dropped the tray for sure, covering at least six people with clam and marinara sauces.

Dev laughed and took a gulp of beer before answering. "I didn't know for sure until just now. Thanks, Odelia, for confirming my suspicions."

To my left, Greg swore softly under his breath. Clark joined in Dev's laughter and held his glass of club soda up to him in salute. "No flies on you, Dev," Clark said as Dev lightly clinked his beer glass against Clark's icy tumbler.

"Come on now," Dev said to the entire table. "I am a detective, after all. And a pretty good one, I might add. You were all just a little too secretive about Clark's job, so I took a stab at my suspicions."

"So are you going to interrogate Clark until he gives up Willie's location?" I asked with concern.

"Go for it," Clark said with a grin, "be-

84

cause I honestly have no idea where he is physically."

Again, Dev laughed. "Bringing Proctor in would be a nice way to cap off my career, but I know he's your friend and has helped you out of trouble on numerous occasions. He's also paid back all the money he stole, so let the feds find him. Frankly, I don't care. I just wanted you folks to know that I was on to you." He took another sip of beer. "I have just shy of two weeks left on the job, and I intend to slide right through them by cleaning up old cases and completing reports. I swear, I'm going to shoot anyone who even thinks of committing a homicide in Newport Beach before I leave."

I was going to point out the contradiction of his words, then thought better of it.

"Then it's a good thing Odelia was in Long Beach when that body was found in her car," my hubs said with a chuckle. "Better Fehring than you, right, Dev?"

"I'll drink to that," Dev said, taking another swig of beer. "Although what's up with that?"

Our waiter returned and took our orders. We were at the Macaroni Grill in Seal Beach, a favorite restaurant for everyone at the table. Dev chose this specific location because it was convenient for us. After dinner, the plan was to head to our place for dessert and coffee. Little did I know that this might also be his going-away party.

Excusing myself from the table, I went to the ladies' room and called Zee and told her what was happening. "So if you and Seth want to come by our place in about an hour or so, please do," I told her. "It might be our last chance to say goodbye to Dev."

I heard her say something to Seth. A few seconds later she returned to our call. "We'll see you then," she said. "Thanks for letting us know. We love Dev almost as much as you and Greg do. And don't rush dinner. I'll use my key and start the coffee when we get there. What else do you need?"

"Nothing," I told her. "I pulled out the regular coffeemaker for tonight. It's on the counter. There's cheesecake and a fruit salad in the fridge."

When I ended the call, I tried to think of others who might want to congratulate Dev and say goodbye. He may not want a big deal made about his retirement and move, but this wasn't about him — it was about people who cared about him. He would just have to suck it up for an evening. I called Greg's parents and Sally and Jill. All said they would be there. Jill said she'd bring something to add to the table; I didn't argue. I'll take her baked goods anytime they're offered. It was too bad Steele and Mom weren't available. After a short hesitation and a quick pee, I called Fehring.

"Odelia," she said, answering on the second ring. "Don't tell me: you've found another body, this time buried in your back yard."

"Cute, Andrea, but no. This isn't an official call, hence the use of your first name." I paused, then jumped right into the purpose of my call. "Did you know that Dev is moving to Seattle in about two weeks?"

There was a long pause. "No, I didn't. When did you find that out?"

"Just now. Greg and I are out to dinner with him. My brother's here too. Dev just dropped the moving bomb on us."

"Wow," was all she said. "Is he getting back together with Beverly?"

"Yes." I cut to the chase. "But here's the thing." Quickly, I told Fehring about the impromptu going-away party, and just as quickly she said she'd be there.

"Did you fall in?" Clark asked when I returned to the table.

Greg snorted. "You've been single too long, Clark. You never ask a woman that." I gave my husband a peck on the cheek for being such a smart boy.

Shortly after I returned to the table, our salads were served. "We can fill you in, Dev, while we eat," I told him. Our salad dishes were cleared and our entrees served by the time I finished telling Dev the details of finding Zach Finch and his background.

"I remember when that kid went missing," Dev said with a shake of his head when I finished.

"I do too," added Clark. "Every law enforcement agency in the nation was on the lookout for him. It's always been assumed the kidnappers killed him after getting their payday."

"The question is," Dev said, a bite of spaghetti with Bolognese sauce dangling from his fork, "where has he been all this time?"

"And why was he dumped naked?" I asked, tossing my question out there for consideration along with Dev's.

"The naked part could have something to do with him not being traced," Clark explained to Greg and me while Dev nodded. "Clothing can sometimes be used to track someone's last few locations through brands, fibers, and things like that, not to mention a catch-all for trace evidence from the murderer."

"Tell me, Odelia," Dev said. "Did you see

any noticeable marks on the body?"

"You mean like bruises or stab wounds?" asked Greg.

"Yeah, those," Dev clarified, still looking at me, "or maybe a tattoo."

Greg dug out his cell phone. "Here's the pic of the body that Grace sent me." He handed his phone over to Dev, who examined it while he continued eating. Nothing like a dead body to spark an appetite. Made me wonder what went best with a corpse — red or white wine?

I closed my eyes to think about the brief glimpse I saw of Zach Finch, then shook my head. "I didn't notice anything specific, but I wasn't exactly given a chance to examine the body. I was in a lot of shock, and he was folded like an origami crane. I do remember his skin being very pale. And his hair was dishwater blond."

"Wasn't he grabbed in Illinois?" Dev aimed this next question at Clark as he handed the phone back to Greg.

"Yeah," Clark confirmed. "I looked up the case last night. He disappeared after a football game at his high school." We ate on autopilot while Clark gave us the rundown he'd found on the kidnapping. "According to reports, Zach went to the game with friends who were old enough to drive. Just a bunch of high school guys, no girls. They said they dropped him off at home after the game, but Zach's parents claim he never came home that night."

"But there was a ransom demand?" asked Greg.

"Yep," said Clark after swallowing some eggplant parmesan. "The kidnappers demanded two million dollars. The whole thing was kept pretty quiet media-wise during that time. The parents paid the ransom, and the kid was never returned. That's when the whole thing went public."

"So who exactly are this kid's parents?" I asked as I doodled in the sauce of my mushroom ravioli with the tines of my fork.

"His father is Alec Finch. He's a big finance mogul. His company owns several mortgage companies, investment firms, stuff like that," Clark said. "At the time of the kidnapping he headed an investment company that specialized in backing international construction, some of it questionable. One of the theories was that some thugs from overseas grabbed the kid, but that was never proved." Clark wiped his mouth with his napkin. "Even with the two-million-dollar hit on the ransom and the economic downturn, it hasn't slowed Finch down. He's expanded his holdings over the years."

"I think I've read about him in the *Wall Street Journal* or someplace like that," said Greg. "He keeps a very low personal profile, doesn't he?" He'd stopped shoveling chicken cannelloni into his mouth and was reaching for more bread. Generally, my husband keeps a sharp eye on his weight to make it easier for him to be more mobile. I knew that tonight's feast would be paid for by extra time in the gym over the next few days. Greg had the discipline I lacked when it came to fitness, but he never got on my case about it. I thought about grabbing more bread but changed my mind. Extra exercise time wasn't a price I was willing to pay, and there was dessert waiting at home.

"Yes," Dev answered. "From what I've read about this Finch guy, he's a big wheeler-dealer but likes to remain behind the scenes pulling strings. He almost never grants interviews." He turned to Clark. "Is that the same guy?" Clark nodded.

"Something's been bothering me," I announced to the table.

"You mean something besides finding a dead body in the trunk of your car, sis?" Clark stared at me with amusement. "Or are you getting used to this sort of thing?"

Dev nudged Clark with his elbow. "Just wait for it, Clark. This is normal procedure for Odelia."

Next to me Greg laughed, but when I shot him a death ray glance, he shoved a bite of food into his mouth.

"We're all ears, Odelia," Dev said, urging me to continue.

I continued toying with my food as I formed my thoughts into a clear picture. "If this Zach was kidnapped so many years ago and his father is such a big deal, why hasn't his death been on the news yet? All they've said is that an unidentified body was found in a car in a Long Beach car wash. It's being treated almost as non-newsworthy as a kitten up a tree."

"Are you complaining that your name's been kept out of it?" asked Dev with surprise. "Wasn't it enough that your backside and car were all over the news last night and today?"

"No, not at all," I quickly added. "The more they forget about me, the better. But the finding of a kid, long missing and thought dead, is very big news. Look at all the media around those kids that pop up years after they've been abducted."

"I'm not involved in this case," Dev said after taking a drink of his beer, "but I can offer up a possible explanation." Our attention turned to Dev, giving him the floor.

"Nothing about Zach's identity would be given to the press until his family is informed of his discovery."

"Dev's right," Clark agreed. "From last night's digging, I also learned that Zach's mother went into a deep depression after the kidnapping and committed suicide a couple of years later. So until they can reach Alec Finch, the identity of the body will not be released to the news."

"Is that why they've kept Odelia's name out of the news too?" asked Greg.

"Most likely," answered Dev. "She knows it's Zach from the questioning, but the police don't want the press hounding her for information." Dev looked at me. "You didn't tell anyone about Zach, did you, Odelia?"

As I thought about the question, I felt a blush creep up my neck and over my face like a quickie fever.

"Uh-oh. From the look of her," said my husband, "I'd say she did."

Now everyone's eyes were on me. "Yes," I said, confessing to my sin. "I told Jolene and Jill at work, and Zee." Then I quickly added, "But I told them all not to say anything to anyone. And Mom knows, of course."

"I'd say you can count on Jill and Jolene

telling their spouses," said Dev. "What about your mother, Odelia? She has that gossipy blog."

"I threatened to lock Grace up if she blogged about it," said Greg with pride.

"And I reminded her before she left our house last night," I added, "that she could not talk about it on her bus trip today either. She wasn't happy about any of our warnings, but if we're lucky and she's smart, she'll comply."

Clark snorted. I turned to him. "What?"

"Nothing," Clark said and pushed the last of his meal between his lips and chewed.

"Considering that the press has yet to come calling on Odelia," noted Dev, "it might be safe to say that they still don't know about Zach, but that won't last long. Someone somewhere is going to talk. It might even be a leak inside the police department or another video could pop up with a clear photo of Odelia or of the corpse. Hopefully, they've been able to contact Alec Finch by now, so expect the news to explode any time."

"And Odelia's name with it?" asked Greg with concern.

"Maybe. Maybe not," answered Dev. "Depends on how much information is released." Dev looked at me. "Do the car wash people know your name?"

I nodded. "Maybe not off the top of their heads, but I'm a regular and belong to their frequent wash program, so I'm in their computer system. If they go through that day's sales, they could figure it out."

"A few dollars slipped to one of the car wash people and your name is out there, sis," said Clark. "So expect it to go public at some point."

I put my fork down and played with the stem of my wine glass. I needed to get my mind off of future media harassment. So far my name had been mentioned very little when it came to my escapades, and I wanted to keep it that way. I brought up another subject. "Maybe this does have something to do with Willie." The three men kept eating on autopilot, but their eyes were on me. "I mean," I continued, "if Zach's dad was some big mover and shaker in investments, maybe he and Willie did cross swords at some point. It still doesn't explain why anyone would know my connection to Willie, but it might be something worth looking into."

Clark shook his head and swallowed his food. "Willie's never met him. I checked." He shot a sideways grin at Dev before continuing. Dev looked at him without so much as a blink. "He says he knows of the guy," Clark continued, "but they've never met in person or on a business level, so he can't imagine this having anything to do with him. But he did say this Alec Finch has a far reach." He looked around the table at all of us. "Willie is as concerned and perplexed by the kid ending up in Odelia's car as the rest of us."

"And what about the other possibility?" asked Greg. "Any word there?"

"None," Clark said. "We're still working on that connection."

"And what, pray tell, is that connection?" asked Dev. He put down his fork, wiped his mouth with the napkin from his lap, and waited. Dev was not someone who could be sidestepped. I knew from experience that he wouldn't budge until he got an answer.

Clark started to say something, but I held up a hand like a low flag. "It's no secret," I said to Dev. "It's something Fehring and the FBI are also looking into." Dev's blue eyes settled on me with expectation. "It's Elaine Powers," I finally admitted in a low whisper. "They're wondering if this has something to do with her."

A hush fell over the table as if I'd just tried to conjure up Beelzebub in a dark room. After nearly a full minute of silence, Dev picked up his fork and took another bite of his food. Greg chewed on bread. Clark drank some club soda. Finally, Dev asked, "And?" I remained still, hoping Clark would field this one.

"And nothing," my brother answered. "We're trying to contact her, but no one has a direct line of communication." Everyone turned to me, even Greg.

"I have no idea how to reach her," I answered, a smidge of defensiveness in my voice. "She just seems to pop up in the oddest places and at the weirdest times." Finished, I pushed my plate away. "But like I told the police, this really doesn't sound like her."

"No, it doesn't," agreed Dev. "Hitmen don't advertise their work, not to mention she seems oddly protective of Odelia." He paused. "Unless someone is trying to flush Powers out."

"That's another theory," I told Dev. "Since there doesn't seem to be a direct connection to me yet, the cops are wondering if someone is trying to force Elaine or Willie out of the shadows."

"The cops are also going back and looking at all of our past run-ins with criminals," Greg told him. "Just to see if anything clicks there."

Also finished with his food, Dev pushed his plate away and took a sip of his beer. Clark and Greg finished their meals, and the waiter came and cleared our plates. When he asked us about dessert and coffee, we waved him off. The check came. Greg grabbed it, but Dev snatched it out of his hand. "I did the inviting," he said to Greg. "I'll do the paying." We knew better than to argue.

After the waiter took the check and Dev's credit card, Dev turned to me and said in a quiet, even tone that meant business, "Willie is one thing, but if I catch sight of Elaine Powers, she's going down. Got that? And I won't care if it's on my final day on the job." He swiveled his head around the table, letting his eyes rest on Greg and Clark in turn before finally coming back to me. "You all got that?"

SEVEN

The next morning as I was cleaning up from the impromptu party of the night before, Clark showed up at my front door. "Got some coffee, sis?" he asked as soon as I let him in.

"It'll just take a sec," I said as we headed into the kitchen.

Clark took a seat at the kitchen table. "I'm assuming Greg's off to work already since Wainwright wasn't at the door."

"You assume correctly," I said with a smile as I started a cup of coffee for him. "It was tough getting Greg out of bed this morning, but he was a trooper."

Clark eyed me up and down, taking in my sloppy attire. "Nice outfit," he quipped. "I can see why Greg has the hots for you."

I stuck my tongue out at my brother. "You want that coffee or not?" That shut him up.

The party had been fun and had lasted past midnight in spite of the fact that most of the guests had to be at work this morning. But at least today was Friday so they only had to suffer through one day before the weekend. The surprise guest the night before had been Steele. He'd called from Switzerland to give Dev his personal good wishes after receiving an email from Jill about Dev's retirement and move. For Steele it was early morning, and he sounded fresh and chipper voicing his congratulations over the speaker on Jill's cell phone. In spite of saying he didn't want any fuss made, I could tell that Dev was touched by the outpouring of affection from the small gathering.

Near the end of the party I saw Clark, Dev, and Fehring in a corner, their three heads together, brows furrowed with concern. I had no doubt it was about Zach Finch and my involvement, since every now and then one of them would look my way. Had Clark not been in the mix, I would have thought for sure that Dev and Fehring were discussing me as the top suspect. I also wondered if Clark was picking up anything useful. He might once have been a cop and he might be a close friend of Dev's, but the bottom line was that he was no longer law enforcement in the legal sense. Whatever they told him would only stretch so far.

"So what was that pow-wow about last night?" I asked Clark as I placed a mug of fresh coffee in front of him.

"What pow-wow?" Clark asked before taking a large gulp of the hot coffee without so much as a flinch. His palate must be made of the same stuff used to line oven mitts.

I grabbed a mug of my own and joined him at the kitchen table. "I saw you, Dev, and Fehring clustered together in a corner last night."

"Just swapping war stories, sis." He looked around the kitchen. "Got any eggs on ya?"

I blew over my coffee and took a small sip before getting up. "If you wanted breakfast, you just had to ask," I told him. I went over to the fridge and pulled out a carton of eggs. "Omelet? Fried? Scrambled? Name your poison."

"Scrambled with some onions and mushrooms, if you've got them." He gave me a wide smile. "Any bacon in that fridge?"

I turned to my brother. "Did you see a Denny's sign in front of this house?" Instantly, I was reminded of Special Agent Shipman's snotty remark to me about Starbucks. Oh well, what can I say? I'm a plagiarist.

In response, Clark's smile turned upside down. "Mom only has high-fiber cereal and soy milk on hand for breakfast."

"And that's why she's skinny and we're not," I shot at him as I grabbed a few veggies, bacon, and some cheddar cheese from the fridge to go along with the eggs. "Sourdough good for your toast? And we only have turkey bacon." Clark nodded and winked at me. He knew I wasn't really peeved at being pressed into service as a short-order cook. I loved spending time with my half brother, even if it did mean wielding a spatula. I chopped some onion and sliced a couple mushrooms, throwing them into a skillet sizzling with a bit of butter and crushed basil. Before I cracked an egg into a bowl, I zeroed my eyes in on Clark's. "Eggs for information."

"What information?" he asked.

"What were you, Dev, and Fehring talking about last night?" I tapped the egg gently on the side of the glass bowl, emptied its contents into it, and grabbed another egg. "Two or three eggs?"

"Just two, sis." He patted his middle. "Gotta watch my girlish figure." My brother wasn't skinny, but neither was he fat. When we first met, he was battling a hefty bulge around his middle. Since then he'd lost his gut and had settled into a stocky but solid physique that he maintained with regular exercise and semi-healthy eating. "Oh, what the hell," he said, "let's live dangerously. Make it three."

I gave the cooking veggies a stir and beat the eggs with a little milk, hot sauce, salt, and pepper. The bacon was the precooked microwavable kind. I placed a few slices on a paper towel and slipped it into the micro-wave. As soon as I had the eggs in the pan, all I had to do was poke the button to get it going.

A few minutes later, I placed Clark's breakfast in front of him, refreshed his cof-fee, and joined him again at the table. While I'd been cooking, Muffin came in from the bedroom, where she'd been having her first nap of the morning, and said hello to Clark. The small animal loved attention and my brother, and she had whined until he'd put her on his lap and stroked her until his food came. When he put her back down on the floor, she went in search of a suitable place for her next nap. Being a much-loved and well-fed cat in our house was exhausting business requiring no fewer than a dozen long naps a day.

"So," I prodded, "what was the pow-wow about last night?"

Clark swallowed the eggs in his mouth and looked at me. "Tell me, sis, would you mind terribly if I asked Andrea Fehring out?"

My coffee cup was to my lips and coffee was flowing into my mouth just as his question hit my brain. I didn't know whether to spit the coffee back into the cup, try swallowing it without choking, or just spray it all over my brother. It was a toss-up, with door number three in the lead. At the last minute I swallowed the coffee in my mouth slow and easy to avoid a coughing fit. The exercise took several starts and stops while Clark continued shoveling eggs into his mouth like he hadn't eaten in a week — or just dropped a big-assed bomb in the middle of my kitchen table.

"You're kidding me, right?" I finally squeaked out.

He shrugged like he couldn't see the problem. "Dev says she's currently unattached, and I think she's pretty interesting and attractive."

I put my coffee cup down on the table and stared at my brother with my right eye closed as if that might help me focus better. Obviously, one of us was seeing a box of demons and the other a fistful of daisies. "The fact that you live in Arizona and Fehring lives here aside, you don't see even a teensy-weensy bit of a conflict?" I leaned back in my chair and crossed my arms over my chest. When he didn't answer, I tacked on, "You know, like the fact that she's trying to nail my ass for murder?"

Clark tore off a piece of buttered toast and popped it into his mouth. He chewed and washed it down with coffee. He held up his mug. "Got a refill?"

I got up and fetched the glass carafe from the coffeemaker. Day to day Greg and I used our little Keurig coffeemaker, but since our bigger coffeepot, the one we used for large gatherings, was still out from last night, I had brewed a whole pot when Clark showed up this morning. I knew my brother was a coffee hound. Now I was considering using the heavy glass pot as a weapon to knock some sense into his thick skull. That would really give Andrea Fehring something to question me about. As if reading my thoughts, Clark held out his coffee mug to me but leaned his head and body backward as if offering a placating treat to a growling dog. I poured the coffee and put the carafe back in the kitchen to remove any temptation to violence.

"Andrea is not trying to nail you for that murder," Clark said after taking a swig from his full mug. "It's pretty clear to both Dev and me that she doesn't think you did it, though I can't vouch for the feds. If Andrea had any proof at all about your involvement, you wouldn't be here making me breakfast."

I returned to the table with my ears pricked with interest. "Did she say they are no longer considering me a suspect?"

"Not in so many words," Clark answered. "One thing is for sure: I don't think she likes that Greg Shipman much."

"That makes two of us," I huffed. "What did she say about him?"

"Again, not much. It was more of what she wasn't saying. I got the definite feeling Andrea is being shoved aside by Shipman on this investigation. Dev got the same feeling." He polished off his eggs and wiped his mouth with a napkin he pulled from the holder we kept on the table. It was a blue and white ceramic windmill with *Solvang* printed along the bottom. It didn't match anything in our kitchen, but we'd picked it up on our first day trip together after we'd gotten married — a kitschy but useful doodad representing our new domesticity.

"Did you tell her last night that Willie had nothing to do with this?" I asked.

"I wasn't sure how to," he answered, "without tipping her off that I might be connected to him, along with you and Greg." He selected a banana from the bowl we kept on the table and started peeling it.

While he bit off a third of the banana with one bite, I went back to staring at him in disbelief. "And you don't think that little bit of information — you know, your connection to Willie Proctor — might be a deterrent to your dating life?"

He shrugged. "Could be if anything came of it." He took another bite, chewed, and swallowed. "I was just going to ask her to dinner, Odelia, not ask her to move to Arizona and live with me. Besides, I work for a solid and legitimate company. I don't work for Willie directly."

"Right." Again I crossed my arms and gave him a one-eyed stare, wondering how such a smart and accomplished man could be so dense. "Do you think, Clark, that maybe you could put your libido on hold until after I'm no longer a suspect in a murder investigation?"

"Sure, sis," he answered with a grin. "But I really don't think you're a suspect. At least I don't think you're near the top of the list, if there is one. Besides, I didn't plan on asking Andrea out immediately. If she's half the cop I think she is, she'd never say yes while all this was going on." He tossed the banana peel onto his plate and wiped his mouth again.

"Nice to know," I said with thick sarcasm

as I picked up his plate and took it to the kitchen sink. On my way back to the table, I asked, "Is that why you came over this morning — to ask my blessing in your pursuit of Detective Fehring?"

He grinned. "I also wanted a home-cooked breakfast." He leaned back in his chair, stretched out his legs, and patted his full stomach. "And there's something else."

I raised my eyebrows in anticipation. "You found out more about Zach Finch?"

He shook his head and took another swallow of coffee. "No, but I did get a lead on Elaine Powers."

I sat up at attention. "You've made contact with her?"

"Not exactly, but I found out how to make contact — or at least how potential clients make contact." When I waved my hand in a circle of encouragement, he continued. "Most of her jobs come from referrals."

I nodded. "She told me that once."

"And also from a guy who works at a dive bar in Redondo Beach."

"Redondo Beach?" I asked with surprise.

"Yep. I'm betting this guy isn't the only contact Powers has out there," Clark said. "She probably has a few other slimy associates throughout Southern California that help her connect with potential clients, but

I uncovered the one in Redondo."

My skin crawled at the thought of a killer hotline. "Did you see this guy and ask him to have her contact us?"

"It doesn't work like that." Clark sat up straight. He was moving from casual into a more serious mode. I'd seen him do it many times when he was about to say something he wanted to make sure people heard and understood. "We pay him to place an ad."

"An ad? Where?"

Clark shrugged. "Who knows. It's probably some online message board. Anyway, we ask this guy to place an ad explaining what we want."

I felt the top of my head levitate in disbelief. "Right out in the open, people say 'hey, I got someone I need to have whacked; call me'?" I held a hand up to my mouth and ear like I was holding an old-fashioned phone.

"Not exactly," Clark said, chuckling softly. "I'm sure the guy has some special code or wording to fit the types of jobs requested. If Powers is interested, she'll make contact with us through the ad, but there's no money-back guarantee she will."

"What does it cost?"

"A couple hundred just to place the ad and hope she answers," Clark said.

I got up and went into the kitchen. Turning on the water in the sink, I rinsed Clark's breakfast dishes and those I'd used to make the food and placed them in the nearly full dishwasher. I added dishwasher detergent, shut the door, and turned the knob to get the machine going. Then I stood in front of it thinking while I listened to the water flowing into the stainless-steel box.

"Are you thinking, sis, or taking a nap?" Clark asked from his perch at the table.

I turned around and leaned back against the counter. "Let's place that ad," I told him.

"And what should we say?" He drained his coffee and got up to bring the mug to me. I motioned for him to bring mine, too. He grabbed it and placed both on the counter. I opened the dishwasher, put them both on the top rack, and shut the door with determination.

"Just say," I told Clark after turning back to him, " 'Mother, call Dottie. Urgent.' "

"Dottie?" Clark asked. His left eyebrow arched with curiosity.

"Elaine once told Greg and me that I reminded her of Dottie, her dead sister," I explained. "She'll know immediately it's me."

EIGHT

After Clark left I was antsy. The house was clean and everything back in place thanks to Cruz. The debris from the party the night before was gone. Even our laundry was up-to-date. What to do? What to do? It was rare I was alone with such a large chunk of free time. Grabbing my Kindle, cell phone, and a jacket, I went out to our back patio and settled on a chaise to read. Muffin followed me out.

The weather was damp again, reverting back to the cloudiness of a few days before. There was even a forecast of more rain over the next few days. The warmth and sunshine of Wednesday had been just an oasis in a series of storm fronts coming at Southern California. Living so close to the beach, it was particularly damp in our area. Overhead, the sky was ash gray and the clouds moved with purpose, but I still enjoyed being outside and would stay until it got too chilly to sit still. Muffin was in my lap, curled into a tight little disk. I could feel the warmth of her body and feel the vibration of her purring through my pants. It was as comforting as a hug or a basket of Jill's scones.

I read a few pages in my book but couldn't concentrate. I tried switching to a different book, but that didn't help. The idea of contacting Elaine Powers weighed on me like a lead apron used by dentists for X-rays. Clark had said that the bar opened at ten. He was going there straight from our house to talk to the bartender before the place got busy and see if he could place the ad per the instructions one of his shady contacts had given him.

Would Elaine answer? More importantly, was she involved in this mess? My gut still said she wasn't, but it wouldn't hurt to check. And once the ad or message posting was done, how long would it take for her to answer? I put the Kindle down on the small redwood table next to the chaise and closed my eyes. While my right hand stroked Muffin on autopilot, I played out the events of the past few days in my head like a movie, the commentary being the information we knew so far about Zach and his disappearance all those years ago.

Picking up my cell phone, I scanned my emails for the photo of Zach in my trunk that Greg had sent to me so I'd have it handy. I studied the photo of the naked kid, although he wasn't really a kid anymore but an adult in his mid-twenties. I enlarged the photo. He looked healthy enough — lean but not skinny. I couldn't see his chest, just a side angle, but his limbs, especially his thighs and upper arms, appeared well-defined and muscled like he spent a good amount of time working out. Wherever he'd been, he hadn't been shut away in chains in a dark room and left to rot.

"Where have you been, Zach?" I asked the photo out loud. "We need to know." In my lap, Muffin raised her head and looked at me with sleepy eyes. After a long, wide-mouthed yawn, the cat lowered her chin back to my cushy thigh and closed her eyes again. She obviously didn't have the answer and didn't give a damn about being clue-less. I, on the other hand, didn't like being in the dark, especially in things that con-cerned me directly. I glanced at the time on the phone. It was almost eleven. Clark would be at the bar now trying to leave a message for Elaine. I stared at the phone, willing him to call me with an update. Bug-ging Clark with a text or a call was out of the question. He'd specifically told me before leaving this morning not to do that, that he would get in touch with me if something happened. In response, I'd stuck my tongue out at him for the second time. Even at my age, you could still do that to your brother.

I ran a hand through my hair and scratched my scalp. It felt itchy. It was my nerves, I knew that. My nerves and feeling powerless to do anything. Before a full-blown breakdown could occur, my phone rang. It was Greg.

"I just wanted to check up on you, sweetheart," my husband said in a concerned voice. "How's your day going?"

"I'm about to jump out of my skin with nothing to do," I told him. "I just want to find out more about Zach, but there's no trail for me to follow."

"Why don't you give Zee a call and go shopping or something?"

"She's off doing something for her church today or else I would," I told him. "I'm almost thinking about going into work, but I don't have that much to do there either. And Mom won't be back until around dinnertime." I paused. I hadn't gone on my usual walk this morning because of waking late and needing to clean up from the party.

"I wish Wainwright was here. I'd walk the bejeebers out of him."

"You don't need the dog to take a walk, Odelia, although he missed today's walk too. He's always a bit antsy when you two don't take one."

"Maybe I will go for a walk," I said. "It's just more fun with Wainwright."

From the muffled sound on the other end, I knew Greg was softly laughing. "He feels the same, believe me. Go for a long, long walk, sweetheart. It will do you good."

"By the way, Clark stopped by this morning shortly after you left. He traded me information for breakfast. He got a lead on how to contact Elaine. It's not a direct contact or guaranteed, but he thinks he found out how to at least send her a smoke signal."

"Good," Greg said. "Hopefully, we can soon rule her out and move in another direction."

"That's the problem, Greg," I whined. "There *is* no other direction. Usually we have something more to go on: coworkers to talk to, family members, favorite hangouts. This kid comes with absolutely no threads for us to pull, unless we go to Illinois and start nosing around his old high-school classmates."

"Do you have the information on the Finch kidnapping that Clark and your mother found?" Greg asked after a short pause. In the background I could hear the industrious buzz of Ocean Breeze Graphics, his printing and graphic design business. Greg and his staff were always busy, even when the economy tanked, and over the years he and his partner Boomer had grown the company from one shop in Huntington Beach into three. The other two were Mountain Breeze Graphics, which Boomer ran in Colorado, and Desert Breeze Graphics, which Boomer's brother ran in Phoenix. There had been talk of a fourth store opening, possibly in northern California or even Seattle, but it had been shelved until the economy turned around. Personally, I was hoping to see an Island Breeze Graphics open in Maui and had volunteered Greg and I to go over to set it up and get it running.

"Yes," I answered, "Clark emailed me everything he found on it." I knew where Greg was going with this. He was going to suggest that I go through it and research anything I could find that looked interesting. It could be busywork — or maybe not. I'd thought of it myself but honestly was just in a pity-party mood.

"If you haven't yet, Odelia," Greg said in an almost schoolmarmish voice, "why don't you read through it and see what you find? Maybe you can do some online research on the names of the kids he went to the game with, if they're mentioned. I'm sure wherever Zach's been, he wasn't using his real name, but I'll bet those kids are still around."

Bingo! Told ya.

"I'm sure the feds have already reached out to them," I said. I shifted my legs, careful not to wake Muffin, although why I bothered escaped me. She sure isn't shy about waking us when she wants something.

"Maybe they have or maybe they're waiting until Zach's identity is released." Another pause. I heard someone say something to Greg and Greg answer. Then Greg said to me, "Sweetheart, I have to go and take care of something in a minute. If you're bored and feeling helpless, then do something to take control of the situation. Do some research. Make some calls. Just be careful not to tread on Shipman's toes too much. We don't need the FBI as an enemy. Fehring might forgive you, but I'm not sure the feds would." Another pause, but this time I didn't hear anyone interrupt him. "It's not like you to be so passive and at a loss for ideas in such a situation. What's really up?"

I gave it some quick thought. "I don't know. I think I'm kind of bummed about Dev leaving."

"Yeah," Greg said gently. "Me too."

"And I don't like that I was specifically targeted in this."

"Yeah, me either," he agreed. "So get to work on it as much as you can and we'll discuss what you find tonight." Another pause, then Greg said, "By the way, I talked to the insurance company. There isn't anything they can do about your car. It's not a loss claim or a damage claim. Their thinking is that we'll get the vehicle back when the cops are done with it, so for now it's in limbo."

"So I keep leasing the car I'm using until the police decide to release my car back to me?" I didn't like the sound of that one bit. "That could get very expensive, especially if the insurance company isn't going to cover it."

"Yep," Greg confirmed. "So how about you and me going car hunting this weekend — maybe look at one of those hybrids? We've discussed getting you one before."

"But I liked my car," I whined.

"Then we'll get you another just like it,"

Greg said, placating me. "We'll sell yours when we get it back. It's paid for, so it's not a big deal. You really didn't want it back, did you?"

"No, I really didn't." I shivered but not from the chill in the air. "Whenever I think about it, it kind of creeps me out. It would be like driving around with a ghost in the car."

Greg softly laughed. "That's what I thought you'd say. We'll go look at cars this weekend, unless you want to start window shopping today on your own."

"A hybrid would be nice, but I'll wait for you. I might look up some models online though." I smiled at nothing in particular. "You are so good to me, Greg."

"It's my job, sweetheart; my main career. This graphic design and printing stuff is just a hobby."

NINE

"The deed is done," Clark said when I answered my cell again. "Now we just have to wait it out." The call had come shortly after I'd hung up from Greg. I had tried to go back to reading, but it was of no use. It was also starting to rain. Very small but steady drops hit the roof of our patio, making a light tapping noise.

"I'm not good at waiting, Clark," I told him, as if he didn't already know that about me. "It drives me nuts." Muffin had woken up at the sound of the ringing phone and was now nudging my hand to be petted. I rubbed her behind her ears. She started purring again, lowered her head, and went back to sleep.

"Isn't your middle name Patience?" Clark asked.

"Mom slapped that on me as a joke. I'm sure of it."

He laughed. "What are you up to now?"

120

"I don't know," I told him. "Greg suggested I do a fine-tooth combing of the information you found on the kidnapping to see if I can find any of Zach's friends from back then. I also thought I might walk down to the beach, but right now it's raining. What are you up to?"

"Not sure. I have some work to do for the office, so I might go back to Mom's and take care of that."

"Come on over later for dinner," I told him. "I'm thinking of either throwing a beef stew into the slow cooker or making meatloaf. It's that kind of day, and I have the stuff on hand for both. Mom should be back by then, so bring her along if she's not too tired. Have you heard from her?"

"Yeah, just a few minutes ago. She said she won two hundred dollars playing a video poker machine." He laughed. "Figures. She hardly gambles, and when she does, she wins. I also checked her blog, and there's nothing there about the body found in your trunk. She posted about her windfall in the casino and about the show she saw last night, but that was it."

"Good," I said and meant it. "Although once the news breaks about Zach's identity, she might decide to blog about it, seeing that it will be out in the public arena."

"Yeah, I'm betting that too," Clark said with a sigh. "But as long as it's *after* the story goes public. I also checked to make sure there's no way to track her physical whereabouts on her blog. I was pleased to see she's been pretty careful to keep that private. All it says is that she's a transplant from New England."

I shuddered. "That's all we'd need right now — some ghoulish crackpot becoming a fan of Mom's."

The rain was coming down harder, and it was getting colder. Still on the phone, I tucked my Kindle under one arm and Muffin under the other and made my way inside. The cat didn't protest. Unlike Seamus, Muffin enjoyed being carted around like a furry sack of bones. "It's getting pretty nasty out," I told Clark once I was inside and had put the cat down on the floor. "I might not make that walk."

"Then I think going through the details of the kidnapping information will be a good job for you today," Clark said. "That and making a nice big pot of beef stew."

"I gather you're voting for that over the meatloaf?" I smiled as I spoke.

"It's not even a contest," he answered. "Any of that chocolate cake left that Jill brought last night?"

"Yep," I said after double-checking the fridge just in case Greg had taken the leftovers into work. Once again, I marveled at my husband's intelligence. He'd taken the leftover store-bought cheesecake and left Jill's cake for us. "Be here around seven."

"Okay then," Clark said. "I'll see you then, with or without Mom. Can I bring anything?"

"How about some crusty rolls or French bread?"

"I'm on it. Just call if you need anything else or come across anything interesting in your research." He hesitated. "And call me if you hear from Elaine Powers."

I saluted the phone and ended the call.

After talking to Clark, I prepared the ingredients for the stew and threw it all into my slow cooker. It would be perfect by dinnertime. Then I stretched out on the recliner with my laptop on my lap and kicked the foot rest up. Not happy with my lap being occupied, Muffin curled up on the back of the chair behind my head, purring a soft lullaby into my ear as I read every word of the information on Zach's kidnapping that Clark had been able to get his hands on.

As Clark had said the night before, it had happened after a Friday-night football game. Zach had gone to the game with three buddies. After the game, they had stopped off at a local pizza place to celebrate their team's win. All three of his friends confirmed to the police that they had dropped Zach off at home between 10:40 and 10:50, before his curfew of eleven. One friend told the police he remembered Zach letting himself in through the side door by the garage. None of the other boys remembered seeing any evidence of Zach's parents or sister when they left Zach.

Sister? I didn't recall anyone — the police or Clark or even my mother during her short research — mentioning a sister. I continued reading, looking for other signs of her. She showed up several pages later in the report. She was two years older than Zach and had graduated from high school earlier that year. At the time of Zach's disappearance, she'd been attending a local community college and lived at home. Her name was Jean Finch. I did a search of the report for her name and located the report of her questioning. The night of Zach's disappearance, Jean had gone out with her boyfriend, Ryan Wright, and another young couple to the movies. She'd returned home before midnight and claimed she'd gone straight to bed after saying hello to her mother, who'd been waiting up for her children. Jean reported that her mother had asked if she'd seen Zach while out because he was late, and Jean responded that she had not.

I searched again, this time looking for the mother's testimony. Her name was Maryanne Finch. She'd told the police that after Jean came home, she had remained in her chair, watching late-night TV and waiting for her son. She didn't remember when she fell asleep, but she woke up around sunrise. Thinking Zach had come in but had not wanted to disturb her, she went to his room to check on him but found it empty and his bed not slept in. That was when she woke her husband. According to Mrs. Finch, she was the parent who had stayed up late waiting for their children, stating that her husband kept long hours at the office and was often too tired in the evenings to stay up much past ten.

Attached to Clark's report was a photo of the Finch family taken from a newspaper. Maryanne Finch looked like the typical Midwest wife of a wealthy man. Her hair was honey blond and coiffed in a beautifully cut style that I remembered as being in vogue during that time period. In the photo she was wearing tennis togs and looked fit and confident. The rest of the family was also dressed in tennis clothing. The caption read that the Finch family had captured first place in their country club's annual family tennis tournament. It had been their second win in a row, and from the ages of the kids, I guessed this photo had been taken shortly before Zach evaporated. It was possibly the summer between then and his sister's high-school graduation. Next to his wife, Alec Finch was tall and tan and held his racket like a weapon at the ready. Mr. and Mrs. Finch were flanked by their offspring. Maryanne had her arms around the waists of both her husband and son. On the other side of Alec was Jean, who looked a lot like her mother but with her father's strong jaw. Both kids held their rackets in both hands like their father. All four flashed smiles of perfect white teeth and looked ready to beat off anyone who threatened their tight-knit family.

But someone had threatened the family and torn it apart by grabbing Zach, and tennis rackets and tournament-winning backhands had not been able to stop it.

Toggling from the screen with the report, I brought up a clean page and started typing out the names of the players: Alec Finch, Maryanne Finch, Jean Finch, and Zach Finch, for starters. I put the names in a table I created first and in a column headed *Family.* Then in a column with the heading of *Friends,* I added the names of Zach's friends who'd been with him that night: Chris Cook, Ben Myers, and Nathan Glick. I also added Ryan Wright, Jean's boyfriend, since he was mentioned in the report. I wanted to look them all up and see if I could find out where they were today.

According to Clark, Maryanne Finch had died by her own hand a few years after Zach's disappearance, so I didn't need to check on her. Still, I dug a little deeper into Clark's information until I came across the notation about Zach's mother. Despondent after her son's kidnapping, Maryanne Finch fell into a downward spiral of depression, booze, and drugs until she finally took her own life two years later. She'd been dramatic about it. Using her husband's handgun that he kept in the house for protection, Maryanne had shot herself in the head while sitting in her favorite chair in front of the TV. It had been on the anniversary of Zach's failure to return from the football game. The report made me shudder.

Several years before, one of my friends had shot herself in the head. It had been the event that had brought Dev and Greg and I together. It had been filmed by her webcam, and I still have nightmares about watching Sophie kill herself.

Pushing that horror out of my head, I started the search on the various players, then remembered Barbara Marracino, a woman who did professional online searches to supplement her retirement. Her late husband, Larry, had been a corporate investigator, and Steele and I had used him a great deal over the years. Barbara was still running the online search business but not the fieldwork her husband had done, since she had trouble moving due to arthritis in her back and legs. Her research business didn't just involve investigations but also research for writers and other people who needed unusual or historical information but didn't have the time to do it themselves. We had used Barbara several months ago off the books, and she had come up with amazing results and was quick as a bunny about it.

I picked up my cell phone and scrolled through my contacts, hoping I'd had the presence of mind to save her number. I had, and I called. As soon as Barbara answered, I said, "Barbara, it's Odelia Grey. How are you?"

"Not bad for an old broad with one foot in the grave." She followed up her words with a throaty laugh. "It's nice to hear from you, Odelia. How are you doing, and how is Mr. Steele?"

"I'm fine, thanks," I responded, "and Mike Steele just got married."

"Seriously?" she asked with another short laugh.

"Yep. He's on his honeymoon as we speak." I paused to form a short gap between the pleasantries and the purpose of my call. "Barbara, do you have time to do a few searches for me?"

She paused too, but hers was longer, and I don't think it was to change subjects. "I'm no longer in the business, Odelia. In fact, by the end of this week I'll be moving into a rest home."

I was taken back, but not that much. While Barbara was younger than my mother, who lived in her own place and was always on the go, she was not in the same good physical condition as Mom. This move probably meant her condition had deteriorated. "I'm very sorry to hear that," I told her.

"I'm not," she said in a voice filled with relief. "It's really getting difficult for me to move around. My mind is still sharp, but my body can't keep up, and lately my emphysema has worsened. I'm in a wheelchair now, but I'm a long ways from being a spitfire like that husband of yours." She laughed. "My son's house is too small and has too many steps inside and out for him to take me in, but he found a lovely place close to his home that can give me the care I need. I'll actually be able to see him and his family more often now." Her tone brightened at the last bit of information. Another pause, a tight raspy intake of breath, then, "But I had to give up the research biz. I hated to do it because it kept my mind focused, but them's the breaks."

In spite of her trials and tribulations, Barbara had an amazing upbeat attitude. "I'm sorry to hear that, Barbara, but happy that you'll be well looked after," I said, trying to keep the disappointment out of my voice. "Do you have anyone you can refer me to?"

"Why not do it yourself?" she suggested. "You're a smart cookie and probably used to doing legal research. I don't work magic. I just know and subscribe to a bushel of specialty sites that you're probably not even aware exist."

I used search sites all the time, but mostly legal sites or free ones or the ones that allowed you to pay per use instead of requiring a subscription. "Can you send me the links to some of your favorite sites and I'll look into it?"

"Tell you what, Odelia," Barbara said. "I'll do you one better. You and Mr. Steele have always been good to me and to my dear Larry. I still have several months left on my various subscriptions that I won't use, and they don't do refunds for unused time. How about I send you the links and the pass-words, and you can use them until the time on them runs out?"

Now that was an offer I couldn't refuse. "That's very generous of you, Barbara." I gave it some quick thought. "But I have a counter offer. How about I pay you for the remainder of those subscriptions, then when they come up for renewal I'll let them lapse and set up my own subscriptions for the services I think I'll use going forward?"

"You don't need to do that."

"I'd like to," I told her with conviction. "I'm sure you could use the refund money, and I'd consider it a training period without having to pay full price. When you email me the information, also email me your new address. I'll drop a check in the mail."

There was silence on the other end of the phone while Barbara considered the deal. Finally, she said, "Here's my final offer, Odelia. You check out the sites and just send me the money for the ones you think you'll need. I don't want you paying for subscriptions just to be nice."

"It's a deal," I agreed, knowing the check would include payment for sites I would use and those I wouldn't.

"I'll compile and send you the information in an email as soon as we get off the horn," she said. "My son and grandson are coming over tonight to dismantle my computer setup and move it to their house. My grandson will be using it for school, so I need to remove anything personal and sensitive. I'm going to be getting a tablet or small laptop for what little Internet access I'll be needing once I'm in the home."

Wow, talk about timing. If I'd waited to call Barbara, I might not have reached her. The information she'd be giving me would be very valuable, both for my own snooping as well as what I did for the law firm. After we said goodbye, I put a reminder in my calendar to send flowers to Barbara's new place to wish her well in her new home.

While I waited for the information from Barbara, I continued reading the report. The morning the Finches discovered that Zach had not slept in his own bed, his parents had called his friends and learned nothing except that they had dropped him off the night before. They called other friends of

Zach's, including a girl he'd been dating off and on, but no one knew anything about Zach's whereabouts. His buddies had dropped him off, watched him go into the house through the side entrance, and then he had simply vanished down a rabbit hole, never to be seen again — until he ended up as a corpse in my trunk.

Why now? Why *my* trunk? I didn't know this kid or his family. I needed to trace his journey from that night in Illinois until now in Southern California. I read on.

The Finches received a call from the kidnappers later that same day instructing them to leave two million dollars in a specific spot by six the next evening. The money would buy their son back. No police were to be involved or Zach would die. Once the money was delivered to the designated dropoff, the Finches were to wait until ten that night. At that time they would be given instructions on where to find Zach unharmed. According to the report, Alec Finch had gathered the money from various accounts and delivered it to an abandoned barn several counties away from their home. Zach had not been at the barn, nor did any instructions arrive as to where they could find him. The next day, the Finches waited again for more information, but none came.

That night they finally called the police and reported the crime.

I stopped reading and tried to put myself in the shoes of Zach's parents. Were they stupid or exercising caution by not involving the authorities sooner? Even though I did not have children of my own, I couldn't imagine the horror of a child gone missing. Tragically, it happened all the time. Sometimes the children were found shortly after. Sometimes they surfaced years later after escaping their abductors. But usually they weren't found at all or, if they were, they were identifiable only by their skeletal remains. Their disappearances remained unsolved mysteries and crimes while parents held out hope and prayed for signs of life or even signs of death, some believing that knowing their child was dead was preferable to the hell of limbo. To those parents, learning of the death of their son or daughter was closure — a deep, ugly, jagged wound that would never heal but could now stop bleeding.

It was too late for Maryanne Finch, but Alec Finch could now have that closure. If I were in Mr. Finch's shoes, I wouldn't stop until I learned the truth. I was searching for the truth myself, but I needed to find out what had happened to get my big butt off the short suspect list and the limelight off of Willie and Elaine. To do that, I had to find out the connection between the Finches and me. There had to be one. I seriously doubted that whomever had dumped the body was walking down the alley behind our home, spotted my car in the carport, and said to themselves, "Hey, this looks like a great place to dump a body!"

No, there had to be a connection between me and the Finches or whomever had dumped the body knew of my gift for finding corpses. It was too much of a coinky-dink, as Dev would say, that Zach's body had showed up out of the blue. I just had to find that connection and poke at it until it revealed the truth, and the sooner the better.

I got up and used the bathroom, then checked on the stew, giving it a good stir. It was lunchtime, so I made myself a fluffer-nutter — a peanut butter and marshmallow sandwich. My mother used to make these for me when I was a kid, and I've never lost my taste for them. Clark loves them too and it wasn't until I found my mother in Massachusetts that I realized that's where she'd picked up the recipe, not that there really was one. But, like lobster and whole-bellied fried clams, it is definitely a New England delicacy.

Due to their sticky nature, fluffernutters go best with hot beverages, and so do rainy days. I took my mug of hot tea and my sandwich and settled down at the kitchen table, positioning myself so I could look out our sliding doors into our cheerful backyard and patio, beyond which was the carport that now housed our rental car. We had a roomy garage, but that usually housed Greg's van. With all its customization, we couldn't afford to have it vandalized or broken into. Not that we lived in a bad neighborhood — we didn't — but why take the chance with something so valuable? I could easily get a rental if something happened to my wheels; Greg could not. And if both of our vehicles were in the garage at the same time, Greg could not easily transfer between his wheelchair and the van. Did whoever had dumped the body know that my car was always parked in the carport? Or had it been just dumb luck on their part to find it out in the open when they needed to get to it?

So many questions were whirling around in my head, it was beginning to bang and clank like an unbalanced washing machine.

I ate my sandwich and drank my tea and made the decision to follow the timeline of

Zach's disappearance from the date and point of origin. I could either follow the dots from the beginning of his ordeal or from the end, meaning my car trunk, but the end led me smack into a brick wall. At least it gave me something to do while I waited for Elaine to get my message and call me back . . . if she called.

After putting my dishes in the sink, I retrieved a yellow legal pad and pen from our home office and returned to the kitchen table. I plucked an apple from the fruit bowl on the table and took a big bite. Holding the fruit in my left hand, I turned the page horizontally with my right and got to work sketching out the timeline between bites.

Zach had gone missing eight years and four months earlier. I printed that date in small neat characters to the far left. Next to it I noted that the ransom had been paid but no Zach returned. On the far right I printed the date he'd been found in my trunk. The gap between yawned at me like a hungry mouth waiting to be fed. By the time I'd eaten my apple down to the core, I still hadn't added anything to the time gap.

My frustration with having no information was interrupted by my laptop dinging to tell me I had a new email. It was from

Barbara and contained all the information and passwords she had promised.

TEN

Barbara's email contained information and passwords for five different sites. Three of them I already knew something about, having used them myself a few times but never as a subscriber. The other two looked to be more for professional use and were accessed on a subscription-only basis. In fact, out of curiosity, I ran a Google search for them and came up with nothing. These were research sites not publicly listed on web search engines. I knew there was a deep web out there — a dark and often scary part of the Internet hidden from the general public. I didn't think these sites were part of the bowels of the Internet but maybe somewhere between where I usually poke and prod and the deep underground. At first review, I could see where these sites, particularly the stealthy ones, would be of great use.

I opened the first site unfamiliar to me

using Barbara's password and went to the user profile. As she had noted in her email, Barbara had changed the attached email address on the account to mine so that any search reports would come straight to me, but she had left her name and phone attached so that the folks running the site would think it was still her using it. She'd explained that she didn't want my information out there unless and until I decided to continue the subscription. She was being cautious, and I was thankful for that.

First I visited each site under Barbara's user name and jotted down the subscription information — the cost of each and how much time was left on the subscription, calculating the prorated amount I wanted to pay Barbara for their use. The three common search services had anywhere between one and two months left on them and were minimal in cost. From the use history of these search sites, it looked like Barbara hadn't been utilizing them much lately, probably because they were for amateurs. One of the deep search sites had less than a month left, and the other still had eight months to go on its subscription. Both of these were much more expensive. From their search histories, it looked like Barbara had discovered and been using the one with more time left the most in the past few months. It had obviously become her favorite. It was called, simply, Marigold. There wasn't a single thing about its name that indicated it could unlock information about anyone anywhere. Instead, the name conjured up thoughts of gardening tips or florists. I could even see a bakery with this name.

After jotting down the cost of the deep sites on my notepad, I paused and wondered if my brother and other people Willie employed used these sites. They always seemed to know a lot about people, even as much and often more than the police. And if these deep sites were not open to public search engines, someone would have to refer the site to you for you to even know about its existence. I could even see Elaine Powers using these powerful know-all Wizard of Oz sites for her dark dealings.

To test it, I put my name and birthdate into the Marigold search engine and waited. It had asked for more personal information to help the search along, but I wanted to see what the minimal brought up. A message popped up saying that the search was in progress and would be delivered to my email within two hours or less. It wasn't instantaneous, as I had hoped, but then a thorough search shouldn't be. I was almost afraid of what it would turn up. Not that I had anything to hide, but the more personal information the search uncovered, the scarier and less secure I would feel personally — yet, on the flip side, the more useful I would know this site to be for my snooping purposes. It was very expensive and I wanted to be sure it would be worth it. Barbara had thought so, and it looked to be the only site she'd been using lately for information on individuals or companies. She'd even noted in her email that Marigold was the best, in her opinion.

After drumming my fingers on the table for nearly a minute, I checked my email. Nothing. Not for the first time, I thought about what a joke my middle name of Patience was and how it mocked me.

Not wanting to waste time, I started plugging in the names of Zach's friends and family and got those searches going. Since Marigold was the priciest of the sites, I was determined to get my money's worth. All I had was names to go on, but I made a stab at birth years based on the ages they had been when Zach disappeared. One of the filters was place of birth. Since the kids were young, I inserted Illinois in on all of them. One after another, messages popped up letting me know each search was under way and would be delivered to my email box in two hours or less. That seemed to be the standard response time.

Once those searches were started, I checked my email. Still nothing, but only about fifteen minutes had passed. I got up and made myself a mug of hot chocolate. It was still raining, and the sky was gloomy and gray. Even though it was warm inside the house, I shivered and rubbed my arms through the long sleeves of my sweatshirt. It was a favorite of mine. It was the kind of clothing we all have — too old and raggedy to wear outside the house but as comforting as a fluffy afghan, so we never gave it up. I had a few of these, and so did Greg. Today's comfort ensemble was a maroon sweatshirt with *CAMBRIA* emblazoned across my chest in large white letters. It was embellished with pale green paint stains from when Greg and I had repainted the guest bathroom last year. I'd paired it today with equally worn and beat-up yoga pants. My hair was dirty and pulled back from my makeup-free face with a wide elastic headband; no wonder Clark had made that crack. Maybe I should use the two hours or less promised by the search site to shower and clean up.

Twenty minutes later, freshly showered

and shampooed and dressed in jeans and a nice casual V-neck sweater in teal over a white camisole, I checked my email again to find the search results for myself waiting.

I sent the report to the printer in our home office. Reading it online was easy enough, but I found I paid more attention to details when reading in hard print — and this thing I wanted to read in great detail. While it printed, I stirred and nuked my forgotten hot chocolate, then sat down with both and a yellow highlighter to see exactly what Marigold had found out about me.

Holy crap! It contained everything about me except which molar I had capped last.

Using the highlighter, I took note of my social security number, my place of birth, parents, education history, employment history, and all of my residences since I came into the world. My driver's license was noted, together with all vehicles I'd owned, along with their registration information and all tickets I'd received. Even my income was listed. I highlighted them all, including my notary commission information. I stopped reading when my eyes caught on a list of the crimes with which I'd been involved. They were noted under a heading called Criminal Activity. Not that I'd committed any of these crimes, which the report clarified by simply calling me "an interested party."

I scanned the list again and wished I'd had something stronger than cocoa in my mug. These were the murders and nefarious activities I'd stumbled upon in my capacity as a corpse magnet. Each contained a small summary, a list of involved individuals, and the outcome. If I ever had a memory lapse of all the trouble I'd gotten into over the years, here was the cheat sheet to remind me. I'd stored each one in a separate compartment in my brain, keeping them apart and shrouded in denial of their severity. It was my coping mechanism. But seeing them like this — in one bunch like overripe bananas, dark yellow and spotted with black — was a shock to my system, and a cold, icy stream started to run through my veins. I drained my mug and thought seriously about the bottle of scotch we kept in the cupboard.

There was even a reference to the person I'd shot and killed several years earlier. That entry was summed up with the words *determined self-defense.* The only crime not listed was the murder of Zach Finch. But hey, that was just a few days ago, and it was a bit comforting to see that Marigold wasn't on top of things as they happened.

So who or what is this Marigold? Was it a super program that pulled information from all available databases everywhere? Or was there a team of nerds sitting in a dark room in front of computers who took the search requests, then hacked into whatever database was needed to harvest the information? I looked over my report again. None of this information was a secret. It was all out there, mostly scattered through various government agency databases. For example, my notary commission was listed with the California Secretary of State. My license, driving record, and vehicle information was kept with the California Department of Motor Vehicles. It was some comfort to see that my medical history wasn't listed anywhere, only my blood type. My marriage to Greg was noted, but, again, that was public record.

As I said, none of this information is top secret, but much of it would be difficult for Joe Blow off the street to obtain, especially in such bulk and with such speed. Whoever or whatever Marigold is, it had access, legally or illegally, to pretty much every database on which personal information was stored. I knew better than to expect much personal privacy anymore with surveillance cameras recording our every move and the monitoring of citizens by the government, but this blew me away. Was the NSA behind Marigold? Or maybe one of their researchers had found a way to cash in on his or her skills on the side. Whatever it was, I was darn sure it was also noting and saving each of the searches I was doing.

I took a deep breath and wondered if I should continue using the search engine. Putting down the hard copy of my report, I checked my email. The search reports for a couple of the people I was investigating had arrived, and I knew I was hooked. A quick look and I knew that my limited search parameters had hit pay dirt and found the right people. Whatever this Big Brother search engine was, I was going to jump in feet first because I might learn something about the body left in my trunk. In this case, as I had with others, I was choosing "the end justifies the means" approach.

The first completed report was the one on Jean Finch. Opening the attachment, I took note that she was now going by the name of Jean Utley. She could have gotten married or changed it for other reasons. If the name change was due to marriage, it meant she hadn't married her college sweetheart Ryan Wright, or she had and divorced and remarried in short order.

Scanning the report, I kept my eyes open for her current whereabouts. It looked like she finished college and moved to Chicago, where she took a job as a project manager in a large company. At this point it looked like she was still Jean Finch. The next bit of information on Jean's report grabbed my attention. Three years ago she'd moved from Chicago to California and was now living in Studio City, and that's when her last named jumped from Finch to Utley. There was no mention of any husband. There were other addresses listed in California before the Studio City one, but it didn't look like Jean had stayed at any of them long.

I checked the summary of her stats in the upper right-hand corner. In my eagerness to read the trail of her personal history, I'd missed them. It gave her birthdate and her current age of twenty-six. It was nice of Marigold to tell me that instead of making me do the math. Sure enough, listed right under Jean's birthday was her marital status: single, not divorced.

My paralegal side kicked into action. I knew that in order to change your name legally, a petition for a decree had to be filed with the court. If Jean made the change a legal one and was living in Studio City at the time, that would mean she would have filed the petition with the Los Angeles Superior Court; that petition, once granted, would have to be published in a public periodical and would become public record. Marigold knew that too. Under a section that gave more detailed personal statistics, like her height and general weight (probably obtained from driver's license records) and which schools she attended, was a notation that she had changed her name legally. The date of the action was just months after she arrived in Southern California. She hadn't wasted any time dumping the Finch name.

Why had Jean come to California? Did she know her brother was here? Had she known all along? More importantly, did she know he was now dead and why? And why did she change her name after leaving Chicago?

I really needed to speak to Jean, and pronto. There was a phone number listed with her current address. I thought about calling her, but if she knew about her brother's recent past and current status, it might spook her into taking off. And why did she choose the name Utley? Maybe it was her mother's maiden name or the family name of some ancestor.

I'd also asked Marigold for a report on

Alec Finch and found it waiting in my email. I opened the attachment and checked his marital status. His was listed as widowed. I scanned his report until I found when he had married Maryanne. Her maiden name had been Worthington, not Utley, so that theory was shot. Alec's report listed his parents' names as Helen and Daniel Finch. Next to siblings, it said none.

What I needed to do was make a sneak attack on Jean. I went back to her report. Her occupation was listed as actress. From there I went to the website IMDB, a database that lists actors, films, and TV shows. I put in Jean's name and up came a nice head shot with a short list of TV appearances. It looked like she'd been getting some small parts here and there in the past couple of years but certainly nothing steady enough to support herself. Her professional bio said nothing about being born in Illinois as Jean Finch. I saved her head shot to my computer and printed it out for a current reference, as well as sent it to my phone. I looked again on the Marigold report for some indication of another more steady job but found none of the usual barista or waitress or temp secretary jobs that many actors work while trying to break into show business.

If Jean didn't work another job, then she

150

might be home most of the time between auditions. Or maybe she worked from home doing something that paid under the table and which would not show up in reports garnered from the usual databases. No matter who or what was behind Marigold, I doubted it was a boots-on-the-ground type of investigative outfit. But that was something I could do, although in my case it was sneakers on the ground.

I looked at the clock in the lower right-hand side of my computer. It was just past two thirty, and Studio City might as well be on the moon considering it was about forty-five to fifty miles away and I'd have to go straight through the heart of Los Angeles to get there. Traffic heading that way and back would be horrendous on a weekday. Maybe Greg and I could check her out early tomorrow morning when the drive would be easier. He had worked at the shop last weekend, so this weekend someone else would cover it. Not to mention, I liked having my hubs by my side when I snooped. He's the muscle and often the brains of our partnership.

I put Jean's report aside and looked at Alec Finch's again. It was the size of a phone book for a small rural village, which was no surprise. Deciding to print it out and read it thoroughly later, I opened the other reports I'd requested, starting with Christopher Cook.

After high school, Chris Cook had gone to college in Colorado, then returned home to marry a local girl and quickly crank out two little girls who, by the birthdates in the report, would be barely out of diapers. Chris then went into his father's insurance business, and that's where he was today and probably would be for the rest of his working life. There was a photo attached, and it showed a man in his mid-twenties. He was nice looking, with a slightly crooked smile, a square chin, and thinning blond hair. Even though still young, he already looked settled and stodgy; in a few years he would probably have a paunch, be bald, and serve as president of the local Rotary Club.

Next up was Ben Myers. It was a short report and a sad one. The year after Zach had disappeared, Ben had been killed in a snowboarding accident when he hit a tree and sustained a fatal concussion. The report claimed his blood alcohol level had been quite high when he made that last run down the mountain.

The last of Zach's pals was Nathan Glick. He'd also gone on to college, but where he went after piqued my interest. After college he had gone to work for one of the companies owned by Alec Finch. His education had been funded by a scholarship provided by the same company. The company was called Aztec Investments. It was headquartered in Chicago, and it looked like he was still there. That didn't necessarily mean anything foul was afoot. Alec might have recognized special qualities in Nathan and given him the opportunities he'd wanted to give his son. According to the report, Nathan lived in Chicago and was single.

But something about Aztec nagged at me; I'd seen that name before. Going back to Jean's report, I checked it over again. Sure enough, there it was: when Jean had lived in Chicago, she'd worked for Aztec Investments.

Quickly I did a search for the corporate entity of Aztec Investments. It was a publicly held company domiciled in Delaware with its home office in Chicago. According to its website, which was very professional but contained only the barest bones of information, Aztec invested mostly in overseas construction projects. Further digging showed it going public less than two years before Zach's disappearance. I didn't know if that made any difference or not to my timeline, but I noted that information just before the date Zach went missing. I also made little hash marks along the line for his sister's move to Chicago and her move to California and name change. I did the same for Nathan Glick's employment with Aztec.

I studied the photo attached to Nathan's report. Unlike his pal Chris, who was already showing signs of going to seed, Nathan looked fit and confident in what was probably a professional shot for his job. His hair was very dark, wavy, and well styled, as was his suit. He had a cherub face that made him look younger than he was, but his eyes didn't sparkle with youth. They were brown and hard. He looked directly at the lens, almost challenging anyone who dared to look at him. I couldn't make up my mind if his gaze displayed offense or defense.

I'd also requested a report for Zachery Finch. Like Ben's, it was very short, stopping the day he had gone missing. It included his birth, family, schooling, and sports involvement until that time, and, of course, the fact that he had been kidnapped. There were no subsequent employment records, marriages, or name changes. Wherever Zach had been since, he'd been totally off the grid.

ELEVEN

The sound of my cell phone ringing woke me.

After reading all the reports except for Alec Finch's, I'd collected his from my printer and settled back into the recliner to read it. Muffin had wedged herself onto my lap between me and the report and promptly fell asleep. A few pages into the report, I followed her lead.

After taking a few seconds to orient myself, I grabbed my cell from the table next to the recliner. It was a blocked number. I almost declined the call, but at the last minute the fog of sleep fell from my eyes as I realized it might be Elaine Powers calling.

"Is this Odelia Grey?" a woman asked after I said my hurried hello. It wasn't Elaine.

I answered with a fair amount of caution, just in case Elaine was using a go-between.

"Yes. And you are — ?"

"My name is Emma Whitecastle. Grace Littlejohn — I believe that's your mother — asked me to call you."

My heart nearly stopped. I sat up straight, dislodging Muffin. "Is Mom okay?"

"I sure hope so," the woman answered. "But don't you know?"

"She's out of town right now," I responded. "I thought maybe you were calling with an emergency."

"I'm so sorry to have alarmed you," she said with sincerity. "I actually called because she emailed me a couple of days ago and asked if I'd speak with you." There was a short pause, then she added, "I don't usually call when fans write." The woman named Emma Whitecastle laughed. "But frankly, her email was so interesting and entertaining, how could I not?"

Fans?

"I'm sorry," I said after taking several quick deep breaths to calm my nerves, "but I'm stumped. Who are you again?" I put the phone on speaker to talk easier while I got up and made my way to the kitchen table and my computer. After turning up the volume, I put the phone down and quickly pecked out her name in a search engine. A ton of stuff popped up, including some photos. I went to her Wikipedia page and quickly scanned the information.

"My name is Emma Whitecastle," the woman explained. Her voice was on the husky side but patient and pleasant. The deepness of her voice didn't quite match the photos before me of a gorgeous middle-aged blond with short cropped hair. "I have a cable TV show on the paranormal," she explained.

Her name sounded vaguely familiar, and what she said coincided with the information on my computer screen, but I didn't keep up with things that go bump in the night — and I didn't realize that my mother did.

"And my mother wrote to you to call me?" I asked, even more surprised. "Whatever for? I'm not into ghosts or stuff like that at all."

"Obviously, she didn't tell you," Emma said. "I'm so sorry I sprang this on you."

"That's okay. I'm just sorry she wasted your time. Do you know why she wanted you to call me?" I asked again, sinking fast into a quagmire of confusion. "My mother often does peculiar things without telling me."

"I looked up her blog. She sent me the link in the email. It doesn't sound like she's having trouble with her mental capacity."

"Not my mother," I said with emphasis. "She's in her seventies and sharp as a tack. Odd, yes. Senile, no way."

"My mother too," Emma commented with another small laugh. "Except for the odd part. I should be so clear-minded now, never mind when I'm her age."

"I hear ya," I replied with my own chuckle. I was kind of liking this lady, even if it was sort of like a blind date set up by my mother. "My mother's problem is that she sometimes oversteps boundaries. It's exactly like her to write to you about calling without giving me a heads-up. She likes the element of surprise, especially when it involves blindsiding either me or my brother."

"Hang on a minute," Emma said. "I have her email right here. It's quite amusing. Grace definitely has a way with words."

"Yeah," I quipped, "she's a regular Stephen King."

My comment evoked another laugh. "That's quite funny," Emma said, "considering it's about a dead body in the trunk of your car."

Oh. My. God. Mom may not have blabbed on her blog, but she'd written about Zach in an email to someone with a TV show. Greg just might lock her up after all, if I didn't kill her first.

"Yes, unless there are other bodies being stashed in trunks all over the state," I joked. "When did she send that email?"

"Let's see," Emma began. "It looks like she sent it late Wednesday night, but I didn't see it until early this morning because I only go through this account and answer the emails once or twice a week. It's the contact email account for fans of my show."

"And my mother is a fan?"

"That's how she starts off," Emma said. "She says she's a big fan and never misses it, not even the reruns. Then she says that I have a lot in common with her daughter Odelia. That's you, yes?"

I shook my head in continued confusion. What did I have in common with a beautiful, blond TV personality who chases ghosts? "How so?" I asked.

"Grace goes on to explain that both of us get mixed up with and solve murders, and that she thinks I could be of help with this latest body you've discovered." Emma paused. "She said you found it Wednesday and she doesn't want you to go to jail, so she wants my help."

"So you're a corpse magnet, too?" I asked as I started to piece together Mom's logic behind the email.

"A what?" Emma asked, taking her turn at confusion.

"A corpse magnet. It's what my friends call me," I explained. "I seem to have a gift for finding dead bodies on a somewhat regular basis." Grabbing the phone and my cocoa mug, I went into the kitchen, where I rinsed the mug, then refilled it with clean water. I took a long drink before continuing. "The body in the trunk is my latest hidden treasure."

"I see." She wasn't laughing now. "I don't find dead bodies, Odelia," Emma clarified. "Mostly I stumble upon spirits of people who have been murdered or who are trying to warn the living of mortal danger."

"But you've solved murder cases?" I asked.

"I've been involved with resolving some, yes."

Now it was crystal clear where my mother was going with this. "Knowing my mother," I said, "I'm thinking she wanted you to help figure out how the body got into the trunk of my car."

"You're right," Emma confirmed. "In the email, Grace asked me to meet with you and see if we could contact the spirit of the man who died and question him."

"Can you do that?" I put my mug down and leaned against the kitchen sink. If it

160

was this easy to question the dead, why hadn't I gone this route before?

"Do you believe in spirits, Odelia?"

"You're answering a question with a question," I pointed out.

"Yes, I am, but it's important. I can't help you if you're going to mock my work."

"Can't help or won't help?" I asked.

"I like your directness, Odelia, but even if I do contact the spirit of this poor man, what good will it do you if you don't believe me?"

"Excellent point," I admitted. I moved from the kitchen and went to stand in front of the patio slider. It was still raining but not as heavy as earlier. I stared past the patio and yard and peered through the decorative privacy slats of the fence separating the yard from the carport. That was likely where someone had stashed Zach into my trunk. I really did need to get to the bottom of this, and as soon as possible. As with using Marigold, the end might justify the means.

I turned away from the window and took my seat again at the kitchen table. "What if I just keep an open mind about all this? My mother obviously believes in your skills. Maybe she'll have to do the heavy lifting in the belief area for both of us."

"So you do want my help?" Emma asked, looking for confirmation.

I again scanned her Wikipedia page, then loudly inhaled and exhaled before answering. "Frankly, Emma, I am a bit concerned about your agenda. I mean, you're famous and have a TV talk show. And you were once married to Grant Whitecastle, the king of sleazy talk shows. Maybe you're thinking this corpse magnetism of mine would be a creepy topic for one of your episodes."

"I thought you didn't know who I was."

"Wikipedia," I answered. "I'm a quick study, with quicker keyboard fingers. I may not have known about your show, but I do remember now seeing footage on TMZ of the public knock-down-drag-out brawl you had with Grant Whitecastle. Trust me, Emma, rich people behaving badly is *not* my thing."

"That wasn't a public brawl," she snapped, the pleasant tone replaced by defensiveness. "It was a disagreement that took place in the driveway of my parents' home."

"Whatever."

"Argh," she grunted. "My daughter says that to me all the time. I hate it."

It was my turn to laugh.

"Seriously, Odelia," Emma said, returning

to an even tone. "I'm not interested in putting you on my show. You're a corpse magnet and I'm a ghost magnet. As Grace pointed out, we both get embroiled in death and crime. Don't you find that a big responsibility? One that you never asked to have?"

I took another deep breath before answering simply, "Yes."

"For some reason," she continued, "we've both been chosen by fate, God, or some other unseen force to help the deceased and their loved ones get to the bottom of things."

"Or maybe it's some big cosmic joke and we're just pawns of the universe?"

"Maybe, but I enjoy helping people who can't help themselves. Unlike you, I've never been a suspect in a murder. From my research, you've been involved a lot more directly with the crimes than I ever have been."

I went on alert. "How do you know what I've been involved with?"

"My fiancé is a lawyer," she answered. "He researched you before I called. Anyone with a lick of sense would."

I looked down at my laptop and wondered if her fiancé had used the usual legal search engines or knew about Marigold. "Fair enough. Did my mother tell you anything about the body in the trunk?"

"No, just that you found one. Is this the story on the news the other night — the one about the car wash in Long Beach? They haven't released the victim's name yet, have they?"

At least my mother had kept mum about Zach's identity. "Yes, it's the same one, and no, they haven't. It's a very complicated situation." I hesitated, then said, "So you think you can contact the ghost of the guy in my trunk?"

"I don't know, but I can try." There was silence except for Emma's breathing. "Besides Grace's way with words, something in my gut told me to reach out to you. I do think a spirit is trying to reach you, Odelia. I don't know if it's the dead man or someone else, but I have a very strong sense that I need to connect the two of you."

The hair on my arms stood as straight as mini flagpoles. I relied on my gut instincts all the time, but never had they told me I had a voice mail from the other side. I made a quick decision, even though I knew I should talk it over with Greg first. "Let's meet."

164

TWELVE

An hour later, I opened my door to Emma Whitecastle.

Even though I hadn't wanted to drive to Studio City today, I offered to meet Emma in Pasadena, where she told me she lived. But instead, she offered to come to my home, especially after I told her that the police thought the body had been put into my trunk while the car was parked in the carport.

"You really didn't have to rush down here," I told her, showing her in. Very tall and slim, with a glowing complexion, Emma Whitecastle was just as lovely in person as in her photos. From her bio online, I knew she was in her late forties, and she had the fine lines around her eyes to prove it. Even though it was none of my business, I was happy to see she hadn't had any plastic surgery to tweak them like most TV celebrities. Still, I was very glad I'd showered earlier and had even slapped on some makeup after we'd hung up from our call.

"It was no problem," she told me. "I was about to leave for San Diego for the weekend, so I'll just head there from here."

"My husband and I love San Diego," I told her. "We go quite often. Is this a special weekend?"

"My fiancé has a condo there," she explained, taking a seat after I directed her to the sofa. "I live up here and he lives down there, and we both have homes in Julian, which is where we usually spend our weekends. This weekend, however, we have to attend a charity event on Saturday night in San Diego, so we'll stay there."

"Julian is another place Greg and I love." I sat on the edge of the recliner. "We go every year for the apple festival."

Emma and I politely smiled at each other. I got the feeling she was trying to look *into* me. I, on the other hand, was trying not to let my nerves get the best of me. Until an hour ago, I'd only vaguely known this woman from Hollywood gossip shows and magazines when she was going through a very messy public divorce. Now I knew she was a famous medium with her own TV show. I didn't know which Emma Whitecastle made me more nervous.

"Relax, Odelia," Emma said with a smile. "I'm not going to bite." She shrugged off her leather bomber jacket and laid it neatly on the sofa next to her. Muffin came out from one of her many hiding places to greet the visitor.

"Hi, cutie pie," Emma said to the cat, scooping her up to pet her. Muffin was in kitty nirvana. She loved guests.

A nervous laugh escaped my lips. "Can you see the future?"

Emma responded with a laugh of her own as she continued stroking Muffin, but unlike mine, it was confident and not the least bit self-conscious. "It's complicated, kind of like the body you found. I don't tell fortunes, if that's what you mean, but sometimes spirits tell me things and sometimes I can sense things that might happen. Working with spirits is not exact."

"In your gut?" I asked. "You get a lot of gut feelings?"

"Yes," she answered. "I work a lot on my gut instincts, mingled with what I gather from the spirits."

"Then tell me, Emma," I said, leaning forward, "when I kill my mother tonight, will I get off with a plea of insanity?"

She tilted her head back and laughed heartily, then said, "Grace was just concerned about you and thought I might be able to help."

"So is it the dead guy who is trying to contact me through you?" I asked, still unsure of what to expect. "You said you felt someone was trying to connect with me."

She nodded and put Muffin down on the floor. "I'm not sure who it is, but I sense his spirit is here with us now." She was still and tilted her chin up. It reminded me of Wainwright when he's checking for scents borne on the air, but in her case she seemed to be listening, not smelling. "But I don't think this is the man found in your trunk. This man passed over a few years ago, not recently." She tilted her head to her left. "He says his name is Horten."

I nearly peed my pants, then remembered that she could have researched me as easily as I did her.

"That's your father, isn't it?" she asked.

I nodded. "But that's public record."

She gave me another warm smile. "I can see, Horten, that we have a tough customer here." She was still again, then told me, "He says he's sorry about the pig." She looked at me, puzzled. "Did you have a pet pig?"

I shook my head.

"Not a pet," she continued, her chin tilted again, "but a plastic pig. A pink plastic pig that your father . . . no, someone named Gigi gave you as a gift."

I held my breath. I had turned fifty shortly after my father died. For my birthday, my evil stepmother Gigi had given me a pink plastic pig that went into the fridge and oinked when you opened the door. I despised the thing and had smashed it to smithereens with a mallet. But I didn't let on to Emma that she'd hit a bull's eye.

"He says he's sorry," Emma continued, "and doesn't blame you for destroying it."

"He saw that, did he?" I asked, not sure what to believe. It was then that I noticed Muffin cautiously walking toward the area off to Emma's left. Her sharp little nose was close to the ground, and she was wary but not frightened or defensive.

"Yes," Emma answered. "He says he was here when you did it." She paused and tilted her head again. "He also says that he's glad you found Grace, and he's very sorry he didn't help you do it years earlier. That's what he wanted me to say to you — he wanted me to apologize to you for that. And he said you're to stick close to Grace. She may not tell you, but she loves you and needs you, and you need her. She'll be your strength when you need her the most."

I sniffed and widened my eyes in an attempt to stem the tears that were threatening to gush. I loved my father and had been close to him. When he died, I was crushed. I glanced at Muffin. She was now lying on the floor and showing her tummy to whatever was over there. It was a gesture of trust and greeting she often made to good friends of ours. This time it was really freaking me out.

"He's fading, Odelia," Emma told me. "Do you have anything quick you want to ask him?"

"Yeah," I said, not wanting to walk down a painful memory lane. "Who put the dead guy in my trunk? Was Dad hanging around then?"

Emma glanced over to her left and asked the empty air about the body in my trunk. After a few moments she turned back to me. "He said he didn't see anything about the body," she relayed. "But he wants you to be very careful. He's worried about your safety and Greg's."

Join the crowd.

"He also said he probably won't be back."

"What?" I asked with surprise. "This was a one-time offer?" I didn't know what to believe, and it was starting to make me angry. "You're saying my father popped in and is now gone for good?"

170

"It's not uncommon, Odelia," Emma explained, "for a spirit to take its leave permanently once he or she has said what they've been waiting to say."

I slouched in the recliner like my bones had disintegrated into dust. Mentally and emotionally I was exhausted and not understanding anything that had just happened. I didn't know whether to believe this hooey or to thank Emma for passing along the message like a note in school.

Muffin had gotten to her feet and was inspecting the area again. Only Greg and I knew about my smashing that pig. There was no way Emma Whitecastle could know that. Not even the know-all, see-all Marigold would know that. Either my home had been under surveillance or Dad had been hanging around at the time like Emma claimed. I laughed inwardly. Wainwright knew I'd done the deed. Maybe he squealed like that dog in the baked beans commercial on TV. It was the only logical explanation, and it was ridiculous.

I pointed at Muffin. "Could she see him?"

Emma smiled at the little animal. "Most animals are very sensitive to spirits. If Muffin didn't see him, she at least knew he was there. Our dog senses spirits all the time and tries to get them to play with him."

171

I ran a hand through my hair, dislodging the headband. "I honestly don't know what to make of this, Emma. I'm torn between thanking you and asking you to leave my home."

"That's not an unusual response."

Emma sat on my sofa calmly and patiently, obviously used to scenarios like this. I, however, was not. Should I offer her coffee or punch her lights out? I liked the idea of my father hovering about from time to time — at least I hoped it was only from time to time. It was comforting to think about. But I didn't like the idea that now that I had had a taste of his company, he was gone — *whoosh* — like he'd never been there at all. A sense of loss was creeping over me as if he'd died a second time. I tried my best to shake it off and turn my attention back to Emma.

"So now what?" I asked. I sat up straight like a grown-up, deciding that throwing a punch was not the way to go.

Emma shrugged and looked at her watch. "I still have time before I have to head down to San Diego. How about you showing me where the body was left? Maybe I can pick up something."

I got out of the recliner and showed Emma the way out through the sliders to the patio. Unlocking the back gate, I led the way to the carport.

"Is this the car?" she asked.

"No," I answered, "that's a rental. The police are holding my car, but it was parked right here when the police think the body was dumped."

Emma closed her eyes and took several deep breaths as if absorbing the energy in the air.

"Would you like a cup of coffee or something?" I asked when she opened her eyes.

She smiled at me. "A cup of coffee would be nice. I take it black, no sugar." She studied the area, then added, "It's not too chilly out, so how about we have it out here on the patio just in case a spirit presents itself. Sometimes they linger near the place where they died."

I had taken a step back toward the house but stopped and turned toward her. "The police don't know exactly where he died. He could have been killed and his corpse left here."

She shrugged. "Maybe. But I think he died here or shortly before he got here."

Not for the first time, a cold river ran through my veins. Without a word, I headed into the house to make the coffee. When I returned, Emma had taken a seat at our patio table. She'd propped the gate open and was seated so she could see into the carport. I placed the two mugs of coffee on the table. I had slipped into a thick hoodie and had Emma's jacket slung over one arm. "You might need this," I said, handing her the jacket.

"Thank you. I was just about to go in and fetch it." She slipped into her jacket and wrapped her hands around the coffee. Before taking a sip, she asked, "So you didn't know your mother watches my show?"

"Not a clue," I said after sipping some hot coffee. "But no surprise there. Mom keeps her private life pretty close to her chest. She's on a senior citizen tour to one of the Indian casinos right now. Neither my brother or I knew she'd taken them before, but apparently she does and just didn't say. She's always been secretive like that."

Emma took a drink of her own coffee. "It's too bad I won't get to meet her."

"Serves her right for pulling a sneaky stunt like this and not telling me."

We sipped our coffee companionably. I wanted to ask Emma a bushel of questions but didn't want to disturb whatever vibes people like her got, if that was even how all this mumbo jumbo worked.

"Grace didn't tell me anything about the man who died," Emma finally said, breaking the silence, "but I get the sense that he was quite young."

"She really told you nothing?" I asked with surprise.

"Not a word, except that it was a male. But I think he was young and lost for a long time." She looked at me, holding my eyes with hers. "And newsworthy, more than just the usual dead body. Am I correct?"

"You got all that from just sitting here?" I closed one eye, giving Emma my dead-eye stare.

"Not the newsworthy part," she answered. "I got that just by my own summation. Grace didn't say who he was. Neither did you, even though I'm pretty sure you know his identity. The police also have not given that information to the media yet. Whoever this young man is, it's going to be a big news story."

"Yes," I said, releasing the breath I was holding and relaxing my closed eye. "A huge story, but we're not at liberty to talk about it on orders of the police and the FBI."

"The FBI," Emma said with surprise. She'd been about to take another sip of coffee but stopped and turned her eyes again toward the carport. "Very interesting." We went back to silently sipping our coffee again, but Emma never took her eyes off the carport, almost willing it to cough up its secrets.

My mug was empty and so was Emma's when she turned her attention back to me. "Would you like more coffee?" I offered.

"No, thank you." Her words were pleasant and polite, but her face was clouded. "I have to be going, but there is something I need to tell you."

I leaned in closer, almost abandoning my skepticism of earlier.

"You've heard the phrase 'killing two birds with one stone'?" she asked.

"Of course," I answered. "It basically means getting two things accomplished with only one action."

"Exactly," she confirmed. "That phrase — killing two birds with one stone — is going around and around in my head. But here's the really odd thing."

The really odd thing? This whole encounter was surreal.

"I'm getting the feeling that this man's name has something to do with birds. Maybe his name is Robin or Sparrow or something like that."

Or Finch.

She looked at me for confirmation, but I

forced my face to remain still and my mouth closed — an amazing feat for me on both counts.

"But whatever his name," Emma continued, "the phrase 'killing two birds with one stone' doesn't refer to his name. I think it refers to the reason the body was left here."

"What?" I squeaked out.

"I may be wrong," Emma said. "Sometimes messages are hazy or cloaked in multiple meanings, but I definitely think whoever killed this person was taking care of more than one problem."

"You mean the killer was multitasking?" I snorted at the absurdity of it, yet inside I was burning what Emma had said into my memory for later reflection.

"Yes," she said with a finality that signaled it was time for her to leave.

I walked Emma through the house to the front door. Along the way she said goodbye to Muffin and grabbed her bag from the coffee table. From her expensive designer bag she extracted a PR photo of herself and handed it to me. It was autographed and made out to my mother. "Tell Grace I'm sorry I missed her."

"She'll like this a lot," I said, looking down at the photo, which was nice but nowhere near as lovely as the real thing. "Thank you for everything, Emma. I'm still not sure what I believe, but I found the thing with my father, real or not, quite comforting, and it contained a lot of closure."

At the door she didn't hold out her hand to shake mine, as I expected, but wrapped her arms around me in a warm hug. I embraced her back and meant it. It wasn't just a gesture for gesture's sake. I really did like the woman and found her to be genuine in her warmth and concern.

"Just be careful, Dottie," she said to me after the embrace ended.

The shock on my face must have made her realize her mistake. "I'm sorry, Odelia," she said with a short laugh. "I don't know where the name Dottie came from."

But I did.

THIRTEEN

I waved as I watched Emma Whitecastle drive off in a Lexus hybrid SUV and wondered if maybe I should test-drive one of those myself. Greg would be okay with the hybrid part but not the Lexus part, citing it as being out of our budget. But it wouldn't hurt to look.

After I went inside, I remembered that we'd left the back gate to the carport open. I knew Muffin hadn't made a break for freedom because while we had left the glass slider open, we'd closed the screen slider, and the doggie door was always locked when Wainwright wasn't home. Also, Muffin was now on the sofa, curled up for another nap. I went to her and scratched her behind her ears. She started purring in her sleep. "Guess you're all tuckered out from playing with ghosts, huh, Muffin?" She yawned and curled up tighter.

Just as I turned to head through the dining and kitchen area to shut the gate, I caught a glimpse of someone on our patio — at least I think I saw someone skulking back there just before the figure disappeared off to the right of the slider, behind the kitchen wall. I looked down at the sleeping cat. She was useless. Wainwright would have been all over this even with his failing hearing. Even in old age, his nose was still one hundred percent functional. Even Seamus would have alerted me to the stranger's presence by dashing through the house to hide. But not Muffin. Unless the stranger entered the house, she could care less. And even then, she'd probably show them her tummy or beg for a treat.

My first instinct was to run out the front door. My second instinct wanted to know who was back there. Was it the murderer coming back to check on things? Maybe he thought the body would still be in the trunk, and he'd come to reclaim it. But if he saw the news, he'd know that wasn't possible, so I dismissed that idea. I mean, if I had murdered someone, I'd be checking the news for updates.

I picked up my cell phone from the table next to the recliner and called Greg. My plan was to act as naturally as possible and throw the person off-guard while also having a lifeline open. Unfortunately, my call went to voice mail.

"Hi, honey," I said loud enough for someone lurking close to hear. Voice mail or not, I wanted the intruder to think I was on the phone with Greg. "I just had an interesting visitor here at the house," I continued even though the voice mail beeped to say my recording time had run out.

I spoke calmly as I walked into the kitchen and posted myself near the patio door. From here the lurker could hear me but not see me unless he came in full view of the slider. Next to the door, a baseball bat leaned against the side of a counter. Greg and I didn't care for guns, but we did like baseball bats, and both of us could and would use one if necessary. We also kept one in the bedroom. Switching the phone to my left hand, I slowly reached for the wooden bat and grasped it tightly in my right. I thought about calling someone else, but changing calls might alert whoever was out there.

"Would you believe my mother contacted a medium to see if we could connect with the ghost of the dead guy?" I forced a laugh. "She showed up here today." I forced another laugh. "Yeah, a medium came here

181

to the house. She left just a few minutes ago."

Just then I saw a hand come creeping into view on the other side of the screen door. It wasn't front and center but off near the side. It held something. At first I thought it was a gun, and panic rose from my gut into my throat, threatening to gush into a scream. But it wasn't a gun, unless guns now came in a flat rectangle shape. It was a cell phone, and from the way it was being held it was probably recording a video or at least audio. Seeing the phone, I was glad I hadn't mentioned Emma by name, but who knew how long that person had been out there listening. Since the story about Zach hadn't been released yet, there was a good chance this person had been following Emma.

"No," I said into the phone, continuing the ruse, "Mom doesn't know she was here." I scooted even closer to the screen and wished it was open so I could take a quick strike at the phone with the bat. I laughed again, then said into the phone. "When she does, I'm sure there will be hell to pay."

I turned slightly to my left and raised the bat in my right, still keeping it out of direct line of sight of whoever was out there. "She did leave a signed photo for Mom," I said into the phone as I took a firmer hold on the bat and pulled it back across my chest. "Maybe that will mollify her." I paused. "What, honey? I didn't hear you." I paused for effect.

The intruder's phone moved closer to the screen and more away from the edge, getting bolder in its presence. That was my cue. I moved closer to it on my side. Quietly I pocketed my phone and grabbed the bat with both hands, slowly raising it over my head. "By the way, Greg, Clark and Mom are coming over for dinner tonight. I'm making beef stew."

Using all my weight, I brought the bat down as hard as I could on the screen exactly where the phone was positioned. I hit a homer. The bat tore through the screen and smashed the phone out of the person's hand, causing screams of anguish. Before they could recover from the surprise attack, I flung open the broken screen slider and barreled out with the bat cocked and ready.

"You broke my hand!" a guy writhing on our patio screeched. He clutched his right hand close to his chest with his left. "You broke my hand, you bitch!"

"Who are you and what do you want?" I asked, ready to smash a leg to match his hand.

He tried to sit up, but when he did he vomited down the front of his jacket and the tee shirt under it. He fell back down to the concrete pad, whimpering. I almost felt bad for him. His cell phone had landed near the door. Keeping an eye on him, I picked it up. The glass front was broken but otherwise it seemed in pretty good order. It was still recording. I put it into my other pocket without shutting it off.

"Hey, that's mine!" he protested from his prone position.

"Come and get it," I challenged.

I pulled my own phone out and started to dial 911, but a call came through as I did. It was Greg.

"What's going on?" Greg said. "I was meeting with a client when you called. Your message was so weird."

"I'll explain the call later," I told him. "Meanwhile, I captured an intruder. This creep came into our back yard."

"Your freaking gate was wide open, Odelia," the guy on the ground protested. He sat up again and wiped his mouth with his good hand. He seemed steadier but didn't try to get up.

"He's still there?" Greg asked. "Why haven't you called the police?"

I was stunned into inaction, torn between

184

explaining the situation to Greg and shocked that the skinny little creep on the ground knew my name. I decided to handle Greg first. "I was about to call the police when your call came through," I told my anxious husband.

"No," the guy said. "No police." He'd stopped sniveling and was shaking his head with vigor. "Please."

"What's he saying?" Greg asked. "Put me on speaker." I did.

"Why were you following Emma White-castle?" I asked the guy on the ground, who couldn't have weighed more than 130 soaking wet.

"Who's Emma Whitecastle?" Greg asked.

"That was Emma Whitecastle?" the guy asked, seeming genuinely surprised. At least the news got him to stop whining. "Wow. I really hit pay dirt."

"What's he talking about, Odelia?" asked Greg.

Hearing Greg say my name brought me back to my original concern. "How do you know my name?" I asked the guy. "Greg, this creep called me by name. He isn't here for Emma; he's here for me. I caught him recording me with his phone through our patio door."

"Who's Emma?" Greg asked again.

"The medium Mom contacted," I explained.

"Okay, that part I did get on voice mail," Greg said, then paused. "Hang up, Odelia, and call the police. I'll be there in five minutes. My client meeting wasn't far from the house."

"No police!" the guy on the ground insisted.

"Oh yeah," said Greg's voice through my phone. "There's going to be police, buddy. Odelia, can you hold him until I get there?"

I put my phone down on our patio table and hoisted the bat. "Oh yeah, I've got him," I said, getting a firm grip on the bat. "If he moves, I'll be doing a number on him with the Louisville Slugger."

"Check to make sure he's alone," Greg said.

Keeping an eye on the guy, I edged toward the open gate and glanced out into the carport and alley. I saw nothing but my rental car. Not even a curious neighbor, which wasn't surprising considering the people who lived on both sides of us worked every day. Otherwise, someone might have heard the guy's screech and come running. I closed the gate tight and secured it just in case he did have a partner lurking out there.

"He looks like he's alone," I said to Greg

when I returned to the phone.

The guy was trying to stand. "Stay where you are," I told him. "If you don't think I'll take another swing at you, think again." The guy slouched against a support post.

"Greg," I said toward my phone, "why don't you call the cops while I stand guard."

"No cops, please!" the guy begged. "I am alone, but please — no police. Let me go, and I'll never bother you again. I promise."

"Not gonna happen, buddy!" Greg yelled from the phone.

A few minutes later, Greg pulled into the alley and parked behind our garage. I unlatched the gate so Greg wouldn't have to unlock it from his side and opened it, then went back to watching over my captive. It was another minute before Greg maneuvered himself into his wheelchair and into our back yard. When he did, he was seething. Wainwright came in with him and stood ready for a command, his usual friendly face curled in a protective snarl.

The guy was sitting upright now, still propped against one of the supports of our patio roof, with his legs sprawled out in front of him. He was cradling his right hand but had stopped whimpering about it. He wasn't very old, maybe in his mid to late twenties. He was skinny, with *geek* written all over him from his wild, unkempt red hair to his pale skin and thick glasses.

"Did you call the police, honey?" I asked Greg.

He shook his head. "Not yet. I wanted to hear what this clown had to say for himself first."

Said clown was staring at Wainwright with raw terror. Our dog is a big old yellow teddy bear, but one word from Greg or aggressive movement toward me or Greg and he'd attack any troublemaker. "Call off your dog," the guy begged. "I won't do anything stupid. I promise."

After a few seconds, Greg said, "Down, Wainwright." The obedient dog stopped growling but remained on alert. To the guy, Greg said, "Hand over some ID."

The guy turned and started to reach into a back pocket with his right hand but flinched. "I can't get it with my hand. I think she broke it." He glared at me as he said it.

"You're lucky that's all she did," Greg snapped. He turned to me. "Odelia, see if you can get his wallet."

I handed Greg the bat. He gripped it tight and moved a little closer, positioning himself between the guy and the back gate. Wainwright moved a few steps closer too. The dog's presence nearly sent the guy into a cold sweat. I went behind the post, keeping it between the guy and me for some security, and reached into the rear right pocket of his jeans. He leaned forward to make it easier for me.

"Steady now," Greg warned.

I pulled out the wallet and went back to the patio table, out of reach, to check its contents. The wallet was a cheap polyester trifold with a Velcro closure, black, with comic book superheroes on the outside. I held it out for Greg to see, then said to the guy, "What are you, six years old?"

"What?" he said with false bravado. "It's a collectible."

The wallet contained no photos but did hold a couple of crisp twenty-dollar bills that looked fresh from an ATM. In slots in the middle section were a credit card, a library card, an employer ID, and an insurance card. On the clear plastic side was a California driver's license. I pulled it out and reported to Greg, "John Seymour Swayze. Lives on Sixth Street in Long Beach." I checked the birthdate and did a quick calculation. "He's twenty-four years old."

"So, John Seymour Swayze," Greg said to him, "what brings you to intruding on our privacy? You do know that it's against the law to record people without their knowing, don't you?"

While we waited for an answer, I checked out the employer ID card. I showed it to Greg. "Honey, he works for the *LA Times* — that's why he's here."

"You're a reporter?" Greg asked. "So were you spying on my wife, as she suspects, or were you following that medium?" Greg turned to me. "What's her name?"

"Emma Whitecastle," I told Greg, "and she's quite famous. Maybe this guy's a stalker — another thing that's against the law."

"I'm not a stalker." John Swayze took a deep breath. "And I wasn't following White-castle." He adjusted himself on the ground. "Can I get up? This concrete is hard and cold."

"No," I said, "you'll stay there until the police take you away."

"No police, please!" He took another deep breath. "Look. If I tell you the truth, will you let me go and *not* call the police?"

"Why don't you want the police involved if you've done nothing wrong?" I asked.

"Nothing wrong?" Greg parroted to me. "He trespassed onto our property and recorded you without your knowledge.

That's hardly nothing."

Remembering John's phone, I pulled it out of my pocket and checked it. It was still recording. The picture was dark from being in my pocket, but the sound was good. I stopped it, then started going back through the photos and videos stored on the device.

"Hey," John protested. "That's private property."

"You mean like this house?" Greg shot back.

"Greg, look at this." I turned the phone toward Greg and restarted the video that had grabbed my attention. Greg watched with wide eyes, then glared at John. There was no doubt now who the creep was following.

"You're the one who took the video of the body in Odelia's car and gave it to the media," Greg said with disgust to the wimp on the ground. "I should kick your ass for that alone."

"But this showed up on the local TV news," I noted. "Why not put photos in the paper?"

"Look," John began, "I do work at the *LA Times,* but not as a reporter. I'm in office services."

"You mean the mail room?" I asked.

"I do a lot of stuff, but yeah, the mail

room, gopher, stuff like that," he admitted. "I was at the car wash when the body was discovered and took the video. A lot of people were snapping photos," he said defensively. "I tried to show that to my bosses, hoping they might consider me for a better position, but they only laughed at me, so I took it to a friend at the news station. She said if I got more, there might be a job for me there."

"Who at the station?" Greg asked. "The cute little blond who did the reporting on the video that night?"

"Gloria Conners," I said. "I think that's her name."

John lowered his head and nodded.

"Did you really think she was going to make good on that, John?" Greg asked, his voice softening a tiny bit. "I'll bet you've been dogging her for months trying to get a date or something, haven't you?"

Again, John Swayze nodded. "I never showed that to the *Times*," he confessed, his eyes down on the ground. "I have tried to bring them stories before but they just laughed at me, so this time I showed it to Gloria. She didn't laugh." He looked up at us, his eyes bright with hope. "She took me seriously."

I tossed his wallet on the ground in front

of him. "She'd take you more seriously if you carried a grown-up wallet."

"Please," he said. "No police. I was in a scrape just a few months ago when I tried to get a story. If I get into trouble again, I might lose my job."

"The library card is from a town in Idaho," I noted. "Is that where you're from?"

He nodded. "Yeah. I moved here a couple of years ago. I just never got rid of it." He shrugged. "It's kind of like a piece of home."

"How did you find out where we lived?" Greg asked.

"I paid someone at the car wash to give me your information," John admitted. It was exactly what Clark had suspected might happen.

"What else did you find out?" Greg prodded.

"Nothing, I swear," John said. "That's why I came here. The police haven't released the name of the guy in the trunk, so I figured it might be a big news story. Gloria thought so too and said if I could get more information, it could be my big break."

"More like *her* big break," I said with thick sarcasm. I turned to Greg. "So what should we do with him?"

"He's not the first fool to do something

stupid for a woman, and he won't be the last," Greg said. "Maybe we should take pity on him and let him go."

John picked up his wallet with his good hand and struggled to his feet. We didn't stop him, but neither did we help. "I promise I won't bother you again." He cast an eye toward Wainwright, still worried about an attack.

"If you do," Greg said, seeing his fear, "that dog will be the least of your worries."

"What about my hand?" he asked, clutching it to his chest. "I think it's broken."

"You have an insurance card," I told him, "use it. Tell urgent care you accidentally slammed it in your car door."

He put his wallet into the front pocket of his jacket. "What about my phone?"

"This we're keeping," I said, holding the phone with the broken front up, "as *our* insurance."

"I need that phone," he whined. "It has all my contacts in it."

"If you're a good boy," Greg said, "when all this is over, we'll return it. If you're not a good boy, it will go straight to the police."

I went over to the gate and unlatched it. While John made his way toward it and the alley, Greg held the bat and Wainwright stood alert. "Where's your car?" I asked.

"And what do you drive?"

"Down on the far end of the alley," he said. "I drive a Prius."

"Huh," I said. "Do you like it? We're thinking of getting a hybrid." John Swayze stared at me like *I* was the geek with the superhero wallet. "Never mind," I added quickly. "We'll do our own homework on it."

Once he was on the other side of the gate, John turned around. "Who *is* the dead guy in the trunk?"

"Do you really think we'd tell you that?" Greg asked.

"For my hand. You owe me," John insisted.

I closed the gate and locked it.

"You owe me," came a cry from the other side, followed by footsteps walking away.

FOURTEEN

"She actually called you Dottie?" Greg asked.

"Yep." I settled myself into a chair across from Greg at our kitchen table. In front of me was my laptop. Over iced tea and a snack, I'd filled Greg in on everything that had happened with Emma. He had been suitably shocked, especially about my father.

"Has Elaine called you yet?" Greg asked. He'd taken Swayze's phone and was fiddling with it. "Damn thing is locked now."

"No," I answered as I plugged away at the keyboard, "and now I'm really worried. Emma Whitecastle is a famous medium. What if Elaine is dead and that was her ghost being channeled through Emma?"

Greg took a swig of his tea before answering. "Do you believe that's possible?"

"After what I saw today, I don't know what I believe. There is no way Emma could have known about me smashing that pig.

196

Or about Zach being young or his name having to do with a bird. So how can those things be logically explained?"

He shrugged. "I have no idea, sweetheart. I'm just sorry I missed it."

"And what about 'killing two birds with one stone'?" I prodded, looking for him to help me with this puzzle.

Another shrug. "If Emma's correct, the killing of Zach and the stashing of him in your car might have accomplished two tasks, yet we still haven't figured out a connection between you and Zach or any of his family." He downed a bite of banana before continuing. "The two tasks could even be unrelated to each other," he finally said. "The killer may have killed Zach for some reason totally unconnected to you, but by leaving his body in your trunk, the killer also tied up another job of some kind."

I stopped typing. "I don't like being the object of a twofer, Greg."

"And I don't like you being one either," he said. "Maybe Elaine and her people were the ones who disposed of Zach. Maybe that was one of their jobs, but for some reason they wanted him to be found — and quickly — instead of his body being disposed of in their usual manner, and thought you might be just the way to take care of that."

Slowly, I shook my head. "I still don't believe Elaine would put me in jeopardy like that. We have a very odd and protective connection."

Greg nodded and downed the last of his banana. "That you do," he said with a full mouth.

"Although," I added, having another thought, "Elaine does have a strange yet strong sense of right and wrong. Maybe she received a hit order to get rid of Zach, but knowing he was a missing kid from way back when, she decided to make sure his body was found so that his family could have closure."

"That would work," Greg agreed after taking another drink of tea. "I wish she'd call you and clear this mess up."

I laughed. "I never thought I'd see the day when you *wanted* Elaine Powers to call me."

He chuckled. "Me neither, sweetheart. Did your research today uncover anything else of note?"

I quickly summarized some of the things I had learned from the Marigold report. "When we have time, I need to show you this search engine," I told him. "It's scary good. I'm running a report on John Swayze right now. I want to know as much as I can about him."

"Sounds like Emma Whitecastle is scary good too." He glanced out the glass slider to the patio to make sure everything was okay and we didn't have any more unwanted visitors spying on us. The back was empty, and it had started to rain again. Greg had pushed the broken screen slider back out of the way as far as possible. "I'm game if you want to visit Zach's sister tomorrow morning. After, we can run by Home Depot and look into replacing the patio screen door."

"It's a date," I said. "We can leave early and grab breakfast somewhere."

Greg turned his attention back to me. "What about Grace and Clark? Are you going to tell them tonight part or all of what you learned?"

"Maybe just the part about Emma's visit," I told Greg. "Especially since Mom was the one who initiated that. For totally different reasons, I don't want either of them knowing we're snooping around on other fronts." I quickly reconsidered that. "I might tell Clark some things, especially about Swayze's visit, but I don't want Mom in on any of that information, especially the stuff about these crazy search engines. Can you imagine if she got her hands on Marigold?"

Greg gave an exaggerated shudder that shook his whole upper body. "I'd love to stay home with you the rest of the day," he said as he slipped his jacket back on, "but I can still get in a few more hours at the office." He held up Swayze's phone. "Besides, I want to take this into the shop. I think one of the guys might be able to break the password."

"Don't worry about it," I told him. "I'll be okay."

He planted a kiss on me. "Keep that bat close, you hear? I don't think Swayze will be back, but just in case, I'm leaving Wainwright with you. He seemed to be terrified of dogs. And if you hear from Elaine or think of anything you want me to pick up from the store on the way home, just call or text me." He sniffed the air with appreciation. "That stew smells great already."

He gave me another kiss before going. "Whether it was real or not, I'm happy that you had some closure with Horten today on some level."

My mother stared down at the autographed photo of Emma Whitecastle, her face contorting with mixed emotions. "I didn't expect her to act so quickly," Mom said, her voice thinly edged with anger like the fine lace on one of her hankies. "Usually I write these celebrities and never hear a word back."

My brother looked at her with knitted brows. "Do you write many famous people, Mom?"

"Sometimes," she answered. "I've even written the president."

"You've written to President Obama?" Greg asked, taking his turn with the questions.

"Not just him," Mom snapped, "all of them fools — every single one since Kennedy. I'm a voting citizen. It's my right to let them know how I feel about things, isn't it?"

My brother tilted his head upward and stared at our ceiling. "I just know Mom's name and photo are hanging on a wall somewhere at the FBI."

"Nah," Greg said with a grin. "If it was, I think it might have come up during questioning by Shipman the other day."

"It's probably on some terrorist list," I suggested as I got up. "Dinner is ready. Come sit down."

As soon as Clark had arrived with Mom, I told them about Emma Whitecastle's visit. I told them everything, including the thing with Dad. Mom had listened enraptured, as if she had a front-row seat to a séance. Clark listened too, but I could see the physical outline of his tongue probing the inside of his cheek as I talked. He was trying to keep an open mind, tough as it was. As a longtime former cop, he didn't dismiss anything but tried to look at each tidbit of information or lead from as many angles as possible — even if it was whacked out.

"So this two birds concept," Clark began after starting on his stew. "Maybe the killer is going to kill two people."

"And dump them both here?" Greg asked with concern, his spoon stopped midair. "That's a daunting thought."

"Maybe Odelia is the second bird," Mom said. After dropping that bomb, she looked down at her lap and adjusted her napkin as pretty as you please while we all stared at her.

Greg put down his spoon and covered my free hand with his. He looked straight into my eyes. "That thought occurred to me too. In fact, it's scaring the crap out of me." I squeezed his hand. I hated to see him so worried, even though I was also worried.

"I don't know," said Clark. "I think if the killer was going after Odelia, she'd be dead already. He's had plenty of opportunities. Take today, for instance. Most of the day she was here alone."

Greg snapped his eyes in Clark's direction. "Is that supposed to be comforting?" Then he looked at me. We hadn't told them about John Swayze; we were saving that for Clark's ears alone. They had come through the front door and hadn't noticed the broken patio screen yet.

Greg and I had briefly discussed whether or not John Swayze was the murderer or had come to the house to hurt me physically. We came to the conclusion that he was exactly who he said he was: a guy trying to impress a girl and looking for a better job. When the report on him came in from Marigold, I sent it to Greg at his office. It showed nothing to put us on alert otherwise. He was just a boring guy from Idaho with limited potential who'd been raised by his aunt and uncle, Mary and Edward Young.

Clark didn't back down on his theory that I was safe for now. "Yes, Greg, it is. I think Odelia is being used in some way here, but I don't think she's necessarily in danger, unless it's the danger of being charged with Zach's death." He stirred the stew in his bowl around, then added, "I think it's someone who is well acquainted with Odelia's history of solving crimes. It could be a criminal from her past throwing down a challenge to her — playing with her."

"Like that hitwoman," suggested Mom. "Everyone thinks it's her."

"But I don't," I said with conviction.

"Neither do I," added Greg. "She struck me as genuinely liking Odelia. I don't think she would do that unless she was reaching out for Odelia's help, but she didn't seem the type who would ask for help."

Greg's words did not go over the heads of Clark or my mother. Both of them stopped eating and stared at him. "Wait a minute," Clark said. He pointed his spoon across the table in Greg's direction. "You've *met* Elaine Powers?"

Oops. Elaine had met Greg only once, but it was something neither of us had mentioned to anyone. We knew if we did, the police would be all over him like they are on me when anything about her came to the surface.

"Yes," Greg answered truthfully after realizing his mistake. "She paid me a visit when I was in the hospital after I was shot. It was the only time I've ever laid eyes on her."

"She wanted to make sure he was okay," I added. "She even brought flowers."

"A contract killer brought you flowers?" Mom said, her eyes glowing with excitement behind her glasses. "Wow, I'm impressed. I wish I'd been there. Contract killers . . . famous mediums . . . how come none of this happens when I'm around?"

Clark, Greg, and I exchanged looks. "Maybe, Mom," Clark ventured, "because people are worried it would end up on that blog of yours."

"Speaking of which, Grace," added Greg, looking at Mom with steely narrow eyes, "you do not mention what I just said to anyone. Not on your blog. Not to your hairdresser. Not even to my parents. You got that?"

Mom looked to me for support and found none. "He's right, Mom. You can't breathe a word of it to anyone."

"Wait a minute," Mom said, narrowing her eyes back at Greg. "If that Elaine woman knew you'd been shot, does that mean she was involved in that murder with the rugby player?"

Clark looked surprised. "Hell, even I hadn't made that quick leap."

"She had nothing to do with that," I assured them both, slightly fibbing. "But she'd heard about Greg and was concerned, so she slipped into the hospital to make sure he was okay. That's all it was. She was there something like thirty seconds."

I looked at my husband and he nodded

with confirmation. "Trust me," Greg said, "Elaine Powers and Odelia are not book club buddies, and they don't exchange recipes. There's just this odd and haphazard connection." He turned to look directly at Clark. "Every now and then Odelia connects with the oddest people. Isn't that right, Clark?"

Everyone at the table except for Mom knew Greg was referring to Willie Proctor. "Yeah," Clark agreed with some reluctance. "She does have an unusual way with some folks. Damndest thing I've ever seen."

"So if it's not her," Mom said, getting back to business, "who would want to send Odelia a message or look for her help like this?" She looked at me. "In the past when people wanted your help, didn't they just come to you for it?"

I chewed the stew in my mouth and nodded. "Pretty much," I said after swallowing. "This really has everyone stumped."

"Have the police come around anymore?" asked Clark.

I shook my head. "Nope. After they questioned me and checked out the house and carport, they went silent. I haven't heard a thing more."

"I don't like the sound of that one bit," said Mom with a shake of her head. "On

TV that's usually the quiet before the storm. Just when you think it's all going away, *bam!* The cops come in and arrest you for murder."

I looked at my aged mother like she'd just announced she was from Mars. My father's spirit had said Mom would be a great comfort to me. I was now sure death had addled his brain or he was talking about some other mother. "You're such a little ray of sunshine, Mom. Keep up the positive thinking."

Mom and Clark left shortly after dinner. Mom was tuckered out from her trip, and Clark wanted to get her home. Before they left, Clark sidled up to me and whispered, "Don't go to bed yet. I'll be back in a few minutes."

FIFTEEN

Mom lived about three miles from us, so it was no surprise when Clark was back in our kitchen twenty minutes later.

"You got some coffee, sis?" he asked after making himself comfortable again at the kitchen table with Greg.

I had just finished cleaning up the kitchen from dinner. "You drink entirely too much coffee," I told him.

"I asked for coffee, not medical advice," he said. His comments came with a grin to let me know he wasn't really annoyed.

Knowing he was returning, I had expected the request for coffee and had started a cup for him as soon as he came through the front door. "Okay, but you're getting decaf." I placed the mug of coffee in front of him. "What did you tell Mom when you left her just now?" I asked.

"I told her I was meeting Dev for coffee," he said after taking a sip of the hot brew.

"She almost wanted to come along to say goodbye to him since she missed his party last night, but I convinced her that we'd probably be seeing him again before he left town. Since she was bone-tired from her trip, she didn't argue."

Greg was nursing a beer. I settled down at the table with a glass of wine.

"So," Clark began, "what's really going on with this Zach situation? And don't tell me 'nothing.' " His eyes darted between me and Greg like a ping-pong ball in play. "I know you two too well for that nonsense."

While cleaning up from dinner, Greg and I had decided to come clean with Clark after all. I told him about Marigold and what I'd learned about Zach's sister. "I didn't want to say any of this in front of Mom," I said after finishing.

"Good call," Clark said. "Expensive or not, she'd be all over that Marigold site. Just because you can learn things about people doesn't mean you should."

"It's not that easy to find," I assured him. "You really have to have someone else point you to it."

"Have you ever heard of it?" Greg asked Clark.

He nodded and smiled. "Yes, I have. Willie's people use it all the time. That's who introduced me to it. I don't know who developed it or runs it, but it gathers information from all public sites, not just a few, and from a few not-so-public sites. Your friend Barbara had to have known someone who also used it; by referral is the only way to find it. Now that you have a way in, respect your friend's trust and don't tell anyone."

"Don't worry," I said in agreement. "So it also hacks information from non-public sites?"

"Some," he confirmed. "But you have to be a special customer to get access to that area. Between Marigold and his personal contacts, that's how Willie always knows so much about people."

Greg chuckled. "I'm guessing Willie is one of Marigold's special clients."

In response, Clark just smiled and took another drink of his coffee. "I'm betting Elaine Powers uses it or something like it herself," he said. "In her business, you have to know everything about your targets to be effective."

"We're going to see Jean Utley tomorrow," I said. "And I don't want you to stop us."

Clark surprised me by saying, "I think that's a good idea. Do you know yet if the police have notified her or her family about Zach?"

"Not a clue," I said, "and I'm sure they wouldn't tell us if they did."

"Do you think Dev could find that out for us?" asked Greg.

"I'd rather not get him involved," Clark said. "He has just a few days left on the job and a lot on his plate with the move and all."

"I agree," I said. "Let's not bother Dev."

"No," Clark confirmed. "I'll handle the cops. I might be able to find something out. Cops talk to cops, even ex-ones."

"You can always romance it out of Andrea," I quipped.

"What?" asked Greg just as he was about to take a swig of beer.

I turned to Greg. "It seems that Clark has the hots for Andrea Fehring."

"Oh, come on now," Clark said with disgust. "I don't have the *hots* for her, I just thought she might make a nice dinner companion when I visit."

"She is pretty nice," Greg said between man-giggles. "At least she is when she's not trying to put Odelia behind bars. But don't you think getting close to Andrea might be a little touchy considering your boss? Isn't aiding and abetting a criminal a crime?"

"I said almost the same thing this morning," I noted.

"I'm not aiding and abetting anyone," Clark insisted. "I don't know where Willie is most of the time myself, and I seldom see him." He jabbed the table with a meaty index finger. "And like I told Odelia, I work for a legitimate company, not directly for Willie Proctor."

"Yeah, yeah," I said. "Do you want more coffee?" In response, Clark held out his cup to me. I took it and went into the kitchen to brew him another cup.

"Getting back to the matter at hand," Clark said, "I think we should split up our efforts to cover more ground. You guys tackle the sister, and I'll see what the cops are up to as well as run down more information on that Nathan Glick. It might be a dead end, but you never know. I'll also dig more into Chris Cook."

I brought Clark's refilled mug back to the table. "Didn't one of the boys see Zach enter the house that night?" he asked as I set it down in front of him.

"I do recall reading that in the report you sent over, but I can't remember which one." I went to our office and retrieved the report, skimming it along the way. "According to this report, it was Chris who claimed to have seen Zach enter the house."

"Yeah," Clark said as he turned the hot mug around in his hands. "I want to have a chat with that kid. Maybe I'll hop a red-eye tonight to Illinois." He pulled out his smartphone and started checking flights. "Best to get to these people before the cops break the story to the media, which could happen at any time."

"I'm still surprised they haven't," Greg said.

"It's probably because they haven't reached his father," Clark said, still looking at his phone. "Or the cops are hoping their silence will flush out the killer. One thing is for sure, whoever did this wanted that body found and knew who Zach was. If nothing crops up on the news, they might get antsy because they're not stirring the pot as they had hoped."

"So you're thinking this was all for show?" Greg asked.

Clark shrugged. "It's just one way to go, especially with that note attached to the body. But if it is and the news goes silent after the initial body find, the people behind it might go a little off the rails because they're not getting the attention they expected."

I became alarmed. "You don't think they'd

dump another body on me, do you?"

Again my brother shrugged, making me want to shake the snot out of him for a straight answer. "They might. That's why it's important we get to the bottom of this as soon as possible. The cops, especially the feds, have their own game plan in play. We need to have ours."

"But what about your schedule?" I asked. "Don't you have a job to do?"

Clark looked up from his phone at me. "I am doing it, sis. On my way over here I got a call from Willie. I'm to stay on this until it's over. He's worried about the two of you — and about his possible exposure."

"But I thought you didn't work for Willie," Greg said, grinning at Clark as he drained his beer. Clark grumbled over the rim of his coffee mug in response.

Before Clark left, we came clean to Clark about John Swayze.

"You should have called the cops," he said, not one bit happy that we'd let Swayze go.

We gave Clark Swayze's phone, which had been unlocked by one of Greg's more talented employees. Clark viewed all the videos, not just the ones involving us. "It looks like he really is just a nosy guy looking for a story," he pronounced when he was finished. "See here, he was even watching you before he came into your back yard." Clark studied the video. "Wow, that Whitecastle woman is really beautiful. Maybe I should be asking her out."

"Down, boy," I told him. "She's engaged to a lawyer from San Diego."

"Still," he said in response, "with all the bodies you find, a ghost whisperer might be the perfect addition to our little circle of friends."

Clark put down the phone and looked at me. "Did anything special come up on the Marigold report on Swayze? You did run one on him, didn't you?"

I nodded and put down my wine glass. "Yes, I did. There were a few John Swayzes that popped up in a similar age bracket, but after I eliminated the obvious non-matches and one that was deceased, I was able to narrow it down and match the photo. There was nothing out of the ordinary. In fact, he leads a pretty boring life. No wonder he's looking for excitement."

"Okay," Clark said, "but to be safe, email me the Marigold report on him and the one on Alec Finch. I'll read them on the plane. And promise me you'll call the cops if he bothers you again."

"Don't worry about that," Greg assured

him. "I don't think he'll be back. Odelia did a number on his hand and he's afraid of dogs. I think he got the message that we're not easy targets for such stuff."

Sixteen

The trip to Studio City entailed about forty miles traveled over three freeways across the midsection of Los Angeles County. It took us an hour without much traffic early on a Saturday morning. The same route could take two or more hours during the week. But even on the weekend, you never knew if you'd encounter a traffic accident, construction, or a police chase. That's life in Southern California, and people who live here know they need to build in extra travel time in case of such incidents.

We wanted to sneak up on Jean Utley early in the day but landed in Studio City around seven thirty, way too early to go calling on anyone on a Saturday unless you were a SWAT team. Not knowing what traffic would be like, we held off on breakfast until we reached our destination. We found an IHOP near her place and filled up on pancakes and coffee while we waited. I'm

217

particularly fond of their blueberry pancakes, while Greg loves their omelet and pancake combos. We'd left Wainwright at home today since we didn't know where our road would lead us after we ambushed — uh, visited — Jean.

Zach's sister lived in a large gated condo development just south of Ventura Boulevard. The buildings were painted the usual earth tones with terra-cotta trim common not only in Southern California but throughout the Southwest. The development looked fairly new and was nicely landscaped with drought-friendly plants. Greg and I stared at the electronic gate and keypad, then at each other. So much for the element of surprise.

"Now what?" I asked as Greg pulled off to the side of the driveway to give us time to think.

"I'm not sure," he said as he studied the security set up.

There seemed to be two gates — one for entrance onto the property and one for exiting. We watched a car approach and stop. The driver stretched an arm out his window and punched in a code. The gate opened as if he'd rubbed a magic lamp. The car drove through and the gate closed behind it.

"Can't we just follow another car

through?" I asked.

Greg shook his head. "I don't think so. I'll bet that gate is on an electronic eye and as soon as the first car passes, it will begin to close. In order to fool it, we'd probably have to be right on the other car's bumper, and I don't think the other driver would allow that, especially if he's a resident."

"At least there's not a guard posted at the gate," I noted.

"It looks like even the pedestrian gate is operated on a keypad," Greg said, still studying the gate. "You probably have to have a code to get in but just turn a knob to get out. Same with the cars. I'm sure the exit gate operates on a simple motion sensor." He turned to me. "We might have to just call her and tell her we need to speak with her. If we say it's about her brother, she might cooperate."

"What about deliveries?" I asked, not willing yet to give in to the honest approach. "Would they have the code? If so, maybe we could bribe them to give it to us."

"They would only have it if the owner gave it to the company, and most wouldn't. Delivery people would have to call the occupant, and they would buzz them in."

I grabbed a water bottle from the console and took a long drink from it while I looked the obstacle over. "How about we wait for the next car to either come in or out, and I'll slip in on foot."

"No," Greg said with finality. "You are not going in there alone. Besides, I'll bet there are security cameras trained on both the exit and entrance recording every vehicle and pedestrian that come in and out."

"Cameras maybe," I said after taking another drink. I handed the water bottle to Greg and he took one of his own. "But maybe not a live person watching screens. This is a very nice place, but it's not that high-end. I'll bet the security footage is only viewed if there's a problem. I could slip in," I argued, "and no one would notice unless they needed to check the tapes later."

"No, Odelia. I'm going with you, and that's all there is to it. I've sat in vehicles too many times worried sick about you." He glared at me. It was his look of warning. "And don't you even think about hopping out of this van and making a dash for it. We have no idea if she knows about Zach or is even involved with his death. If she is, she's probably armed."

"It's only nine o'clock on a Saturday," I pointed out. "Jean is probably still in her jammies or maybe even still in bed."

"Or taking a run," Greg suggested.

220

"What?"

"Could that be her?" He pointed to a slender blond dressed in running clothes approaching the pedestrian gate from the property side. "That person looks a lot like the photo you showed me."

I squinted to study the woman making her way through the gate, then from my bag pulled out the photo I'd printed for a comparison. It could very well be Jean Utley, but it could also be anyone else. In Los Angeles, pretty blonds were a dime a dozen, thanks to the entertainment industry. Some were natural; some not. Some weren't even women.

She jogged slowly past the van on my side, oblivious to our scrutiny. Her long hair was pulled back into a ponytail that bounced when she jogged, and earbuds were plugged into her ears. As she ran by, I thought the profile was close enough to pursue it.

I hopped out of the van and took after her on foot. "Hey, Jean," I yelled as I jogged after her, my sneakers heavily pounding the sidewalk in pursuit. But the earbuds were too much competition — not to mention that even with my exercise walking, my lung capacity was not what it should be thanks to my age and size. Walking is not jogging, and in less than half a block I was looking defeat squarely in the eye in the form of her tight butt as it increased the distance between us.

When she reached the corner, I hoped the light would stop her — but the walk light turned green, and off she went across Ventura without so much as a slight hesitation. I gathered my breath for one more shot. "Jean!" My voice got lost in the traffic noise, and I gave up the chase. I bent over, hands on my pudgy knees, to catch my breath. Sweat was pouring down my face and also down my back, pooling in the crack of my butt under my heavy jeans. I was not a pretty sight. Let's face it: I may have the legs in the family, but Greg has the physical fitness.

I was about to stand upright and head back to the van when it pulled alongside me. "Need a lift, sugar?" asked Greg.

"You didn't need to come pick me up," I said as I took deep breaths and felt a catch in my side. "I could have walked the block back."

"You sure?" Greg asked. "You look pretty done-in to me."

I wanted to say something snarky but needed to save my breath to haul my ass back into the van. Once inside, I grabbed the water bottle and drank down the contents. "I really need to exercise more," I finally gasped. Greg flashed me a look that clearly displayed *haven't we had this conversation before?* And we had — on numerous occasions. Greg didn't mind that I weighed about two hundred twenty pounds. But he did mind that I wasn't in the best shape, even with my walking, and kept pushing me to increase my distance and speed and add some weight training, especially as I got older. But I wasn't without my talents. Being pigheaded was something I excelled at. In fact, I was an Olympic champion in the sport — a Gold Medal winner standing at the top of the podium.

"If you hadn't been so eager, sweetheart," Greg said, turning the van around and heading back into the cul-de-sac that led to the gate of the condo complex, "you could have listened to my plan and saved yourself a near heart attack."

"I'm all ears now," I told him with a roll of my eyes. "What's this brilliant plan?" I mopped my forehead with a wad of tissue. If it had been the dead of summer and not an overcast February day, I might have keeled over out there.

He parked the van back in the spot where we had been earlier. "She didn't leave on an errand in her car, Odelia. She's taking a run.

Eventually, depending on how long her runs are, she has to come back, and she won't be going as fast when she does. In fact, she'll probably be walking to cool down."

He was one hundred percent correct. Hearing his explanation made me feel like a big dummy. Not only is Greg the physically fit one in this relationship, he's the logical and sensible one. Some days I wonder how I'd ever survive without him.

"Unless," I said, "she gets hit by a bus. Then your theory goes out the window."

Greg tossed his head back and laughed. Then he leaned close to me to grab a kiss. "I'm all sweaty," I protested.

"I like you hot and sweaty," he answered. He made another attempt, but I stopped him. "Hold that thought while I grab more water from the back."

My bus possibility was shot down when, about forty minutes later, Jean returned. I watched her in my side-view mirror as she rounded the corner walking at a brisk pace, just as Greg had said. This time I wasn't about to run or even walk fast after her. I climbed out of the van just before she reached it and faced her, visually confirming at the same time that she was the woman in the photo.

"Jean Utley?" I asked her. She wasn't

focused on me and still had her earbuds in place. "Jean?" I said a little louder as she started past me as if I were no more interesting than a fire hydrant. One thing was for sure: soreness from my earlier jog was settling in. If she got spooked and made a run for it, I would be as mobile as said fire hydrant. But she didn't. This time she heard me and turned.

"Excuse me?" she said, taking out one earbud. "Did you speak to me?" She took a trusting step closer. I'm sure if I'd been a guy, especially a big guy of color, she would not have been so curious and polite. Sometimes it pays to be a squat white middle-aged woman. I'm surprised more crimes aren't committed by women like me, considering how harmless people consider us. If my hair had been gray, she probably would have also given me a concerned smile.

"Yes, I did," I answered. "Are you Jean Utley?"

She hesitated, her face quickly dropping the look of trust, replacing it with wariness. She checked my hands to see if I was holding something. Maybe she thought I was a process server ready to slap her with a summons. "What do you want?" She took a step back.

"I need to talk to you about your brother,

Zach. It's very important."

Now the other earbud came out. "Zach?" She took another step back.

Please don't run. Please don't run. Please don't run.

"Yes," I pressed. "When was the last time you saw him?" I kept my eyes on hers to keep her focused. I was afraid if I glanced over at Greg, she'd take off.

"I don't know what you're talking about."

Oh, come on, I wanted to say. Even with her name change, I'm sure the police had already tracked her down. Whether or not they'd been able to contact her yet was another story, so I held my sarcasm.

"Your brother, Zach Finch," I said, clarifying my question. "When did you see him last?"

"What kind of dumbass question is that?" she asked, her face darkening with anger. "Do you know who my brother is? Or was?"

"Yes," I assured her. "Zachery Finch. He was kidnapped at age fifteen and never found — at least until a few days ago."

Her mouth dropped open, then quickly she snapped it shut. "What kind of scam are you running?" She glanced over at Greg, who was leaning over the passenger side of the van to see and hear better.

"It's no scam," I assured her. "I'm the one

who found him. Haven't the police been trying to reach you?"

She looked me up and down, then glanced over at Greg as she tried to make up her mind about us. "I was out of town on a commercial shoot until late last night. There were a few messages on my machine from some woman cop in Long Beach. She said it was urgent. I was going to call her back this morning." She stared at me, and I could still see skepticism in her eyes. "Is that what she's calling about?"

"Yes," I told her. "Your brother was found dead."

She noticeably staggered, her eyes huge with shock. A second later, before I could offer support, she got control over herself.

"But it's more complicated than that." I took a deep breath. "Look, my name is Odelia Grey, and that's my husband, Greg Stevens, in the van. We'd really like to talk to you about Zach."

"How did you even find me?" She took another step back and glanced around.

I wasn't about to spill the beans about Marigold, so I said, "Name changes are public information, and I'm a paralegal with a lot of research options at my fingertips. I simply did a search for Jean Finch and up popped Jean Utley. Another search gave me this address."

It was clear Jean was processing everything around in her head, and it was clear she wasn't the stereotypical Hollywood dumb blond. I could almost see her weighing every tidbit I'd given her and quickly deciding her options. It also was clear that — like many actresses — she'd had her boobies enhanced and possibly a nose job.

"What do you want from me?" she asked.

"Just to talk to you about Zach," I told her. Quickly, I came up with a story to peddle. "Until I can prove otherwise, I'm on the suspect list in his death. It's ridiculous, I know. I was nowhere near Illinois when he went missing, but I'm the only lead they have right now since I found the body."

She fidgeted from foot to foot, the sweat on her body glistening in the sunlight, and again glanced around for something or someone. "Where was his body found?"

"His body was found in the trunk of my car," I tacked on, hoping the bizarreness of it would tip her decision in my favor.

SEVENTEEN

Once she made up her mind about speaking with us, Jean punched a code into a box next to the security gate that allowed us to drive through and park in visitor parking. We followed Jean down a walkway, into her building, then into an elevator. Not a word was spoken by any of us the entire time. I glanced a few times at Jean but couldn't tell what she was thinking. She just stared straight ahead, like people do when sharing an elevator with strangers.

She lived on the top floor of a three-story building. The condo development was made up of clusters of such buildings centered around a large sparkling swimming pool and green common areas. When Jean saw that Greg was in a wheelchair, her comfort level went up. Like fat middle-aged women, people in wheelchairs just bring out the trust in people. Outside of the occasional white lie, Greg and I were pretty harmless and believed in doing people good, not harm, but people really shouldn't make that assumption when they see people like us. Really, folks, you shouldn't. A handsome paraplegic and a woman wallowing in menopause can be just as dangerous as any thug from the inner city — maybe more so because they have the element of surprise on their side. But for now, I was glad Jean had decided to take a chance.

After seating us, Jean asked us to excuse her for a few minutes and disappeared down a hallway. The condo was laid out in what I like to describe as the roommate setup. There was a nice size living room and dining area in the middle, with a modern open-plan kitchen off to the back and a balcony with several patio chairs across the front that overlooked the pool. Two hallways branched off the common area, presumably each to a different bedroom and bath. I got up from my seat and started down the hallway Jean had not taken.

"Where are you going?" Greg asked in a hushed whisper.

"To use the bathroom," I whispered back. I did need to pee, but I also wanted to know if Jean lived alone.

As I expected, down this hallway was another bathroom and bedroom. The bathroom was off the hallway, with the bedroom next to it. The bathroom door was open. The other door was closed. After a quick glance back toward the common area, I quietly opened the door to the bedroom.

The room was decorated with dark colors and simple furnishings. The queen-size bed was neatly made, and nothing personal covered any surface. On the wall were several framed prints of old movie posters but nothing else. There was a small desk over which hung a bulletin board. The bulletin board was empty except for a few push pins stuck here and there. The room had a masculine feel to it and felt recently abandoned. I wanted to snoop more but couldn't, knowing I had no time. Still, I quietly eased open the closet door and peeked in. It was also empty except for a few hangers and one pair of men's athletic shoes tucked into a corner behind the door as if forgotten. Closing the door, I took another glance around the room, then tiptoed out and eased into the bathroom and closed that door behind me. The bathroom also had an abandoned feel to it. There were hand towels on the towel rack but no other towels or shampoo or soap except for a small bottle of hand soap at the sink. Everything looked recently scrubbed. I used the facilities and washed my hands. While the water was running, I opened the few drawers, the cabinet under the sink, and the medicine cabinet.

When I returned to the living room, Jean was back and seated on the sofa. She'd changed her top from a tank to a loose tee shirt but still had her running shorts on. She'd also slipped off her running shoes but left on her socks. Just above her left ankle was a tattoo of a blue hummingbird sipping a flower. Her face and neck looked like they had been quickly scrubbed.

"Did you find the guest bathroom okay?" she asked, her face void of any emotion. She'd been upset when she led us up to her place, but now she looked fairly composed.

"Yes, thank you," I answered, taking a seat in an easy chair next to Greg's wheelchair. "Do you live here alone or do you have a roommate?"

"I had a roommate," she said, still without emotion, like she'd taken the time in the back to pull herself together while she washed up. "Until a few weeks ago. He was an actor and moved to New York when he landed a part back there."

"Are you also an actor?" I asked, even though I knew she was.

"Yes, or at least trying to be." Her tone

and face finally changed from deadpan to reveal mild frustration. "It's not easy, but I manage to land enough commercial work and small parts to support myself, although I might have to advertise for another roommate soon."

She got up, grabbed a bottle of water from her fridge, and sat back down. She didn't offer us anything. Jean was ready to listen but not to play hostess.

"Okay, so what about my brother? How did Zach's —" she stopped and swallowed hard, then took a drink of water before continuing. "How did his body get into the trunk of your car if you didn't put it there? And how do you know it's him? If you know anything about my brother, you'll know that he went missing years ago. We've always presumed he's been dead for a long time." Jean asked the questions with a shiver and a slight tremble of her lower lip.

"That's the million-dollar question," Greg said. "We have no idea why someone would choose Odelia's car as a body dump site. We're hoping you might be able to give us some information to make the connection."

"As for the ID," I added, "The police did that. And he hadn't been dead a long time, just a few days." I watched her response and knew Greg was doing the same. Something flickered across her pretty face, and her beautifully sculpted eyebrows scrunched together, but I couldn't tell if it was curiosity or disbelief. "Zach was killed Tuesday night," I continued. "This past Tuesday night or very early on Wednesday."

"Is this some kind of a joke?" she asked, each word climbing in volume as if mounting stairs. "What kind of scam are you pulling?" She hopped to her feet, her trust in us shattered, but made no move to throw us out. Was she playing a part or was this real?

"It's not a scam," Greg assured her. "Those calls you're getting from the Long Beach PD will confirm what we've said. Andrea Fehring is the detective handling the matter."

"Have you gotten any calls from a Gregory Shipman yet?" I asked.

She shook her head slowly. "Just those voice mails from the woman in Long Beach."

"Gregory Shipman is FBI," I informed her. "They're involved in this because of your brother's missing status. Expect to hear from him too. He's not near as nice as Detective Fehring."

I pulled my cell phone out of my purse. "I have a photo of his body right here if you don't believe us." I cued up the photo and offered her the phone, faced down so she wouldn't see it unless she really wanted to.

Jean studied both of us for what seemed like a long time. No one moved while she pulled her thoughts together. She sat back down on the sofa with a heavy thud and shook her head, indicating she didn't want to see the photo. "So where has Zach been all this time?" she asked. "Do you know?"

"No one knows that yet," I answered.

"So he was one of those kidnapped kids that someone kept locked away for their personal amusement?" She shook her head slowly from side to side in disgust. "Like that Dugard girl or those three girls in Cleveland?" She took a deep breath, wrapped her arms around herself tightly as if freezing, and looked toward the balcony. "Every time I saw a story like that on the news, I'd wonder if Zach was out there, still alive, being tormented daily." Tears started to well. "Sometimes I'd hope he'd be found. Sometimes I hoped he was dead and not living a daily nightmare." She looked up at us. "Isn't that awful, to wish your brother dead instead of holding out hope?"

"If it's any consolation," Greg replied gently, "the police said he looked to be in good shape."

"I saw his body myself," I said. "He didn't

look abused or neglected physically."

Jean got up and retrieved a photo displayed on a shelf near the TV. She held it out to us. I took it. It was a hinged frame with two small photos on either side. One showed a little girl and boy, both towheads, mugging for the camera. Behind them was a lake. The other photo was of Jean and Zach in their teens wearing tennis clothing. It looked like it was taken the same day as the photo I'd seen in the newspaper talking about their victorious tennis match.

"You and Zach?" I asked, even though I knew it was. I showed it to Greg.

"Yes," she said, taking the photo back. She sat back down and caressed the memento like an amulet. "The one of us as teens was taken after we'd won a family tennis tournament at the country club with our parents. That was just a few months before Zach disappeared. The other is my favorite photo of us when we were kids. We were on a family vacation." She looked at the photos in her hands and said, "I always wondered what Zach would look like all grown up. He was such a good-looking kid. A lot of girls were after him at school."

"From what I saw," I said, "he looked a lot like that photo of you as teenagers. His hair was still blond, and he wore it long."

"Did he have a girlfriend at the time he went missing?" Greg asked.

Jean closed her eyes as she gave the question some thought. "There was a girl he took to school dances once in a while. I think her name was Courtney or Cathy, something like that. But I don't think they were going steady or anything."

"If your brother was killed here in Southern California," Greg said, "then there's a good chance he was living here, possibly with his captors. Are you sure he never reached out to you? Especially recently?"

Her emotions changed gears as she shifted back into anger. "Don't you think I'd remember that?"

"He might have called you under another name," I quickly pointed out. "Have you had any odd calls lately?"

She visibly calmed at that suggestion, realizing it was a sensible one. She shook her head. "No, except for those from the Long Beach police and the occasional telemarketer. And Zach wouldn't know about my name change or whereabouts, so how could he contact me?" Greg and I both nodded, following her logic, although I couldn't help thinking about Marigold, but I doubted Zach would know about that.

"Why did you change your name and

move?" I asked.

"I wanted a new start. After Zach disappeared, people saw me as that poor girl who had lost her brother. With my father being so well known, people wouldn't forget about it. Every now and then someone would come forward claiming they knew something, and the whole sordid mess would be flashed across the news again. My father had offered a huge reward for any viable information, and that brought out all the nuts. It was difficult enough on my poor mother to lose Zach, but having it publicly dredged up constantly tore her apart even more."

"I believe I read that your mother committed suicide," I said softly. "Was that because of Zach's disappearance?"

"Yes. Every time someone contacted the police saying they knew something, she'd get her hopes up, only to have them destroyed." She put the photo down on the coffee table. "What you might not have read is that after Zach disappeared, Mom became an alcoholic and was addicted to sleeping pills. A couple of years after he was kidnapped, someone contacted the police saying they had seen Zach alive and well in a small town just outside Las Vegas. They wanted the reward, but when the police investigated they discovered it was a hoax. That was the last straw for my mother. Two weeks later she shot herself while hopped up on booze and pills." Jean looked away as her eyes filled with tears.

"I'm sorry this is so hard on you," I said. "We don't mean to cause you pain, but it's important that we find out what connection Zach might have to us."

"I understand," Jean said. "Really, I do." She got up and went back down the hall, returning a few seconds later with a wad of tissue in her hand.

"What about your father?" Greg asked. "When did you last see or speak with him?"

Jean wiped her eyes and nose with the tissue before speaking. "My father and I are not on good terms."

"How recent is that development?" I asked.

She curled her lip a little at the edges, then stopped, as if she thought better of it. "My father and I have always had a difficult relationship. Mom always said it was because he and I were so alike, stubborn and bull-headed. After Zach's disappearance, with everyone's nerves on edge, it got worse. I stuck around because of my mother."

"Is that when you moved to California, after your mother died?" Greg asked.

Jean shifted in her seat. I wondered if she was going to mention working for Aztec. I was dying to know what, if anything, happened there to prompt the move and whether or not she'd mention Nathan.

"I stuck it out until I graduated from college," Jean began after she'd dried her tears. "After that, I decided I needed to start over, so I came to LA. I'd always wanted to be an actress and had taken classes in both high school and college, so why not give it a shot? If it didn't work out, I could always get a job doing something else. Fortunately, it's worked out enough that I don't have to do that yet."

"And your father was okay with that?" I asked. "It seems to me that a man like Alec Finch would want to keep his only remaining child close after everything that had happened. He could have tempted you with a plum job in one of his companies to get you to stay."

"My father was not thrilled with my decision, but he didn't stand in my way," she explained. "Not that he could have. I had my savings and a nice bit of money left to me by my mother. I left for California right after my college graduation. The money allowed me to buy this place." She gave up a thin smile. "If there's one thing I've learned from my father, it's how to manage money."

"So you came straight here after college? Did you know anyone in California?" I asked. "You know, someone you stayed with while you got settled? That's a big change for a young woman on her own." My curiosity was really on alert now.

"No one." She shook her head as she said it. "When I got here I rented a small efficiency apartment in Hollywood and started taking acting classes. I made some friends in the business and roomed with some of them after that. Eventually I landed a few small commercials and some small parts. When the acting work got steady, I bought this place. That was just a year ago."

"No family other than your dad?" I asked. I knew from Marigold that Jean had no kin on her father's side, but I had not pulled a report on her mother.

"No one," she said. "It was perfect for starting over. No loose ends. No people I'd miss seeing at Christmas or Thanksgiving." She was trying to put a positive spin on it, but her voice was coated with sadness. She gave me a small hopeful smile. "But I do hope to have my own family one day."

"Why the name Utley?" Greg asked while I mused over her information. "What's the significance? Is it an old family name?"

She shook her head. "It has no connection with my family. When I was a little girl there was a librarian in our town named Jean Utley. She was always so nice to me. She said we had a special connection because we were both named Jean. When I was thinking of names to use, that one came to mind."

"That's a lovely thought," I said to her. "Does she know that?"

"She passed away when I was in college. Some type of cancer, I think."

I got up. "I guess we've kept you long enough, but I have one more question to ask. What about Zach's friends? Do you know if any of them relocated to California after high school or college?"

She thought a minute. "I don't think so. He was very close to a couple of guys. They were inseparable since grade school. One was killed in an accident shortly after Zach disappeared, I remember that; I don't know what happened to the others. I dated the cousin of one of them but lost touch with everyone after I moved away." She paused, then said, "I preferred it that way."

"Do you know where your father is now?" Greg asked as we moved toward her front door. "I think the police are waiting to talk to him before they release the news about your brother's death to the media. They need to notify family first."

She opened the door for us. As cooperative as she'd been, she looked eager to be rid of us now. Then again, if she didn't know anything about Zach being alive until recently, she'd just been dealt quite a big blow.

"No," she said quickly. "I don't keep track of my father's comings and goings. I haven't spoken to him since I left home after college."

"You haven't?" I asked with surprise. Worried that she would pick up that I might know something I wasn't disclosing, I quickly tacked on, "That's a long time, like four or five years? Especially since the two of you are all you have?"

She shrugged it off. "I wasn't willing to live the life he wanted, so we went our separate ways. Believe me, I don't think he's suffering much because of it. He's too busy being a big shot."

"I'm sure your father will want to reunite with you over the loss of your brother," Greg said, "if for no other reason than damage control. The media is going to be particularly bothersome. A kid missing for a lot of years and now found dead is big news, especially the kid of a famous financier."

"Listen," Jean said, her face turning worried. "I do not want my name connected to this. I don't want to go back to being the daughter of Alec Finch or the sister of poor Zach Finch. I have a new life, and I want to keep it clear of this mess. Understand?"

"That's not up to us," Greg told her. He glanced at me. "Odelia and I won't say anything about you. I can promise you that." I nodded in agreement. "But we have no control over the police or the media."

"Nor," I added, "are we interested in having our names connected to this. When the news hits the fan, my name as the finder of the body is going to go public. That's one of the reasons we're tracking this down on our own. We want to minimize our exposure as much as possible by uncovering as much as we can about what happened to Zach as quickly as possible."

Before leaving, I pulled out one of my T&T business cards and handed it to her. I jotted my cell phone number on the back. "Please call me if you think of anything that might be helpful in figuring out why Zach's body was left in my car. There has to be a connection. Things like this just don't happen randomly."

We thanked her for her time and made our way down the elevator and back across the common area toward the visitor parking lot.

"What do you think?" Greg asked, stopping by the far end of the pool area.

"I'm not sure what to think," I answered honestly as I glanced up at Jean's balcony. "She seemed genuinely shocked by the news of Zach's death, but I'm not sure she was surprised to learn he had only just died."

"You think she knew he was alive all along?"

"I think it's a good possibility," I said. "It was difficult to tell which emotions were real and which were acting. But I do think she knows more than she told us. It was like a mix of truth and lies, and we need to figure out which is which."

"I think the stuff about her father is true," Greg said. "I'm betting they have been estranged a long time."

"Yeah," I agreed. "I think that part is true too. There were several discrepancies in what Jean said about her life compared to the Marigold report I pulled on her." I placed a hand on Greg's shoulder. "Let's talk about them on the way home, honey."

We started again for the van, but as soon as we saw it, we stopped short. We had company. Leaning against our vehicle with his arms crossed was Gregory Shipman of the FBI, and he did not look happy.

EIGHTEEN

Shipman pushed off from the van and stood straight as an arrow, his hands at his sides. He wore shades and a dark blue suit with the jacket buttoned. His chin was tilted up. He looked down his nose at us as we approached, like some ill-pleased despot.

"Imagine running into you two here," Shipman said when we reached him.

"Are you following us?" I asked.

He didn't answer but asked us a question instead. "So what can you tell me about Jean Finch Utley?"

"Who?" I asked back.

Next to me, Greg took my hand and squeezed it. "I think we need to cooperate, sweetheart."

"Listen to your husband," Shipman said. "He's talking sense."

"Well, he's not the one under suspicion here, is he?" I snapped as I stared into the inky darkness of Shipman's glasses.

Shipman lowered his chin and gave me a superior smile that made me want to smack him. "In my book, everyone's a suspect, Odelia, even your mother."

"You leave my mother out of this." I'd become an angry snapping turtle. If Shipman wasn't careful, I might just snap off his nose. Greg squeezed my hand in warning.

"We just asked Ms. Utley some questions," Greg told him. "Probably the same questions you'll ask her."

"I doubt it." Shipman removed his glasses and looked at both of us several times, studying our faces. He finally settled his suspicious peepers on Greg, probably thinking he was the more reasonable of the two of us. He was right.

"Jean Utley claims she didn't know her brother was still alive and in California," Greg told him. "She also said she and her father had a falling out when she moved to California and changed her name."

"She told us," I chimed in, "that she hasn't spoken to her father since then."

"Do you believe her?" Shipman asked.

Greg and I looked at each other, silently comparing thoughts. I gave him a slight nod, letting him know I was onboard with telling Shipman what we knew. "I don't know," Greg answered. "There were some discrepancies in her answers."

"Like what exactly?" Shipman asked, his ears pricked with curiosity as he listened.

"She claims," I said, "that she moved here right after graduating from college, but I don't think that's true. She worked for one of her father's companies after college — Aztec was the name of it. It's located in Chicago. She was there maybe a year or so, then moved to California. That's when she changed her last name to Utley."

"Tell me," Shipman asked, obviously pointing the inquiry at my husband instead of me, even though I'd just given him the information, "how did you two find Jean if you didn't already know her?"

"Name changes are public record," Greg answered, parroting my explanation to Jean, "and Odelia is a paralegal with a lot of research options at her fingertips."

Shipman turned his eyes once again on me. "Even employment records?"

In response, I shrugged. I wasn't about to tell Shipman about Marigold. "The question is," I asked instead, "how did you get inside the security gate? We were invited in."

"You have your ways. I have mine," was all he said. He put his sunglasses back on. "Look, you two, I know you have a bad habit of sticking your noses where they don't belong, but this is not one of those times. The more you get involved, the more the agency is going to think you had something to do with Zach Finch's murder. Maybe Greg here put the body in the trunk and forgot to tell you."

"That's absurd," Greg said, taking his turn at being a snapping turtle.

"You may be in a chair, Greg, but it's easy to see you're a pretty strong guy. Or maybe, Odelia, you didn't realize the trunk would be opened by the car wash people." Shipman said, turning his covered eyes my way.

"I go there all the time," I told him, sticking my chin out in defiance. "Of course I'd know they would open the trunk."

"Frankly," Shipman said, turning his shaded eyes toward the building housing Jean Utley, "I'm thinking one of your crime buddies did it, thinking the corpse would be safe there for a few days until they could dispose of it properly. My money is on Elaine Powers; I believe you call her Mother. Maybe Ms. Utley put a hit out on her brother through Mother's crew, and Mother thought it would be safe to leave the body with her goody two-shoes pal Odelia for the time being. If you hadn't gone to the car wash and popped the trunk, I'll bet that body would have disappeared as magically as it appeared, without you knowing a thing."

"I don't think Elaine did this," I told him with conviction.

"Have you spoken to her about it?" Shipman asked.

"No, I haven't," I answered truthfully. "I have no idea where she is or how to reach her. She just sort of pops up unexpectedly from time to time. You know, like a pimple. And we're not friends." Okay, a little fib, but honestly I didn't know if that cryptic ad would produce Elaine or not.

"She's telling the truth, Special Agent Shipman," Greg told him as he edged his chair closer to him. "Elaine Powers is not someone we have over to dinner."

"But you do have Willie Proctor over for dinner?" he asked with sarcasm.

"You're barking up the wrong tree there," Greg said, giving his voice a sharp edge. "It's true, we have come to know some unusual people in our travels, but we don't harbor or hide them. Watch us all you want. You're going to find nothing." Greg took my arm and edged closer to the van. "Now, if you'll excuse us, my wife and I would like to leave." Greg aimed the key fob at the van and unlocked it, the audible click of the lock's release underlining his words.

Shipman moved and opened the passenger-side door for me with exaggerated gallantry. Greg went around the back of the van to the driver's side. By the time he'd gotten his butt into the van and stored his wheelchair, I was still standing on the pavement having a staring contest with Shipman. He looked into my eyes. I looked into two black holes of expensive sun protection. "Get in, Odelia," Shipman finally said with a low chuckle. "I'm not going to bite or even slam your fingers in the door." He laughed again. "We have other ways to make people talk."

Once I was settled inside and buckled up, Shipman shut the door. Greg lowered the window on my side. "Special Agent," he said, leaning slightly across me, "if we find out anything else important, we'll let either you or Detective Fehring know. We're as eager for this to be over as you are, if not more."

Shipman was about to say something when we heard an ear-piercing scream followed by loud shouts. It was coming from the pool area. There was another sharp shriek, louder and longer than the first. Shipman took off at a run in the direction of the hysteria. I piled out of the van and ran around the other side to help Greg get out of the van faster by grabbing his chair and setting it up so he could just swing his butt into it. Together we made our way back down the path toward Jean's building. When in a hurry, Greg can propel his wheelchair at a pretty good clip. My stumpy legs and fat ass had trouble keeping up with him.

A small crowd of people had gathered by the pool in a circle. They were eerily silent except for two women who were weeping. One was older. She was seated on a bench, clinging to a toy poodle for dear life while others tried to comfort her. "I saw it. I saw it all," the old woman was saying while her dog peddled its tiny legs like an egg beater to get down. "I was walking Cedric and saw her fall," she whimpered to those around her. "It was horrible!" She broke into sobs and buried her face into the dog's fur.

Greg and I made our way to a small break in the circle. I poked my head between two young men, then wedged my way in to make enough room for Greg to see between me and the man to my right. In the center was Gregory Shipman. He was giving orders on his phone while squatting next to the partially clothed body of a woman facedown on the concrete apron of the pool. There was no way she was alive. Her body was contorted, splayed like a rag doll tossed to the floor by an angry child. Her head, with its long blond hair secured by a barrette, was surrounded by a pool of blood. She was barefoot and wore nothing but a short terry cloth robe.

I didn't have to see the face to know it was Jean Utley. On the dead woman's left ankle was the tattoo of a blue hummingbird.

"I really don't want to seem callous in light of what has happened to Jean and her brother," I said to Greg as I climbed into the van next to him and buckled up, "but I am so over being questioned by the police."

Greg glanced over at me after he backed the van out of the visitor parking at Jean's condo and headed for the exit. "Does that go for the FBI too?"

"It goes double for the FBI." I pulled my cell phone out of my purse and checked for messages. It had rung a few times while we were being questioned, but they wouldn't allow me to answer or even look at it while being interrogated. "I know they're doing their job and I want to get to the bottom of what's going on just as much as they do, but why do they have to keep asking the same questions over and over and over like a broken record?"

"They did the same to me, sweetheart. I

think it's their way of checking for discrepancies and slip-ups. They want to make sure what we tell them is the truth."

"But did you get asked if we said anything to Jean to make her jump?" That particular question, posed to me by Shipman, almost sent me for the man's throat, except that I remembered he carried a gun. "The very idea that we would even try to do that is ridiculous."

In spite of the severity of the situation, Greg chuckled. "Yes, I got asked a similar question by another agent."

Studio City is not an actual city but an area in the humongous city of Los Angeles. Units from the Los Angeles Police Department had swarmed the condo complex, along with agents from the local FBI office called by Shipman. While waiting in the community room of the complex to be questioned, I'd overheard Shipman saying to one of the LAPD officers that Jean's death was part of an ongoing FBI investigation and therefore they would have jurisdiction and be in charge of the matter. The LA cop did not look pleased, but a call into his office caused him to back down and cooperate.

There were three calls I'd missed during the couple of hours we were tied up with questioning. One was from Clark. I listened to the voice mail he left and reported to Greg. "Clark just left a voice mail saying he's in the town where Zach grew up and is trying to find Chris Cook. Cook's office is shut for the weekend, and no one seems to be home at his residence. Clark will check back in later." I called Clark's phone but only got voice mail. I left him a message bringing him up to speed with Jean's death.

The next call and voice mail was from Andrea Fehring. I put it on speaker and played it for Greg.

"I just heard what happened in Studio City," Andrea said in her message in a tone so sharp it nearly sliced my inner ear. "As soon as you're done there, you're to come straight to my office. You hear? No detours. No wild goose chases. Straight to the Long Beach PD. That's an order!"

"Should I tell her we're on our way?" I asked Greg.

We'd just turned onto the freeway and were starting our long freeway journey back to that neck of the woods. At least the Long Beach Police Department was close to home.

"Yeah," Greg said, "but before we get there, let's stop at Gino's and pick up some sandwiches for lunch. It's right by the station. Knowing the police and their long-winded questioning, we'll need to come stocked with provisions for the long haul." He checked the clock on the dashboard. "It's already well after one. Better yet, call her back and see if we can pick up something for her. It couldn't hurt in the brownie points department."

"Sounds good," I agreed. "Even though I don't have an appetite after seeing Jean's brains splashed on the pavement just moments after seeing her alive."

"Me either." Greg reached over and gave my knee a comforting pat. "But better to be prepared just in case. I don't think Andrea is calling us in for a short, casual chat."

I nodded in agreement as I texted Andrea back that we had just left Studio City and were heading her way. I asked her if she wanted something from Gino's, knowing that almost anyone who lived or worked in Long Beach would know that menu by heart. A message quickly arrived saying to forget the food and get in there. I read it to Greg.

"Ha! There's no way I'm showing up there without my lunch," he said in response. "Let her stop me."

The final call was from my mother and had come in just before we were released by

Shipman. She left a short, simple message, which I also played on speaker: "Call me. Urgent."

"She doesn't sound upset or worried," Greg noted.

"No," I agreed. "I wonder what that's about and if it can wait until after we see Andrea." Before he could answer, I called Mom, thinking I'd tell her we'd be there after we saw Fehring. She answered on the first ring. "Mom, it's me," I said as soon as she said hello. "Greg and I had an errand this morning. We're on the freeway heading back now. What's so urgent? You okay?"

"I'm fine," she said calmly. "It's just that a friend of yours stopped by, and I think you should come to my place as soon as possible."

For the life of me, I couldn't think of who might have visited Mom, but she did seem genuinely delighted. "Who is it?"

"It's a surprise," Mom said.

I sighed. "Mom, Andrea Fehring is demanding our presence at the Long Beach Police Department ASAP. That's where we're heading now. Can this mystery person wait or come back later?"

Mom hesitated. "I don't think she can. You need to come here first. Tell Detective Fehring you'll meet her later. I'm sure she'll understand."

I remembered Andrea's tone and doubted seriously that she would tolerate any holdup. "She was pretty adamant that Greg and I meet her now," I said. "Something very serious has happened, Mom. I'll tell you about it when I see you. But for now there's no way we can stop by your place before we go to Long Beach."

I could hear Mom relaying my words to whoever was there. I racked my brain but couldn't think of who it could be. I raised my brows in question at Greg, but he only shrugged. Who did we know who would stop by Mom's if they didn't find us home? Who besides our closest friends even knew where Mom lived? I thought about Willie, but Mom did say it was a woman.

"Mom," I called into the phone. "You still there?"

"Here," Mom said. "You talk to her."

There was a brief moment during which Greg and I could hear fumbling and voices as the phone was passed along to someone else. Finally came a familiar voice. "Dottie, is that you?"

My eyes snapped in Greg's direction. He also recognized the voice and was having trouble keeping his mind on his driving. The van swerved slightly, and the guy next to us laid on his horn.

"Elaine, what are you doing at my mother's?" I asked, not even trying to hide my shock.

"You contacted me, remember?" she said, her voice filled with amusement.

"Um, does my mother know who you are?"

"Affirmative."

"And — ?" I prodded. I looked over at Greg. He was staring straight out the windshield and shaking his head in disbelief.

"And we're drinking coffee and eating banana bread fresh out of the oven while playing gin rummy," Elaine reported. I looked over at Greg. His eyes grew wider and wilder as he urged the van to go faster. "Grace makes great banana bread," Elaine added.

"Why my mother, Elaine?" I asked. "I contacted *you.* Why get her involved?" I wanted to ask her how she found Mom, but after using Marigold, I realized that might be a waste of time. There might be several deep search engines like it on the net. Let's face it, individual privacy is a ship that sailed a very long time ago. All we private citizens can do is wave goodbye to it with hankies while it disappears into the horizon.

The next question was, how did Elaine

get into Mom's retirement community? It was gated and, unlike Jean's complex, had a guard at the front gate. Did Elaine simply say who she was and Grace told the guard to let her in? It would be something my mother would do.

"True, but you have way too many police buddies for my comfort," Elaine explained. "That's all I'd need is for that Fehring woman or Dev Frye to show up at your door while we were having a heart to heart. It might get messy." She paused to let the full impact of her words sink into my thick skull. "And it seems I made the right decision, considering what your mother has told me. The cops *and* the FBI? Odelia, you've come up in the world since I last saw you."

"Mom told you about . . . um . . . the body?" I looked up out the windshield and realized for the first time how fast Greg was going. For a guy without the use of his legs, he sure had a lead foot — at least today.

"Yes, she did," Elaine said, "and the guy's identity, which is why I wanted to see you sooner than later. Come straight here, Odelia. Make some excuse to Fehring to put her off, but come straight here. It's important for you and for Fehring. I'll be waiting."

As soon as I hung up, I texted Andrea

Fehring and told her we had to make a small detour — a family emergency that had just cropped up — but that we'd be at her office as soon as we solved the crisis.

She texted back immediately: YOU HAVE TWO HOURS TO GET IN HERE. DON'T MAKE ME COME AND GET YOU!

Family dinners would be a laugh-a-minute if Clark got involved with this woman. I texted back, assuring her that two hours should be plenty of time.

"Forget Long Beach," I told Greg when I was finished with my phone. "We need to stop by my mother's first."

"That's where I'm heading," Greg said, keeping up the speed and deftly weaving in and out of traffic.

"Are you deliberately trying to get a ticket?" I asked.

"I'm trying to save your mother's life," he answered, not taking his eyes off the road.

I chuckled. "Relax. You heard Elaine. They're drinking coffee and playing gin rummy."

"That's the problem," Greg snapped without looking at me. "Grace cheats at cards."

On my side of the vehicle, I nearly pushed my right foot through the floor board.

NINETEEN

When we got to Mom's, she was still alive. The two of them had abandoned their card game and were sitting companionably on Mom's patio enjoying the fresh air. They looked like a couple of old hens gossiping about the neighbors. The patio ran across the front of Mom's townhome and was bordered by a waist-high concrete block fence. It was accessed through sliders in the living room. They waved to us as we approached the front door. "The door's open," Mom said to us as we came up the walk.

By the time we entered the house, both Mom and Elaine had made their way back into the living room. "Let's talk inside," Elaine said as she closed the slider to the patio. "No sense taking the risk of someone overhearing us."

"You two want some coffee or tea?" Mom asked us.

"Just some water, Mom," I said.

"Coffee would be great, Grace," echoed Greg. "Thanks. And do you have any of that banana bread?"

Leave it to my hubs to think of his stomach, even while in the presence of a killer.

Mom went into the kitchen, which was separated from the living room by a short counter. She would be able to see and hear everything from there, otherwise she might have not have offered us drinks. Meanwhile, Elaine and I stared at each other, neither making a move to sit. I wasn't sure if I should give her a hug like I would one of my usual friends, or even Willie. Willie didn't scare me. Elaine Powers terrified me. She made the decision for me.

"Come here, Dottie," Elaine said, holding out her arms to me. I tossed my bag onto the counter and went to her. We shared a short warm hug. Elaine called me Dottie because I reminded her of her deceased sister. If Elaine hadn't been the mastermind of a successful crew of hitwomen, I think we might have been normal friends. She's smart and funny and genuine. But it was kind of difficult to overlook the killer part.

After releasing me, Elaine held out her right hand to Greg. "Nice to see you looking so fit, sport."

Greg eyed the hand, not sure what to do

with it. Even more than me, he had personal conflicts when it came to being chummy with murderers. The first and only time he'd seen her was after he'd been shot, when she'd visited him briefly in the hospital. In the end he caved and shook Elaine's hand.

"I didn't see Lisa outside," I said to Elaine after we each took our seats and Mom had delivered our drinks. Then Mom scampered back to the kitchen to retrieve a plate of sliced banana bread and napkins. She handed a slice on a napkin to Greg before sitting down in her recliner. Grace Littlejohn wasn't about to miss a thing.

"Some things are better done solo," Elaine said with a brief smile. "It attracts less attention, especially in a place like this where people have nothing else to do with their time but be nosy."

"You've got that right," agreed my nosy mother.

Lisa was a pint-size killer who usually rode a sleek, high-powered motorcycle and often accompanied Elaine as her bodyguard. I wasn't sorry Lisa wasn't present, and I certainly would not have given her a hug. She didn't like me one bit, and the feeling was mutual. The first time we met she wanted to put a bullet in my brain. The last time we saw each other she called me dumber than a box of rocks, but at least no guns were involved. Maybe that's measurable progress, but I still didn't like her.

"But rest assured, Lisa isn't too far away. She never is." Wiping the smile off her face, Elaine got down to business. "Do they know anything about Zach Finch yet?" she asked. "Like who killed him?"

"Not yet that we know of," I told her after glancing at Greg. His mouth full of banana bread, he gave me an encouraging nod to go ahead and tell Elaine what we knew.

"Maybe that's what Andrea wants to talk to you about," chimed in my mother. "She said it was urgent." Mom leaned toward Elaine. "Even though she's a cop, Andrea Fehring is quite nice socially. I think my son Clark is a little sweet on her."

Elaine laughed at the thought. "Considering Clark's connections and yours," she said to me, "that could be a very interesting pairing."

"My son used to be a police officer, you know," added Mom. "In fact, he was chief of police in our town. They'd have a lot in common." Elaine looked at me and winked when Mom finished.

Right then and there, I understood that Elaine knew a lot about me and my family and friends that I hadn't disclosed. I was also pretty sure now that Mom didn't have a clue about Clark's true employer but that Elaine had more than a clue. Next to me, Greg started tapping the fingers of his free hand nervously on his leg as if sending me a message in code.

"Andrea's good people," I confirmed. I looked Elaine in the eyes and slightly shifted mine toward Mom, hoping to send her a warning to tread lightly with information. Elaine gave me a tight-lipped smile and blinked once — message received.

"The police think you might have had something to do with Zach Finch showing up dead in Odelia's trunk," Greg said. He'd stopped drumming his fingers, so maybe he'd caught my silent little tête-à-tête with Elaine.

"Not me, sport," Elaine answered.

"My name is Greg," Greg informed her with a face so tight it could crack. Even his beard, a tidy van dyke, looked ready to splinter and fall off. Years ago Greg and I had come across a criminal named Gordon Harper who had called Greg *sport*. He has hated it ever since, no matter who used it. Elaine paused a moment, and I held my breath. Mom looked uncomfortable too.

"That it is, Greg," Elaine finally said to him. "My bad, and I apologize." She smiled at him, and he nodded acceptance of her apology.

"Getting back to Zach Finch," Elaine continued, "my crew had nothing to do with killing him or with stashing him in Odelia's trunk. Even if we did do the job, I would never put you all at risk like that. We're not that sloppy, for one thing, and I don't treat people I like with such disrespect. Odelia here gets in enough trouble on her own without me throwing gasoline on the fire."

"You've got that right," my mother said half under her breath.

After shooting my mother the evil eye, I turned my attention back to Elaine. "There's been another development just this morning, which is what I'm sure Andrea wants to discuss with us." I took a deep breath and a drink of water, then jumped in with both feet. "We just came from Jean Finch Utley's place — that's Zach's sister. Right after we spoke to her, she did a swan dive off the balcony of her third-floor condo onto concrete."

Mom gasped. "What did you do to that woman, Odelia?"

"We did nothing, Mom," I assured her. "We asked her a few questions about Zach and her family and her move to California in the past few years. When we left her, she was dressed in running clothes. When she fell, she was naked except for a short terry robe. The police found her shower running when they went to check her apartment. She must have been getting ready to take a shower when she was murdered."

"Murdered?" Mom asked. "So it wasn't suicide?"

"Nothing's been determined yet," I said, "but why get ready to take a shower, then change your mind and jump from the balcony? The police and FBI aren't sharing information with us, so we don't know if they found evidence of anyone in the condo unit after us. After we left her, we were hijacked by Special Agent Shipman at our van and questioned. There was about twenty to twenty-five minutes between the time we last saw her and her death."

"Plenty of time for someone to slip in and push her off the balcony," noted Elaine, "especially if they were already in her place or nearby."

I filled Mom and Elaine in on the information we'd gotten from Jean. After, we were all silent for a bit. Greg snagged another piece of banana bread and took a big bite. I loved my mother's baking, but right now the sight of the bread turned my stomach.

Elaine broke the silence. "We were contacted about the job," she admitted.

"Zach or Jean?" Greg asked after swallowing his last bite of bread.

"Both," Elaine answered.

In shock, we all snapped our heads in her direction in expectation of more information.

"I received a request, but when I got the names of the targets," Elaine explained, "I turned it down as too much exposure for the crew."

"Exposure?" asked Greg.

"I do my homework on targets before I give the green light to a job," Elaine explained. "Zach Finch was a live grenade, even dead. The kid of a powerful man goes missing for years, then shows up freshly dead? The police and the feds would be all over that like a bloodhound after a coon, which they apparently are. We could dispose of the body somewhere, make it disappear, but even that's tricky. We kill pests; we don't dispose of the remains. As for Jean, just being Zach's sister would put a spotlight on that."

"So who tried to hire you?" I asked.

"I don't know," Elaine answered. "All inquiries about our services are anonymous until I agree to take the job. The less I know about the employer, the safer I can keep my crew and me if I turn down the job and it blows up later." She paused, then added, "Like this one did."

"So when do you find out about who hires you?" asked Greg.

Elaine hesitated before answering, then with a shrug gave up the information. "First I get a cryptic message, like how Odelia contacted me this week. Then I contact that person using a burn phone. One burn phone per job. When the job is done, the phone is destroyed. We discuss the job by phone. If I'm interested, I ask for information about the buyer to confirm who he or she is. Once I'm convinced that it isn't a set-up and the target is legit, we move forward with payment arrangements and the job. All I remember about this job request is that the person on the phone was male, with no strong accent — either international or Southern or even from the Northeast — that I could decipher."

"What do you mean by a legit target?" Mom asked, leaning forward as if taking notes.

"I don't kill for the sport of it, Grace," Elaine told her. "There has to be a good reason for the target to be taken out for me to take the contract, like maybe he's a pedophile or wife beater. Or maybe it's a woman who abuses her kids or murdered them and got away with it. I fancy myself an exterminator of vermin. And I have other business endeavors that don't involve killing, which I have to protect." She winked at me, reminding me of how I last came across her. She'd been running a financial scam on the aged mother of one of my bosses.

"It's still murder," noted Greg with his eyes fastened tightly on Elaine. "Even though you've helped Odelia out a few times and even saved her life — and for that I'm very grateful, believe me — it's still murder."

Elaine got up and started for the kitchen. As she passed Greg, she gently patted him on the shoulder. "That it is, Greg. I don't deny it, and I don't deny that I deserve to be damned to hell for it."

Elaine continued to the kitchen. She was wearing loose black knit pants and a bulky knit pullover, also in black, with a cat print around the hem. On her feet were bright blue Crocs and rainbow socks. When I last saw her, Elaine's hair was a soft brown. Since then, she'd let it go to a natural shiny dark gray shot with silver, which she wore clipped into a perky tousled pixie. She looked like she'd lost weight since our last encounter, and her skin was pale and her eyes dark. Maybe she just needed a good night's sleep. Being the leader of contract killers had to cause many sleepless nights. As she walked away from us, I could see the outline of a gun tucked under her jersey in the waist of her pants. Greg saw it too and widened his eyes at me. Did he really think she'd come unarmed? At least she'd left Lisa, her churlish bodyguard, somewhere out of sight. Elaine may trust us, but she wasn't in the habit of letting her guard down.

In the kitchen, Elaine started to help herself to a cup of coffee. Mom started to get up to assist her but Elaine waved her back down in her seat. She returned with the pot and refilled Greg's mug. After putting the pot back in the kitchen, she stood on the kitchen side of the counter and sipped her coffee. She was so at home, you would have thought she visited my mother frequently. "Do you know any other professionals in my field?" she asked us.

"If I do," I said, "I'm not aware of it. I mean, I can hardly imagine Zee or Steele or Sally Kipman moonlighting as contract killers." I hesitated. "Well, if any of my friends had it in them, it would be Sally, but I seriously doubt she's taken that path."

"How about William Proctor?" Elaine asked. "Has he branched out from embezzlement and fraud?"

"The police asked me the same thing," my mother said, "but I don't recall ever meeting a William Proctor." Through her thick glasses, my mother looked truly puzzled.

When my mother met Willie, he had been going by the name of Willie Carter and was passing himself off as Greg's cousin. We always thought she'd figured out the truth somewhere along the line but was keeping her own counsel. Once Mom had asked Greg's mother about Willie Carter, and Renee had looked at her with confusion. Greg had quickly stepped in and got the two women's minds onto something else before anyone could compare notes. Later he told Mom that Willie was a very distant cousin, the black sheep in his father's family, and that no one talked much about him.

At some point, she was going to make the connection. My mother is far from stupid, but she can be artfully distracted. So after the Renee incident, Greg, Clark, and I had sat down and fabricated a story about Willie Carter using bits and pieces that Mom already knew and the lies we'd told her. Then we each memorized the story and made a pact to stick to it, come hell or high water. Herding Mom's inquisitive mind in the direction we needed it to go for both Willie's and her protection could be exhausting. She seemed to have pretty much forgotten about Willie until the police questioned her about him this week.

I caught Elaine's eye and telegraphed another warning. Over the rim of her coffee mug, she gave me a slight nod of understanding, barely hiding her amusement, and moved back into the living room to take her seat.

"Wait a minute," Mom said, raising an index finger in the air like she was testing wind direction. She turned to Greg. "Are William Proctor and your cousin Willie Carter the same person, Greg?"

Bingo. Give the woman a prize.

"Yes, Grace," Greg responded, "they are the same person. I told you that Willie is the black sheep in the family, and this is why. I'm the only one who keeps in touch with him, and I'd rather the rest of the family not know that."

"Gotcha," Mom said with a jerk of her head. "Don't worry. I can keep a secret."

"You sure?" Greg asked, looking for confirmation. "This isn't fodder for your blog, you know."

"Nor is this visit from Elaine," I tacked on for good measure.

"I like your blog, Grace," Elaine told Mom artfully and with a smile. "I read it regularly."

Mom looked at Elaine and beamed like she'd just received praise from a rock star. "You do?" I was about to voice the same surprised question.

"Yes, I do," Elaine told her. "I really enjoy An Old Broad's Perspective, but I'd be sorely disappointed in you if my name ever ended up there. Willie's shouldn't either. You understand what I'm saying?"

"Don't you worry, Elaine," Mom assured her. "Neither will."

Elaine glanced at me, and it was my turn to give her a small nod of assurance. My mother could be a bit daffy at times, like asking Emma Whitecastle to pay me a visit, but she wasn't a snitch. Maybe it was because she was the black sheep in our family.

"We've been assured that Willie had nothing to do with any of this," I said to Elaine, getting the conversation back on track. "And he's just as anxious to get this resolved as we are so the police will stop thinking about him."

"Okay," Elaine said. She took a long drink

of her coffee and put the mug down on the coffee table. "Do you know how Zach died?"

"We were told by suffocation," I told her. "The police don't think he was dead very long before he was put in the trunk."

"Interesting," she said, considering the information. "Most hitmen would use a gun. Not always, but usually, unless they were concerned about blood or noise."

"Maybe whoever did this," I said, "wanted to make sure Zach didn't bleed all over the trunk of my car. That's pretty considerate, don't you think?" All three of them shot their eyes at me like I'd gone off the rails. "I'm just joking," I quickly added. "Geez."

"Not considerate," Elaine said, "but careful. Shooting means blood, and blood can leave a trail back to the killer or to where the murder took place. Even a drop can give the police a great deal of information these days. Obviously, whoever did this wanted the boy to be found, and the killer knew you'd be the perfect candidate."

"So it is someone Odelia knows?" asked Greg.

"Not necessarily," answered Elaine. "It could be someone who's read or heard about her adventures in the news. Not all of them have been kept quiet, even if the police have been pretty careful about it. But for

277

sure the killer, whether it was hands-on or hired out, wanted that body found. It could have been a message to Zach's father. And whoever did this knew that boy was alive and being kept somewhere all these years."

Elaine pulled a phone from her pocket and hit a button. "Hi, it's me," she said into it in a low voice. "You know that contract we turned down, the one for Zach Finch and his sister? Well, he turned up dead in Odelia Grey's car, and his sister took a dive off a balcony today." She paused and looked at me, a grin on her face. "Yeah, her again." She turned her attention back to her call. "Quietly dig around and see if any of the other local crews took the job or know anything about it. I'm sure whoever wanted those kids dead went somewhere else after we turned them down." She listened, then said, "Right. Zach Finch and Jean Finch."

"Jean Finch Utley," I added.

"The sister also went by Jean Utley," she said into the phone. "I want to know who did these jobs and why they stashed Zach's body with Odelia. And I want to know *now.*" She sharply ended the call and looked at us. "Lisa's on it. She's good at ferreting out information like this."

When Elaine got ready to leave, I walked her to the door. "My brother is looking into

Zach's friends," I told her. "You never know, one of them might be keeping a secret."

"Good start," she said. "And look into the father as deep as you can. Willie can probably help with that more than I can. Another thing: kidnappers don't usually keep a kid alive after being paid ransom money. I'd say the kidnapping was close to home. If the kidnappers knew the family, they might have kept Zach alive."

"You mean he's been living with them all this time? And not necessarily as a captive?"

She shrugged. "Stockholm Syndrome. Maybe Zach preferred being with them over going home. Maybe Zach took the opportunity to break from home. Look into that family's background and see if there was a reason for Zach not to come home. Didn't you say Jean took off right after college and changed her name?"

I nodded. "Yes, but she also worked for her father for a while, even if she didn't disclose that to us. She said she hasn't had contact with her father in a long time. And their mother committed suicide a few years after Zach's disappearance."

"Match up the timeline," Elaine suggested. "My gut is telling me that you'll see a correlation between the mother's death and Jean running away from home. If Lisa

279

turns up something, I'll let you know."

Without a word, Elaine left, went out to a dark sedan parked curbside, and returned with a cell phone. "Here," she said, handing it to me. "It's a burner with one of my numbers programed into it. Use it if you need to reach me, and if it rings, answer it. It'll be me and only me. Don't use it for anything else, got that? Also, text me if anything significant comes up."

I nodded, and again we gave each other a brief hug. "Thanks, Elaine, for your help," I told her once we broke apart.

"No problem, Dottie." She smiled and leaned in close. "By the way, your mother cheats at gin rummy. She clipped me for $3.75."

"Put it on my tab."

TWENTY

We made it to the Long Beach police station barely within the two-hour time frame. We were taken back and parked in a hallway where we cooled our heels for another forty-five minutes before Andrea Fehring was ready to see us. Plastic molded chairs held people of various genders and description, mostly on the rough-looking side, who had also made it past the front desk and were on hold in this second phase of waiting like cattle queued up for slaughter. As far as I could see, none of the other folks were handcuffed, which made me feel better.

"We forgot the darn sandwiches," I hissed to Greg partway through our wait. I'd spent most of the waiting time anxiously watching for new text messages and catching up on my various Words With Friends games. When that was done, I stared at the scarred linoleum and listened to my growling stomach.

Greg laughed. "Don't worry, sweetheart, we won't starve."

"That's easy for you to say. You scarfed down Mom's banana bread. I should have taken some to go. I don't answer questions very well when I'm light-headed."

"I was just about to put out a BOLO on you two," Fehring said as she came down the hallway to fetch us.

"We made it here within the two-hour time frame we promised," I pointed out. "We didn't even stop for sandwiches. It was *you* who weren't on time for this coffee klatch."

She led us back to an interrogation room. "Sorry, but I was unavoidably detained," she apologized. "Zach's father finally showed up. We weren't able to reach him until last night. He got here just after I heard from you two a few hours ago."

I turned my head in several directions as we walked, hoping to catch sight of the man in question among those waiting, but saw no one that looked like the Alec Finch in the photos I'd found online.

"Quit rubbernecking, Odelia," Fehring snapped. "He's in an interrogation room."

"Should we have a lawyer present?" Greg asked after we entered a room and Fehring closed the door behind us.

"That's up to you, Greg," Fehring said, "but I just want to know what happened in Studio City. Shipman isn't sharing like a good boy." Fehring and I took seats on opposite sides of the table — us and them right off the bat. Greg pulled his wheelchair up to the end like an arbitrator. "I also wanted to let you know that we're about to release the whole story to the media now that we've reached Alec Finch."

"Does he know about his daughter yet?" I asked.

"To my knowledge, he doesn't know she's dead. Shipman asked me to wait on him for that," Fehring told us. "Shipman's on his way back from Studio City now. I did ask Finch about his relationship with his daughter since Zach's disappearance and if he knew both of them were apparently living here in Southern California." She paused, then added, "At least we think Zach might have been living here. Finch said he wasn't aware of his son's whereabouts at all. He always assumed he was dead. As for Jean, he said they didn't see each other much after she moved to California but that they remained close and talked often and she never mentioned her brother."

I threw Greg a surprised look. Fehring caught it and said, "From that look, I'd say you know something different."

"Right before she died," I said, looking back at Fehring, "Jean Finch told us she hadn't spoken to her father since she left home after college."

Fehring did some head calculations. "She was probably about twenty-six when she died, so that would be in the neighborhood of about four or five years, wouldn't you say?"

"The way you said that," I noted, "Jean died years ago instead of just a few hours ago."

In response, Fehring amended her comment. "Jean was probably around twenty-six when she took a nose dive to her death today. That better?"

I rolled my eyes toward the ceiling, then brought them back down to hers. "About that," I agreed. "But the thing is, she told us she left for California right after college to become an actress, but she didn't. She didn't move to California until about three years ago. Between college and then, she worked for Aztec Investments, one of her father's companies. It's located in Chicago. She also lived in Chicago for a while. So while she did move away from home, it wasn't directly to California."

"One of the guys with Zach the night he

disappeared works for Aztec now," Greg added. "Nathan Glick."

"Nathan Glick came here today with Mr. Finch," Fehring told us.

"Aztec even funded Glick's education through scholarships from the company," I added.

Fehring leaned forward. "How do you two know this?" she asked, looking from me to Greg and then zeroing back in on me like a heat-seeking missile.

"I'm a paralegal, Andrea," I answered. "I have access to all kinds of search engines." I was really getting tired of explaining myself, even if it was only a half truth. "It isn't that difficult to go online and piece together someone's timeline from public records. Jean changed her name when she moved to California. Before that she worked in Chicago for Aztec under her real name. But she never mentioned that job when we spoke to her."

"Did you ask her about it?" Fehring asked.

Greg shook his head. "We really weren't there very long."

"But it did look like someone had lived in the condo with Jean until recently," I offered. "She claims it was a guy, another actor who left to take a job in New York."

"Did she say when exactly?" Fehring asked.

"No, but it might have been very recently," I answered. "The furniture was still there, but all personal stuff was gone." From a side pocket of my purse I pulled out something wrapped in tissue. "I did find this." I placed it on the table and carefully unwrapped it. "This was left behind in a drawer in the bathroom. There's long blond hair caught in the teeth. There are also sneakers left behind in the closet of the second bedroom. Maybe Zach was living with his sister. I would have liked to ask the neighbors who were huddled around Jean's body about her roommate, but Shipman hustled us off for questioning before I could get close."

"I would have done the same," Fehring said.

Greg looked at me with surprise. "You didn't tell me you had that." He indicated the comb.

"I forgot, honey," I told him honestly. "After Mom called, my mind was sort of on that."

"What's wrong with Grace?" Fehring asked with concern. "Nothing serious, I hope."

"No," Greg answered before I could. "At

least it turned out to be nothing once we got there. She called Odelia in a bit of a fluster and asked us to drop by as soon as possible."

"That's why we had to postpone coming here," I added, pleased that we stuck to the truth somewhat about Mom. "But she's fine, and the problem's resolved."

"That's good," Fehring said with genuine relief. "Something happening to Grace is the last thing you need right now."

"Tell us about it," Greg said half under his breath.

"Good thinking with this comb, Odelia. I'll take it and see what comes up," Fehring said. "Zach did have long blond hair." She went to the door, opened it, and said something to someone. An officer came in with an evidence bag and carefully scooped up the comb. "Process the hair on this," she told him. "See if it's a match against the Finch kid. And put a rush on it."

"A rush?" the officer said with skepticism. "Everything's on rush."

"Tell them this is for the FBI's Finch case," she said. "See if that can get things moving faster." The officer nodded and started to leave with the comb. "And if it doesn't, let me know," she added.

Before we left, Fehring made us go over

every detail again of our conversation with Jean Utley while she jotted down notes. When we were done, she said, "Do you two have someplace to go?"

"Home?" I suggested.

"Maybe not," she said. "As soon as both of these identities are released, the media is going to explode. Zach Finch's death would be bad enough, but coupled with his sister's death, the whole world is going to go crazy for any tidbits they can get. We'll try to keep your names out of it as best we can or at least minimize your exposure, but that doesn't mean there won't be a leak to the press. A press conference is going to take place in a few hours, so be prepared."

Greg and I exchanged glances that once again put Fehring on alert. "You know, you two," she said with frustration, "if you'd just come in and spill your guts about everything you know, we wouldn't have to go through this little guessing game."

I took a deep breath. "You know that video that showed up on that one newscast showing the car wash and me screaming when I first see the body in my trunk?"

Fehring laughed. "Hard to forget, Odelia. Especially the graceful way you dropped to the wet pavement and almost took Grace down with you."

I curled my lip at her before continuing. "Well, the guy who shot that video showed up at our home, and I caught him taking video through our back screen door."

"Did you call the police?" she asked.

"No," I admitted. "I —" I started, then paused and corrected, "We — Greg and I — let him go. He seemed to be just a geeky guy trying to impress the newscaster on TV. You know, that Gloria Connors. He has a thing for her and also wants to break into TV news himself." I dug around in my tote bag and produced Swayze's phone. By accident I almost handed over Mother's burn phone. "We took his phone and kept it." I pushed the phone with the broken front glass across the table to Fehring. "If you play the last couple of videos, you'll see the one taken at the car wash, a blurry one taken through the slats in our back fence, and the grainy one taken through our screen. None of them are very long except the last one. We kept it on while we were talking to the guy," I explained. "It was in my pocket but the audio was running."

"His phone wasn't secured by a password?" Fehring asked with surprise.

"It was," Greg explained after a sheepish hesitation, "and it kicked in shortly after we took it, but one of the guys at my shop managed to hack it, and we reset it for our use. The new password is *geek.*"

Fehring started to say something, then thought better of it. Instead she played the videos and watched with interest.

"His name is John Swayze. He works at the *LA Times* as a gopher," Greg told her. "There's a photo on there of Zach's body with the note. He must have taken it before the police moved in."

Fehring wasn't studying the last video, but the one before it — the one taken through the slats of our fence. The audio was much clearer than the picture. Fehring listened with interest. "Who are you talking to, Odelia? She looks familiar."

I hesitated, then fessed up. "It's Emma Whitecastle. She's a —"

"I know who Emma Whitecastle is," Fehring said, cutting me off. "Did you call her?"

I shook my head. "My mother did, totally without my knowledge. She's a big fan of Emma's show and wrote and asked her to look into the body in my trunk. I think Mom thought Emma could contact Zach's ghost, so I decided why not talk to her and see what cropped up. I had nothing to lose."

"Do you believe that stuff, Detective Fehring?" Greg asked her.

In answer, she shrugged. "Honestly, I'm

not sure. I've never met the woman myself, but I know that Emma Whitecastle and her mentor, Milo Ravenscroft, have helped clear up a few crimes over the past few years. I have a friend, another detective, who worked with her on a case in Las Vegas. He respects her a great deal. He claims she even shot a guy once to save his life."

"Really?" I asked, surprised. "Did she kill the man?" Maybe Emma and I had something in common.

"No, she didn't, but the guy she shot was about to shoot my friend." Fehring played the video again, this time closing her eyes and concentrating on what Emma had told me about birds and multitasking. "Interesting," she said when she opened them again. "Do you think this Swayze knows who was in the trunk of your car?"

"He gave no indication of it," I answered. "None at all."

"I'm going to be keeping this." Fehring pocketed Swayze's phone. It wasn't a request but a statement of fact.

"And another thing," Greg said, "my guy said there are no other photos or videos on the phone. Usually people have tons of them on their cells. He thinks that maybe it was cleaned off recently because it doesn't look like a new phone. Oh, and the guy lives right here in Long Beach," Greg added. "At least that's what his driver's license said."

Fehring smiled. "Well, that will be convenient, won't it?"

She looked us both in the eye, one after the other. "But next time something like this happens, *call the police*!" Her tone left no room for rebuttal.

After taking a few seconds to compose herself, Fehring patted the pocket with Swayze's phone and said, "This really convinces me that it would be best if you go somewhere for a few days." She paused, then added, "And not just because of the press but for your safety. If Jean was murdered and not a jumper, whoever did it might have seen you there and wonder what you know. Don't make it easy for them to get to you. You were lucky with this Swayze guy. The next intruder might not be so easily handled with a baseball bat."

I looked at Greg. "We could go to my mother's, but her retirement community doesn't allow big dogs, not even as visitors."

"And my parents are remodeling the upstairs of their house right now," Greg remembered. "They're crammed in their downstairs guest room for the time being, so that's out."

"We'll ask Seth and Zee," I said. "Seth's

allergic to cats, but we can stash Muffin at my mother's for as long as we need." I turned to Fehring. "The Washingtons live in a gated community in Newport Beach."

"Even better," she answered. "Go straight home, pack up some things, and get out as soon as you can."

I was about to call Zee when I changed my mind. "If we're in danger, I don't want to get Zee and Seth involved. I don't want to get anyone involved." I looked at Greg and saw that he was nodding in agreement. "Honey, maybe we can go to a hotel for a few days. Something pet-friendly with a kitchen."

"I have a better suggestion," he said to me. "We'll leave Muffin with your mother and Wainwright with my folks and stay at Steele's place. He's out of town for another week, isn't he? I'll bet if you ask, he'll say yes."

"But he has a two-story townhouse," I reminded Greg. "You can't get up to the bedrooms."

"So I'll sleep on the sofa in his den for a few days."

"But you can't shower there. His downstairs bathroom is barely big enough for you to use as it is."

"I have a better idea," Fehring said. Unclipping her phone from her belt, she made a call. "Dev, it's Andrea. I'm here with Greg and Odelia and they're in a bit of a fix." She listened, then laughed. "So true."

Greg and I exchanged looks, understanding that we were the butts of an unheard joke.

"They need a place where they can lay low for a few days and we don't want to get their families or the Washingtons involved. I remember that you have a good set up at your place that might accommodate Greg. Can they stay there a few days until some things clear? I can fill you in a little later."

"But Dev's getting ready to move," I objected.

Fehring held up a hand like a stop sign to silence me while she listened. Then she said, "Okay. They'll be there soon. Oh, and can they bring the dog?" Another pause, then she said into the phone, "Great. I'll tell them." She ended the call.

"Get your stuff, and get yourselves and both the dog *and* the cat over to Dev's place. No arguments. He's waiting for you. Do you know where it is?"

"What about my mother?" I asked. "Should she come with us?"

Fehring thought about it. "How secure is her retirement community?"

"It's gated and has a round-the-clock guard at the gate," Greg answered. "And we can tell Grace to stay put and not leave."

"Will she listen?" Fehring asked. It was a legitimate question since she already knew Mom quite well.

"She will if Greg tells her to do it," I said. "If I tell her not to open her door to strangers, she'll not only open it, she'll go out and round them up out of spite." *Or let in killers.* But I kept that comment to myself.

Fehring gave off a low chuckle that started in her gut. "Mothers . . . I have one. I know the frustration." She paused. "What about Clark? Is he still in town? Maybe he could watch over her or take her to his place in Arizona for a few days."

I shook my head. "Something came up with his job. He left on a red-eye last night. I think he left his car at the airport, so he should be back when he's done with whatever he's doing."

She looked at the large watch on her wrist. "Okay, then tell Grace to stay put behind those gates until further notice, then you two get yourself over to Dev's."

In unison, Greg and I nodded our compliance, then were shown the door like a couple of schoolkids being dismissed by the principal.

TWENTY-ONE

As we were leaving, a man came out of the men's restroom located in the hallway where we'd been cooling our heels earlier. I recognized him right away as Alec Finch. He was tall, with faded blond hair combed back slick over his head, which accommodated a long, narrow face with small blue eyes. Zach looked a lot like him.

The elder Finch was dressed in a suit with hardly a wrinkle. If he rushed to get here, along the way he made sure he was flawlessly groomed, almost like he was readying himself for the news cameras. He moved down the hall in our direction stealthy and alert, his eyes moving to take in his surroundings like a panther ready to jump at either danger or easy prey. He wore power like his suit — tailored and impeccable. He didn't look like he was suffering from grief or even from jet lag. Fehring said Alec Finch knew about Zach but not yet about Jean.

But even with one child dead, even a supposedly long-dead child, you'd expect a little more wear and tear.

"Mr. Finch," I said, approaching him, "I'm sorry for your loss." I was careful to use the singular.

He looked like he was going to brush me off like an annoying gnat, but at the last minute he stopped. "Who are you?" he asked as he looked me over. "You're not a cop. How do you know about my son? Are you with the press?"

"I'm Odelia Grey, and this is my husband, Greg Stevens," I told him.

He held up a hand to stop me from saying anything more. "Odelia? I know that name." Still keeping his hand up, he looked me over again, this time as if looking for a bar code so he could scan me into his memory bank. He lowered his hand and stared into my face with intensity. "You're the person who had Zach."

"Not exactly, Mr. Finch," I told him. "I *found* Zach. I didn't know I *had* him."

He took a step closer, into my personal space, keeping his eyes locked on mine, but said nothing. Greg wheeled in closer. "Mr. Finch," Greg said, trying to get the man's attention, "my wife and I were just leaving. So if you will excuse us?"

"Who are you, and what do you want?" Finch said to me, ignoring my husband, whose head came up only to his waist. "A reward? Sorry," he spat. "I already paid, so tell whoever you're working with to piss off. They're not getting a penny more." Finch said the nasty words without raising his voice, keeping them low and menacing. I backed up a few feet. He might look good on the outside, but inside he appeared to be coming apart at the seams, which is more what I would expect from a grieving parent.

Greg wedged his chair into the space I vacated when I backed away. "I'm down here, Mr. Finch." Greg kept his voice low, too, and added a touch of warning to his tone. "I'm the one speaking to you right now."

A man approached us. Like Finch, he was dressed in a fine suit. I did a double take, recognizing Nathan Glick from his photo. "Everything okay here, Alec?" he asked. He reached out and put a hand lightly on Finch's upper arm.

Finch didn't look at the guy but shook off the hand as he slowly took his eyes off of me and looked down at Greg. "That's better," Greg said once he had the man's attention. "My wife was only expressing her condolences, which is what nice people do.

She had nothing to do with your son's murder. For some unfortunate reason, her car was targeted as the body dump. We're cooperating one hundred percent with the police. If you have concerns, please address those to them." Greg turned to me. "Come on, sweetheart, let's get out of here."

We exited the hallway into the entry of the police station and were heading for the door when Finch caught up to us. The other guy was behind Finch, trying to get him to back down. Again he placed a hand on the older man's upper arm.

"Just a minute, you two," Finch called to us. "I have questions I want answered." Nearby, cops in the entry stood ready to intervene should things get ugly.

"What's the problem here?" asked Fehring as she came through the door from the hallway.

"No problem, Detective Fehring," Greg said. "Odelia expressed condolences to Mr. Finch here on the loss of his son, and he had trouble accepting them gracefully."

Finch yanked his arm away from his keeper and glared at us, waiting for answers to questions he hadn't asked yet. I noticed Fehring was eyeing Finch with caution. The guy with Finch was studying Greg and me. Finally, Fehring said, "Mr. and Mrs. Stevens, you two get out of here before we break the story. I'll call you if we need anything else."

"I want to speak with these people," Finch demanded of Fehring.

"We've already taken their statements, Mr. Finch," Fehring told him, "so let's go back and talk some more while we wait for Special Agent Shipman." As if underlining her request, a uniformed officer stepped forward and opened the door to the back. Finch stared at the door but didn't budge.

While Fehring was trying to calm Finch down, we exited the building and headed for our van, which was parked in a nearby handicapped spot. We were almost tucked inside when Finch came out of the police station in a huff and looked around. As soon as he spotted us, he headed our way, yelling, "I don't give a damn what the police say. I want answers from you, and I want them now." On his heels was Fehring, a uniformed cop, and Glick.

Greg started the engine and started to pull out of the parking spot when someone ran up to Finch. I shook my head in disbelief. It was John Swayze, his right hand heavily bandaged but not in a cast or sling. Maybe it wasn't broken. Greg stopped the van, mesmerized as I was by the turn of events.

"Hey, Mr. Finch," Swayze yelled, holding a phone out in front of him. Obviously, he'd replaced the one we'd kept. "Do you have any comments about your daughter's death today?" The question froze Finch and everyone else in their tracks. Even Greg and I stopped breathing for a few seconds.

Finch found his voice first. "What in the hell are you talking about?" he asked. Fixing his steely eyes on Swayze, he stepped forward until the kid stepped back, as I had earlier. Finch was definitely an aggressive personality used to intimidating people.

"Zach and Jean. They're both dead," Swayze said, his voice not quite as confident as it had been when he started. "Do you think their deaths are related?" Swayze pushed on. "Where do you think Zach's been all this time?"

"Jean?" Finch asked no one in particular. "Jean's dead? That's impossible!"

"Ask the cops," Swayze said. "They know."

People in front of the building had stopped to watch the show but gave the situation cautious room, not wanting to crowd the players in case someone went postal. Greg and I watched the whole thing while seated in the van. It was like watching a close-up drive-in movie, except it was daytime and there was no popcorn.

As Swayze noticed the attention, the ancient fight-or-flight question clearly crossed his face. He backed up, then turned tail and took off. A police officer shouted and started after him, but Fehring told him to hold back. I knew Swayze was the flight type.

Finch turned to Fehring. "Is this true?"

"Let's go inside, Mr. Finch," Fehring said to him. "We have more to discuss."

"I want to know now!" Finch roared. Glick again put a hand on his arm to calm him down. Finch shook it off once again. "Stop handling me," he snapped at Glick.

"Mr. Finch," Fehring said. "Please calm down and come inside. We can explain everything."

"Holy crap!" I said to Greg.

"You got that right, sweetheart."

Fehring noticed us and walked over to Greg's side of the van. I thought maybe she was going to invite us inside for more questioning, but she didn't. Instead, she asked, "I'm assuming from your description that that character is John Swayze. Am I correct?"

"That's him," Greg confirmed.

"I suppose you need us to come back inside," I said, leaning toward Greg's window. Part of me wanted to stay close to the

302

action, but the bigger part of me wanted to get the hell out of Dodge.

Fehring thought about it, then said, "No, get out of here and get yourself to Dev's as soon as possible. If we need you, we'll call you. Right now we need to do some damage control before the press conference."

Once we were on our way home to pack up the animals and ourselves, I turned to Greg. "What did you make of that?"

"I'm speechless," he answered. "How did John Swayze know about Jean or that Finch was even in town?"

"And how did he know the body in my trunk was Zach Finch?" I asked, adding another question to the growing pile. "He gave no indication yesterday that he knew."

"Maybe he pieced it together from what Emma Whitecastle said," Greg suggested. "He did overhear that."

I shrugged in response. "I'm sure Fehring will get to the bottom of it."

"I'd love to be a fly on the wall while Fehring talks to Finch," Greg said. "I'm kind of disappointed that Fehring sent us packing."

"Me too. But I've really had enough of the police. And when Shipman gets there, the shit will really hit the fan. He didn't want Finch to know about Jean until he was present."

"Finch didn't seem all that tore up or surprised about Zach." Greg glanced over at me. "Did he to you?"

"No, at least not at first, but later I could see the cracks the strain is causing. Especially when he almost got nose to nose with me. Everyone deals with grief differently," I noted. "And depending on when the police finally reached him, he might have had time to process it while he travelled here. He looked pretty darn good for a man travelling from who knows where, but I doubt he flew coach. He probably has his own jet."

"I'd like to know when they actually reached him," Greg said. "Fehring said it wasn't until last night, but even if he was in Timbuktu, a man like that is always reachable."

"If he wants to be," I said with emphasis.

"Exactly," agreed Greg. "Steele is on his honeymoon and still able to be contacted. I'm sure the feds were reaching out to Finch via every way possible until they got him on the line. Even if they didn't have a direct number for him, his office would have tracked Finch down pretty quickly when the feds called on Wednesday, when Zach's body was found. Men like that are never far from the pulse of their empire. So why is

Finch just now getting to Southern California?"

"Maybe he was climbing Mount Everest?" I suggested tongue-in-cheek.

"Or in seclusion at an ashram," added Greg with equal sarcasm.

"He didn't strike me as the ashram type, honey."

Greg glanced over at me. "Me neither. I'd like to know when his office or whoever reached him and why he didn't respond right away."

"I'm sure the police didn't tell his office about Zach," I said.

"Maybe not," Greg agreed. His jaw was tight as he spoke. He had taken an instant dislike to Alec Finch; we both had. "But didn't Fehring say he claimed he was close to his daughter?"

"That's what I recall." As soon as I answered, I knew where Greg was going with this. "If he was so close to her," I said, sounding out the thoughts coming together in my head, "then he knew she lived in LA. Most parents receiving a call from the police near where one of their kids live would answer it pretty darn quick."

Greg glanced over at me. "Bingo! Either he didn't know Jean lived in Southern California or he didn't care. Doesn't sound to me like they were close."

I pulled out my phone and started texting.

"Who's that going to?" asked Greg.

"Clark," I answered. "I'm asking him to contact me as soon as possible. He's our eyes and ears in Illinois. Maybe he can find out something about the Finch family dynamics that isn't in that toothy photo taken at the country club."

Greg glanced at me. "And I'm sure the guy with him was Nathan Glick. He looks like the photo you have, and Fehring said Glick arrived with Finch."

"Yes, I'm pretty sure that was Glick."

I pulled out my phone again and got to texting, this time letting Clark know that Nathan Glick was in California. At this rate, my fingers would be worn down to nubs.

TWENTY-TWO

Dev lived in a modest but nicely maintained three-bedroom house in Costa Mesa, the city next to Newport Beach. It had been an easy commute to his job. His house reminded me a lot of our own home in Seal Beach except that all three of the bedrooms were on one side of the structure, where our master suite was on the opposite side from the other bedrooms. But, like our place, the living room, dining room, and kitchen were really just one big great room sectioned off by the layout into separate areas. Even his kitchen was divided from the dining area by a counter, but his counter was of average height, where ours was built lower to accommodate Greg.

When his wife had become sick, Dev had made a few adjustments to the master bathroom and bath to make it easier for her to get around on her own as long as possible as she weakened, including installing a walk-in tub and shower. Fehring had been right about Dev's house being the right place for Greg. Dev even had hardwood floors instead of carpet. Unlike our place, Dev had a large back yard with plenty of grass beyond a small patio, where we had little grass and a huge patio. Wainwright would be in doggie heaven since he usually had to make do with our tiny back patch of the green stuff. We didn't even need to mow ours. It was so small, our landscaper trimmed it with a weed wacker.

Dev was waiting for us when we got there. "Andrea just called and gave me the 4-1-1 on everything," he told us as we unloaded the van with his help. We'd pulled up in front of his two-car detached garage, which was set back to the rear of the property, just behind the house. From there, Greg could enter via a short ramp Dev had built for Janet. He'd never removed it after her death because of the occasional visits we made.

"Thanks, Dev," I said. Standing on tiptoe, I gave him a small peck on the cheek. "You're being such a good sport, but we hope to be out of your hair in a day or so. On the way over here, I called Mom and told her not to leave her retirement place at all until she heard from us that it was okay."

"Do you think she'll listen?" asked Dev. "I

know how headstrong your mother can be." He shot Greg a look, then did the same to me. "Like other people I know."

Greg started chuckling. "Andrea Fehring asked the same question."

"Not so fast, Greg," Dev added. "I wasn't only talking about Odelia. You were included in that comment."

Greg shook his head and laughed again. "I'm in good company, then." He started rolling toward the house. "But I think Grace will listen. She's especially skittish after this afternoon." He stopped and clamped his mouth shut. I went about the business of pulling two small rollerboards containing clothing out of the van, hoping Dev wouldn't ask, but of course he did.

"And what happened this afternoon?" Dev asked Greg with a glance my way.

"Didn't Andrea Fehring tell you about Jean Utley?" I asked, looking surprised. Technically, Jean had jumped this morning and Elaine had showed up this afternoon. I hoped Dev didn't get picky about Jean's timeline and press the matter.

"Yeah, she did," Dev answered. "It was part of the call she made to me while you two were on your way over here. And she told me about that Swayze guy, too, but said you'd fill me in more about his visit to you yesterday." With his free hand he grabbed a handled canvas bag containing bags of both dog and cat kibble and almost dropped it, surprised by its weight. "Man," Dev said, gaining a better grip. "This is almost as bad as couples who travel with a bunch of kids."

"If you haven't noticed, Dev," I said, glad to take his mind off Greg's slip, "these *are* our kids."

Inside the house, a few boxes were in the midst of being packed and for now were shoved off against the wall in the dining area. "I tried to make sure there was plenty of room for Greg to get through," Dev explained. "There are more boxes already packed in one of the spare bedrooms — the one with the closed door."

"Wow, Dev," I said, looking at the bare walls and surfaces once graced by family photos and mementos, "you've really made a lot of progress." The only thing except furniture left in the living room was the flat screen TV mounted over the small fireplace. The house, once warm and cozy, now felt bare and cold.

"I made this decision several weeks ago," he told us, "but only just announced it. I've been packing a little every night, and my daughter did the kitchen. I'm sorry, but there's barely anything left in the kitchen except for the coffeepot and a few dishes and utensils. We've even taken a load of stuff over to the storage unit already. My daughter wanted to have a garage sale, but I really don't have the time for it before I go." He pointed down the long hall. "You guys will take the master suite at the end of the hall."

"Dev," Greg said, "we can't put you out of your own bed."

"It's not a bother," Dev said, "so not another word. That bathroom will be easier for you. I put fresh sheets on the bed just now." He put the cat carrier and the pet food down and took the cat litter box from Greg. "Where should this go?" he asked.

"We usually put it in the spare bathroom," I told him, "but anywhere where it won't be in your way will do."

"The master bath has a vanity with an opening under it," he said. "How about I put it there?"

"Perfect," I told him and he disappeared down the hall, returning a few seconds later.

As Dev washed his hands at the kitchen sink, he said, "You will be on your own tonight. I'm staying at my daughter's."

"Geez, Dev," said Greg. "Now I really feel bad."

"Don't," Dev said as he dried his hands on a kitchen towel. "I had already planned to stay there tonight. My daughter and her husband are going out for their anniversary — dinner and a night in a swanky hotel. I'm watching the kids. I usually stay over when they go out so they can stay out later and I don't have to drive home after." A big smile crossed his face. "The deal is they have to give the kids their supper and their baths and put them in their pj's before I get there, and I'll make pancakes in the morning so my daughter and her husband can sleep in and not rush back."

"You're going to miss them terribly, Dev," I said. "Are you sure you want to move?"

"It'll be tough but doable," Dev said through a determined locked jaw that conveyed his own doubts. He checked his watch. "I don't have to be there for a few hours, so let's get down to business. I want to know what's going on. I have Andrea's side. What's cooking on your side?"

"Speaking of cooking, how about we order Chinese or go out for an early dinner?" suggested Greg. "Our treat and no argument. Odelia and I have been on the run all day and haven't been able to eat since breakfast."

"Yes," I agreed with enthusiasm. "We were going to take sandwiches when we went to talk to Fehring, but we forgot. You know how long the police can keep you."

Dev grinned at my words. "It's part of our interrogation tactics — starve the truth out of them. An early dinner sounds good, but how about Thai instead of Chinese?" he suggested. "There's a great place that just opened up not too far from here."

Once the takeout arrived, the three of us sat around Dev's kitchen table hashing over the day's events while eating Thai food. Muffin had settled down after some exploration, and Wainwright was outside on the lawn. Fehring had pretty much filled Dev in on everything, but he questioned us extensively about our conversation with Jean Utley and our encounter with John Swayze.

"So the dad says they were close, and she said she hadn't seen or talked to him in years," Dev said, recapping what we'd told him.

"Yes," said Greg. "That's what she said. One of them is lying, and I'm betting it wasn't Jean."

"And something is off about that Nathan Glick guy," I added, picking up our dirty plates and taking them to the sink.

"How so?" asked Dev.

Greg leaned over toward Dev. "Here's where we don't agree. Odelia thinks it's odd that Glick is close to Finch and showed up here with him. I think it's only natural."

Dev leaned back in his chair. "Tell me what you're each thinking."

"Well," said Greg. "Nathan Glick was one of Zach's close friends. Why wouldn't Alec Finch help him out with a scholarship and a job if he thought the kid had potential?"

"On that I agree, Greg," I said, returning to the table.

"And," Greg continued, "with Zach turning up after all these years, why wouldn't Glick come along in case the police wanted to question him more about the night Zach went missing. He was one of the last to see him alive that night."

Dev looked to me for a rebuttal. I had nothing. "That makes sense, too," I agreed. "Everything makes sense on the surface, but I still have a creepy feeling in my gut about Glick. He kept trying to calm Finch down, and Finch kept brushing him off."

"Finch was upset," Greg said. "And he's used to handling people, not people handling him. Any attempts to do that would naturally be met with brusqueness. He was also sure we had something to do with Zach's death and was focused on us. He even accused us of wanting some sort of reward or payment."

"Yes." I pointed my right index finger at

my husband. "He did, and the way he worded it was odd, I thought."

"What did he say exactly?" Dev asked, leaning forward again in his chair to listen better.

I took a deep breath and gave it some thought before answering. "He said something like for us to tell whoever we were working with that he'd already paid and not to expect anything else."

"Actually," Greg added, "he told us to tell whoever we were working with to piss off. His exact words."

"He could be referring to the original kidnappers," Dev said after mulling it over. "He could have thought you'd been holding Zach all these years and now were looking to cash in twice."

"Look at us, Dev," I said with frustration. "Do we look like we swooped into a small town in Illinois years ago and grabbed a teenager practically from his front yard? We can barely handle our pets."

Dev was trying hard not to laugh at the thought. "You don't have to be the ones who kidnapped Zach to be working now with the people who took him and held him captive."

"Very true," Greg agreed.

"Getting back to Nathan Glick," I said,

not comfortable with us being in the limelight as suspects, even around the dinner
table. "I was watching him when Swayze
announced that Jean was dead. While Alec
Finch nearly lost his mind, Glick didn't look
surprised at all."

Both men looked at me. "Are you sure?"
Dev asked.

"I was watching both men, and their re-
actions were totally different," I explained.
"Shouldn't Glick be in at least a tiny bit of
shock about the news?"

"You'd think," said Greg. "Unless he was
so intent on keeping his boss under control,
all his energy was spent there."

"This was a woman's sudden death we're
talking about," I went on to say. "Someone
Glick knew well when he was a teen."

Dev leaned back in his chair. "I do think
that's enough to dig deeper into Glick," he
said after a short silence. "Maybe Clark can
help ferret out his relationship with Alec
Finch."

"Clark is in Illinois right now checking on
Zach's friends and the Finch family," I admitted.

Dev only nodded. "I'm not surprised. Has
he learned anything yet?"

"Nothing," I replied. "Chris Cook, one of
Zach's friends who was with him the night

316

he disappeared, is nowhere to be found. His business is closed for the weekend, and no one appears to be home. Nathan Glick we know is currently here. He resides in Chicago, and I believe he's single. The third kid was killed in a snowboarding incident shortly after Zach disappeared."

Dev leaned forward. "Do I want to ask where you got all this information?"

"I'm a paralegal, Dev," I repeated for the umpteenth time in a short period. "I have access to all kinds of search engines."

Dev fixed his eyes on mine and held them for several seconds. He did the same with Greg, then simply said, "Bullpucky."

Just then my cell phone rang. *Saved by the bell.* I left the table to retrieve my phone from my bag. It was Fehring. "What's up?"

"What's up is that the Finch story is about to break," she told me. "The news conference is about to start. Get to a TV if you're interested."

"The news conference is about to start," I told the guys. Dev got up and turned on his TV, and we all moved to the living room to watch it. "Did you ever catch up to Swayze?" I asked Fehring.

"No," she answered. "I sent a unit to the address you gave me in Long Beach. It was a mailbox place."

"How did he know about Jean?" I asked.

"All we can figure out," Fehring said, "is that he followed you and Greg there. Apparently, smashing his hand with a bat wasn't warning enough to stay away from you two."

"How is Mr. Finch?" I asked.

"Still hell-bent on talking to you two, so stay out of his way. In fact, stay put at Dev's at least until tomorrow night. Got that? Now I gotta run."

The news conference was handled by Special Agent Shipman. He stood behind a podium set in front of the police station. In front of him was a gaggle of microphones. Behind him stood several people in business attire, including Fehring, some police officers in uniform, and Alec Finch. Next to Finch stood Nathan Glick. Both men appeared to be wearing the same suits they were wearing earlier. This time Finch did look a little ragged around the edges. Glick still looked poised and in control.

"That's Nathan Glick," I said to Dev, pointing to the left of Finch.

Dev sat down on the edge of an ottoman and leaned forward to study the man while Shipman talked about finding Zach Finch's body after he'd disappeared eight years earlier. He confirmed that it was Zach's corpse found in the trunk of a car at a local car wash earlier in the week. He also talked about Jean's death, noting that both deaths were under investigation through the combined efforts of the bureau, the Long Beach Police Department, and the Los Angeles Police Department, and because of the ongoing investigation he wasn't at liberty to disclose much information. He made no mention of me and kept it short and sweet. As soon as he was done, he was peppered with questions from the press. He pointed at a woman in the front with long, thick brown hair and too much makeup.

"Where has Zach been all these years?" she asked. "Was he living in California?"

"We don't know at this time," Shipman answered and pointed to an African-American woman on the other side.

"Did Zach's sister have anything to do with his disappearance eight years ago?" this one asked.

"We don't know at this time," Shipman again replied. He pointed to a young Latino man standing next to her, granting him permission to ask his question.

"What about the woman who found him in the trunk of her car?" he asked. "You haven't disclosed her name. Is she a suspect?"

"Her name is Odelia Grey," called out a familiar voice that made my teeth clench until they hurt.

Upon being outed by John Swayze, I plopped down on Dev's sturdy leather sofa. This was not how I imagined my turn at fifteen minutes of fame would be. I closed my eyes tight, willing it to go away. Fehring had promised they would do their best not to disclose my name, but she'd said it might leak out. For a fleeting moment I wished I'd hit John Swayze in the head with that bat.

"Is this woman," another reporter called to Shipman, "this Odelia Grey, is she a suspect in either murder?" The camera panned to the gaggle of reporters, and I saw it was Gloria Connors asking the question, her perky elfin face pinched with determination.

Shipman shook his head. "At this time, no, she is not, but I can assure you we are looking into all possibilities."

"I understand," pushed Connors, "that this Grey woman was at the scene when the Finch woman fell to her death." The camera found her again.

"As I said," repeated Shipman as the camera ping-ponged back to him, "at this time, Ms. Grey is not a suspect but we are exploring all possibilities."

"At this time?" Greg yelled at Shipman through the TV. "All possibilities? How about just saying *no, she's not*? Period."

"Calm down, Greg," Dev said, holding out a hand toward him. "It's just standard language."

"I don't give a damn," Greg said to Dev. "My wife's name was just put on TV as a possible murder suspect, no matter how boilerplate the language."

"Honey," I said, finally opening my eyes, "Detective Fehring said something like this might happen."

Greg pointed at the TV. "That little worm Swayze. We should have filed charges against him."

I stopped burying my head in the sand and watched again. More reporters were asking questions, and Shipman was deftly side-stepping them. Swayze didn't put his hand up but continued to push about suspects, especially me, from the edge of the crowd. Connors was in the hunt with him. Shipman ignored both, while Fehring stared in Swayze's direction. It made me wonder if she was silently directing officers to apprehend Swayze.

"Why is Swayze continuing to throw me under the bus?" I asked. "Is he trying to get revenge for my smashing his hand or does he really believe I had something to do with it?"

"He could just be pursuing what he thinks is a hot story," Dev said. "A story he thinks could change his life and give him a chance with Connors, so he's motivated." Dev leaned forward even more toward the TV until I thought he would topple over.

When Shipman was done, Alex Finch stepped up to the podium. He looked at the reporters, moving his head slowly from side to side almost a full thirty seconds as they snapped still photos and ran video, like it was a photo op at a red carpet event. "I want to thank the FBI and both the Long Beach and Los Angeles Police Departments for everything they are doing to bring Zach and Jean's murderers to justice. For more than eight years our family has lived a nightmare, and it is far from over. Two years after Zach went missing, my dear wife, Zach's mother, took her own life because she could not bear the pain any longer." He paused, giving that statement time to soak into the viewer's brains, then looked straight at the camera and pounded his fist on the podium. "I vow that I will not rest," he said, his voice cracking as he choked up, "and I will put all of my own personal resources on the line until I find whoever stole my family from me." He started to say more but was overcome with emotion.

Nathan Glick stepped up and put an arm around the now-spent Finch. Moving him gently to the side a few inches, Glick spoke firmly into the microphone. "What has happened is unspeakable. It would be appreciated if the media would respect the privacy of the Finch family at this difficult and tragic time. Any further questions should be directed to Special Agent Shipman or the police."

The press conference ended and the scene switched to an anchor in the newsroom who talked about Zach's kidnapping eight years earlier. Projected to the side was a toothy photo of a cocky, fresh teenage boy. Next flashed a photo of Jean. It was a beautiful professional headshot, and the newscaster talked about how Jean was cut down at the beginning of a promising acting career. The anchor said anyone having any information about the deaths of Zach Finch or his sister, Jean Finch Utley, should contact the number at the bottom of the screen. A toll-free number was posted, big and bold, at the bottom of the TV screen.

TWENTY-THREE

When the newscast was over, Dev turned off the TV and just stood staring at it. Greg wheeled over to me and took my hand. "Don't worry, sweetheart," he said to me, giving my hand a squeeze. "The police know you're not the murderer." Even though his words were comforting, I could see from the high color in his face that he was still angry over Shipman's words.

"It's okay, honey," I said to him. With my free hand, I stroked his face. "Agent Shipman was just doing his job."

"I'd still like to teach that creep Swayze a lesson," he said.

"Something tells me he's a slow learner." I moved my hand up and brushed the side of Greg's hair back. I loved my husband's hair. Touching it was more comforting than a steaming bowl of mac and cheese.

"Hmm," Dev said, still staring at the TV. "That Glick guy is Zach's age, correct?"

"Yes," I told him. "They were high school pals, but if I remember the report correctly, Glick was a year ahead of him in age and in school. He was the one driving the car that night, so he had to be at least sixteen."

"So he's only about twenty-four now," Dev said.

I gave it some quick thought. "That would be about right."

"Do you know what he does for Aztec?" Dev asked. It felt strangely like he was interrogating someone and I was that person's proxy.

"I believe he's VP or assistant VP of some kind." I got up and went to my laptop bag. I pulled out my computer and fired it up. Soon I was looking at the report from Marigold that I'd saved. I scanned it. "It says here he was seventeen when Zach went missing." I looked at his personal stats, then added, "He was in his last year of high school when it happened."

Dev finally turned away from the blank TV. "So that would make him twenty-five now. That's still pretty young to be a vice president of a major company, isn't it? Not to mention his boss's confidant."

I looked at the report again. "It says here that Glick is Vice President of Public Affairs." I glanced over at Dev. "Would that be like PR?"

"More like public image stuff, media relations, liaison to agencies, etc.," Greg answered. "That could be why he's here, in addition to being a witness in the original kidnapping."

"And a youthful public rep would be a good image to project," Dev conceded. "He's a good-looking kid and well packaged, but he still seems young to have such responsibilities in a major company." Dev looked at me. "Are you sure that doesn't say Assistant VP?"

"I'm sure," I answered.

"Could be Finch fast-tracked him because of their longtime ties," Greg suggested.

"Do you know what Jean did at her daddy's company?" Dev asked me.

I opened the report on Jean and scanned it. "She was a project manager." I looked up. Dev looked tired. Dark circles cupped the bottom of his blue eyes, which drooped now at the edges from the pull of time. He'd probably be asleep as soon as he got his grandkids down tonight. "But that could mean most anything."

"It could," Dev said, rubbing a hand over his craggy face a few times. "But it's not an executive position. Does that report say when Glick became a VP?"

I looked again at the report. "No, it doesn't, but he started there three years ago."

"He might have worked there a couple of years before getting that spot," Greg noted, "and Jean might not have been there long enough to prove herself."

I compared Jean and Nathan's employment records. "Jean told us she didn't know what happened to Zach's friends, but according to this she left Aztec the same time as Nathan Glick showed up at the company. It just gives the years, so they may or may not have overlapped."

"True," Dev said. He still didn't look convinced, and neither was I. There was something about Nathan Glick that nagged at me.

"I'm going to head out now, guys," Dev said to us. "Make yourselves at home. Call my cell if you need anything." He started to walk back into the kitchen area, where a small overnight bag was waiting by the back door. He picked it up and put one hand on the doorknob.

A cell phone rang. It was a generic ring, not one of the ones Greg and I had assigned to family and friends, so it could be anyone. Greg and Dev both pulled their phones out and looked at them and then at me.

"I think that's coming from your bag, Odelia," Dev said. "It's not my landline."

I shrugged in confusion as I went into the kitchen to retrieve my cell phone, even though I knew it wasn't the one ringing. I stared at it, dumbfounded, as another ring broke from the depths of my bag. *Crap.* It was coming from the burner phone Elaine had given me, which was buried in the bottom of my bag. Should I answer it now, in front of Dev, or ignore it? It rang again, then stopped. I let go of the breath I was holding. I turned around in relief, slowly, to give myself time to come up with a story to peddle to Dev. To some people I might be dumber than a box of rocks, but no one who had ever met him thought that of Dev Frye, who was eyeing me like a criminal he was about to cuff. I glanced over at Greg. He was looking at me with wide eyes, waiting to see what harebrained explanation I was going to fabricate. I looked back at Dev and knew I couldn't lie to him. Not only would he see right through it like a sheer curtain, but he was a close friend and helping us.

"That's a special phone for emergencies," I said, grabbing my purse. "If you'll excuse me, I'll take it in the bedroom."

"Oh, no, you don't," Dev said. "Take it here."

"But it's personal, Dev," I said, hoping he couldn't read in my eyes the fear that ran through me like a fast-moving fever. But he didn't read it, he smelled it. He smelled my fear of discovery as clearly as Wainwright smelled bacon on a weekend morning.

"I'll bet fifty dollars that's a cheap burner phone," Dev said, taking his hand off the doorknob and turning his all-seeing, all-knowing eyes on Greg. "Maybe she's cheating on you, Greg, and that's her lover calling."

Greg plastered a lopsided grin on his face. "Maybe."

Dev turned back to me. "Or is that your direct line to Willie Proctor? I always thought you might have one. Kind of like a hotline." He waited, and when no one said anything, he added, "Look, guys, I meant what I said at dinner the other night. I don't give a tinker's damn about William Proctor. If he's able to help with this situation, great. He has my blessing."

The phone in my bag started ringing again. Dev put down his overnight bag and stepped toward me, holding out his hand. "Give it to me; I'll tell him myself."

Greg and I exchanged glances. Like Fehring did earlier in the day, Dev caught it. "What's up, guys? Spill it."

"Yeah, sweetheart, let's tell Dev the truth," Greg urged.

My eyes ping-ponged between them with uncertainty until I was slightly dizzy. "It's not a hotline to Willie, Dev," I finally said, understanding that Greg was right. Like before, the ringing stopped.

"Then who?" Dev insisted. He stepped forward. Towering over me, he latched his eyes onto mine and didn't budge. "Who is on the other end of that phone, Odelia?"

"It's Elaine Powers," I finally confessed.

Dev stepped back and ran a hand roughly over his face. "You said you had no way of contacting her. Were you lying to me?" He turned to Greg. Anger flashed in his eyes. "Were you *both* lying to me?"

"No, Dev," Greg quickly replied. "We weren't. Until a few hours ago, we had no contact with her. She gave Odelia that phone just today."

"Today?" Dev shook his head in disbelief. "This morning, bright and early, you went to see Jean Utley. After she plunged to her death, you were questioned by the FBI. Then you spent a good amount of time at the Long Beach PD and had a bit of a tussle with Alec Finch. After that, you packed your duds and your fur balls and came here. When," he asked with exasperation, "*when*

330

did you have time to have a chat with Elaine Powers?"

Greg wheeled closer for encouragement and gave me a nod. "It was between the FBI and Andrea Fehring," I answered truthfully. "She called and asked to meet with us." I carefully maneuvered around the fact that the face-to-face occurred at my mother's place. "She saw the news about Zach and had some things to tell us."

Dev checked his watch, then took my arm and directed us back into the living room. "I've got a few minutes before I have to go, so let's make this quick — and bring the purse."

Once we were seated in the living room, Dev started the questioning. "So she knew it was Zach Finch in your trunk before the press conference today?"

"Yes and no," I began. "She saw the clip on TV, like a lot of us did, and recognized me. She wanted to offer help if she could. When she was told about Zach's identity, she told us that she had been contacted by someone who wanted to hire her to take him and his sister out. It was a man, but she turned it down before learning who it was."

"She turned down the hit job?" Dev asked with suspicion. "Why?"

"Two reasons," Greg said. "Elaine said a job like this would come with too much media attention, and she was right. But she also said she saw no good reason for Zach and his sister to be executed."

Dev chewed on that for a few seconds in silence.

"Elaine said she's having her people nose about and see who might have accepted the contract and placed the body in Odelia's car," Greg continued, then he reached over and took my hand. "I believe Elaine, Dev, like Odelia does. I know that's nuts, but I believe Elaine is telling the truth here."

Dev stood up just as the phone in my purse rang again. "Persistent killer, isn't she? Answer it," he ordered. "And put it on speaker."

I dug through my tote bag and pulled out the ringing burn phone. "Hello," I said into it after hitting the speaker feature.

"Where in the hell have you been?" Elaine snapped on the other end of the line.

"I'm kind of hiding out," I answered. "Police orders."

"Not a bad idea," she said, calming down. "Well, now that I have you on the horn, I've got some big news for you. Did you see the news conference about the Finch kids, by any chance?"

"Yes, we did," I told her.

Dev was dancing around foot to foot, antsy to talk.

"By the way," I said to Elaine. "Dev Frye is with us, and he wants to talk to you. You're on speaker." I hoped she wouldn't hang up. She didn't.

"Nice to finally meet you, Detective Frye," Elaine said in a cheerful voice. "I feel like I already know you."

"Cut the bullshit, Powers," Dev growled into the phone. "What's going on?"

"First, the little matter of this phone," Elaine said. "Please understand that there is no way to trace my whereabouts from this call or by hitting redial. I'm not that stupid, just to be clear."

"Understood," Dev snapped.

"Did you catch the news conference?" she asked again.

"Yes," I answered. "We all did."

"Well, the guy who tried to hire me to take out Zach Finch was there today," she told us.

"But I thought you hadn't met him," I said at the phone in my hand.

"I haven't, but I heard him loud and clear both times we spoke," Elaine explained. "It's that guy with Finch — the young one in the fancy suit."

"Nathan Glick?" Greg asked with surprise.

"I don't know his name," Elaine answered, "but as soon as that guy opened his mouth, I knew it was him."

"That's a serious accusation." Dev was staring up at the ceiling, blowing out gusts of air at it. "How sure are you?"

"I'm getting old, Frye," Elaine said. "My teeth are all capped and my back and knees are shot to hell, but my hearing is still sharp. I'm 99 percent sure."

"Elaine," I said into the phone, "have your people learned anything yet?"

"Nothing, but they're still on it. I'll let you know if I do find out anything." She paused. "And who was that fool shouting out Odelia's name?"

"His name is John Swayze," Dev told her. "Ever hear of him?"

The other end went silent for a few seconds, then Elaine answered, "Can't say that I have."

A cold chill went through me. "Elaine, please don't kill him."

She laughed. "Who? Dev? Of course not. He's one of the good guys. In spite of my profession, I like the men in white hats. There's not enough of them."

"No," I clarified. "John Swayze. He's a pill, but please don't track him down and take him out. I don't need you to fix this."

"Oh, all right. I promise," she agreed with reluctance. "But it would certainly make your life easier." She cut off the call.

Once again Dev checked his watch. "I've got to get out of here or my daughter will kill me." He picked up his overnight bag again. "I'm going to call Andrea on the way over there and fill her in." He pointed a finger at us. "You two are to go nowhere tonight. Nor are you to tell anyone where you are if you talk to them, and that includes your mother and the Washingtons." He paused in his rant. "Or do they already know where you are?"

I thought about it. "No," I said. "We just told Mom to stay put until everything gets ironed out. We didn't say we were going anywhere. And we haven't talked to Seth or Zee today."

"Good," he said. "Only Andrea and I are to know you are here. Got that?" He was speaking to both of us but pointed a meaty finger only at me. My nose twitched.

We both nodded. I didn't have to consult with Greg to know he didn't want to budge tonight either. We'd had a full day of driving around Southern California and talking to people.

Dev snatched the phone from my hand

and started for the door. "Hey," I said, following him. "Where are you going with that? You heard Elaine — she can't be traced."

"Maybe not," Dev said right before he walked out, "but *you* can with this. I'll bet Elaine is using it to track you right now."

"But what if she learns something about who killed Zach?" I argued.

"Then she'll just have to tell me." He left, slamming the door behind him. It was a crystal-clear message that he was not listening to any additional arguments on the subject.

Dev was barely out the door when my cell phone rang. I held it out to Greg. "It's Clark. Do you mind, honey? I think I'm all talked out."

Greg took the phone and answered it with the speaker feature. "Hey, Clark. How are things going out there?"

"Interesting," Clark said. "Very interesting. But more interesting out there. I caught the press conference about the Finch kid and his sister. Who was that ass yelling out Odelia's name?"

"That was John Swayze," Greg told him. I'd gone into the living room and plopped down again on the sofa. Greg wheeled in next to me while he talked. "Too bad Odelia didn't take out his mouth instead of his hand when she swung that bat at him yesterday."

"Yeah, he's a real jackass," Clark said. "Are you sure he doesn't have an axe to grind against Odelia instead of just being a nosy nerd?"

"We've both given that a lot of thought, Clark," Greg said, "and we've come up with nothing. To our knowledge, we've never come across him or anyone by the name of Swayze."

"I read his Marigold report," Clark said, "and you're right, it's pretty mundane stuff."

"Have you learned anything?" I asked, mustering up some energy.

"Yeah, quite a bit, in fact," Clark said. "First of all, the Finch family wasn't a Norman Rockwell painting of love and healthy living. Seems Mrs. Finch had a bit of a drinking problem long before Zach disappeared. Alec Finch was a very controlling father, overbearing and abusive."

"How did you find that out so quickly?" Greg asked.

Clark laughed. "Seems there's a Jean Utley right here in town. I read about her in a little local weekly newspaper and looked her up on a gut feeling. She's a retired librarian and remembers the Finch kids quite well, especially Jean. At the time I spoke with her, the news hadn't broken yet about Jean's death. I'm sure Mrs. Utley will be quite torn up over it when she hears."

"Jean told me that woman was dead," I said, surprised.

"Far from it," Clark said. "She's quite old but very spry and sharp. When I told her I was a writer looking to write a book about the Finch kidnapping, she opened right up. Librarians love writers."

"You couldn't write a grocery list," I said.

"No, probably not," Clark laughed, "but she didn't know that. Mrs. Utley said Jean used to spend a lot of time in the school library hiding in the stacks, reading. She said she never wanted to go home and once even asked Mrs. Utley if she could go live with her."

"Instead, Jean took her name when she ran away as an adult," Greg noted.

"Sure looks that way," Clark agreed. "I asked Mrs. Utley if she knew why Jean didn't want to go home, and she got very upset. She said it was suspected that Alec Finch abused his wife and kids. When I pressed about how much people suspected it, she confessed it was common knowledge but that no one would do anything because of Finch's power and money. She said she never saw bruises on the kids, but emotionally they had all the signs of being battered, especially Jean. Mrs. Utley said she's always felt guilty about not stepping in herself and stopping it."

"Was any of it sexual?" I asked.

"I asked specifically about that, and she said she didn't think so but did say both kids spent as little time as possible at home. She said Zach was always running around the streets with his friends. Sometimes Mrs. Utley and her husband would see him walking alone late at night or just sitting on the swings in the school yard. The cops knew the situation at home and left him alone because he wasn't a troublemaker."

"How sad," I said, shaking my head.

"What about the happy photos in the paper?" Greg asked.

"I asked Mrs. Utley about that," Clark answered, "and she said Alec Finch often trotted out his family for public appearances. They were well liked, except for Alec, and when he was travelling, which he did a great deal, Maryanne and the kids seemed like a happy and close-knit family."

A new thought, fresh and shiny, occurred to me. "Do you think Zach convinced his kidnappers to let him go, and he went into hiding to get away from his father?"

The two men went silent while they considered my question. Finally, Clark said, "Now there's a plausible thought, although it would be pretty difficult for a kid of fifteen to go on his own without hitting the mean streets as a runaway. If the cops picked him up for any reason, they'd know immediately who he was. And his photo was plastered all over the media, so people might have recognized him, especially since Daddy Finch offered a nice fat reward."

"So who would help him?" asked Greg. "The kidnappers would probably take the money and send the kid packing before they took off. They wouldn't care what happened to him once they got their payoff."

"True," Clark agreed. "Maybe they even gave Zach a few bucks as seed money, but that still wouldn't get him far."

Something buried in my memory was waving at me, and it wasn't being subtle. It was jumping up and down and spinning its arms in the air like a driver stranded on the side of a road. Before it sent up a flare, I focused inward, finally recognizing the tidbit of information so determined to come out.

"Honey," I said to Greg, "didn't Jean mention something about someone reported to have spotted Zach somewhere near Vegas a few years after he disappeared?"

His eyebrows came together as he gave my question thought. "Yeah," he said, "I remember her saying something like that. Didn't she say the police investigated the report and found it not to be true?"

"Yes," I said, "but what if it *was* true, and Zach took off before they could investigate it?"

"Or the witness could have disappeared or recanted," Clark suggested.

"Clark," I said, "I found a comb left behind in the spare bathroom at Jean's. It had blond hair stuck to it. I gave the comb to Fehring, and she's going to have the hair analyzed. What if Zach eventually contacted his sister, and they met up in California? Maybe that's why she left Aztec so soon after she went to work there. Maybe the two of them took the surname of Utley and lived together."

"Jean wasn't exactly in hiding, though, was she?" Clark asked.

"Not really," Greg answered. "She'd cut off ties with her father, but she was an actress. Even though she mostly had bit parts on TV, it doesn't seem like she would have pursued such a career if she had been in total hiding."

"It's going to take the police days, if not

weeks, to process that hair," Clark said, "unless the FBI can put a rush on it." He paused. "Didn't you say Jean claimed another actor lived with her but had moved out recently?"

"Yes," I confirmed, "but they didn't take any furniture, just their personal effects."

"But if it was Zach and not another actor who lived there, what spooked him to make him leave suddenly?" Greg asked. "Do you think he knew someone was out to get him?"

I shook my head. "If he thought he was in danger, then he would have assumed Jean was too, and she would not have stayed behind. If she was hiding him, she would have known too much."

At the same time Greg and I yelled out, "Glick!"

"What?" asked Clark.

"Nathan Glick," Greg responded. "That was the slick dude next to Finch at the press conference — the one who spoke after him."

"What about him?" Clark asked, his voice slow with suspicion.

"Shortly before you called," I said, "Elaine Powers called. She recognized Glick's voice from the TV as the guy who tried to hire her to take out Zach and Jean."

"Elaine Powers got in touch with you?" Clark asked. "Why didn't you tell me?"

"That's one of the reasons why I texted you to call me," I said, getting defensive. "We've been a bit busy with the cops out here, you know." Truth is, I didn't want Clark to know yet that Elaine had contacted us through Mom. I wanted to tell him that in person, just in case he had a stroke and we needed to call 911.

After a short pause, Clark asked, "Okay, so what else did she say?"

"The first time, she talked to us," I began.

"The first time?" I could hear Clark's blood pressure rising through the phone.

I looked up at Greg and he looked concerned. "Tread lightly," he mouthed. I nodded in agreement.

"Yes," I said to Clark. "We've talked to her twice now. The first time, she told us she had nothing to do with the Finch murders but that her crew had been contacted to take on the job. She turned it down even before she knew who was doing the asking as being too much of a hot potato."

"The second time we spoke to her," Greg chimed in, "was just now. She called to say she'd seen the press conference and recognized Glick's voice as the guy who tried to hire her and her crew."

"Does she have any idea who might have

taken the job?" Clark asked.

"No," Greg answered, "but she's having her people look into it."

There was another long pause on Clark's side before he said, "Well, that's very interesting, because I finally tracked down Chris Cook. He and his family returned late tonight from visiting family. I gave him the same cock-and-bull story I gave Mrs. Utley, and he bought it just like she did." He chuckled. "Trusting people must be a Midwestern thing because most people I know on both coasts would have asked for credentials and checked them out first."

His comment made me think about how easily we'd obtained access to Jean.

He paused, and we could hear him take a drink of something. It was probably his twentieth cup of coffee for the day. "I have to tell you," Clark continued, "it really made my job easier not having Zach's death plastered all over the news until just now. None of these people might have spoken to me otherwise. To them it was a cold, sad story and I was just doing research. Anyway, after we went over the usual stuff that happened that night and he confirmed that he saw Zach go into the house, I asked him if he kept in touch with his buddy Nathan Glick, since they were the only two left from that posse. He said they did keep in touch, though less often now that Glick had moved to Chicago and he had gotten married." Clark chuckled. "Seems Mrs. Cook does not like Glick — at least that's what Chris confided in me. Which is interesting because when I asked Mrs. Utley about Zach's friends, she said they were all nice boys except for Nathan."

"How so?" Greg asked. "Was he in trouble a lot?"

"Not really, but she said he was always up to something and could get the other boys to do almost anything. She said he was sneaky and manipulative."

"He was acting more like a handler with Alec Finch today," I said.

"Did you find out anything else about Glick?" Greg asked.

"One last tidbit," Clark said. "And this ties a lot together, especially with what Elaine Powers said. When I asked Chris about contacting Nathan, he said I might have to wait because he left last week for a Hawaiian vacation and would be gone about ten days."

"And now he pops up in California," noted Greg.

"He could have flown back to meet up with Finch when he found out about Zach,"

I suggested.

"But here's the thing," Clark said, and I could almost hear a smile in his voice. "I checked on his flight information."

I wanted to ask how but knew better. Greg caught my eye and shook his head in his own form of surrender.

"Don't tell me," I said into the phone. "He didn't go to Hawaii. He flew to Los Angeles instead."

"Yes and no, sis," Clark said. "Nathan Glick flew to Maui on February eighth with a layover in Los Angeles."

"A layover in LA isn't unusual, Clark," Greg noted. "You can get a nonstop to Maui from LA."

"But a three-day layover?" Clark asked. "According to my source, Glick flew to Maui on the eleventh and checked into an ocean-view suite at the Grand Wailea Hotel for a ten-day stay. He cut his vacation short and flew back to LA on the twentieth, two days after Zach was found dead."

"Those few days before Hawaii would have given him enough time to set up the hit," I said. "I wish Dev hadn't taken that phone because we could ask Elaine what day she got the hit request."

"What phone, and what does Dev have to do with it?" Clark asked.

346

"Elaine gave us a burner phone to use so she could get in touch with us easier in case she found out anything else," Greg explained. "Dev found out and took it away from us."

"Smart man," Clark said. "So where is Dev now?"

"He's at his daughter's, babysitting his grandkids," I told him. "He was with us when Elaine called to tell us about Glick. He said he was going to call Fehring and fill her in."

There was another long pause, then Clark said, "I don't like this one bit. If Powers didn't do this hit, then there is another contract killer out there who did the job and knows who you are, Odelia." I heard my brother blow out a long breath, just short of a whistle. "Any other hitmen on your Christmas card list?"

"Smart ass," I snapped at the phone.

"Well, someone with a gun for hire knows where you live, and that makes me nervous — very nervous."

"If it makes you feel any better, we're not home right now," I told Clark. "We're in hiding for a few days — Fehring's orders. Only she and Dev know where we are. We're not even supposed to tell you and Mom."

"I can live with that," Clark said with

relief. "The question is, can you?"

"Trust me," Greg said. "Wild horses couldn't blast us out of this place. We're going to let the feds and the police handle this."

"For a change?" Clark quipped. "Listen, I was going to fly back to LA tomorrow, but I think I'll stick around and ask about Glick. You two stay put."

TWENTY-FOUR

"Hi, Mom," I said into the phone. "I just wanted to check on you before we went to bed. Everything okay? No more contact with Elaine?"

"Not a peep," she told me. "It's kind of boring."

"Boring is nice and safe," I told her. Greg looked up from his Kindle and shook his head.

We were tucked in for the night at Dev's place. Muffin was on the bed at our feet. Wainwright was on the floor at the foot of the bed. As we have at home, Dev had a TV across from the bed. And just like at home, it was tuned to the late-night news.

The big news of the day was still speculation about Zach Finch's murder and his whereabouts for the past eight-plus years. Jean's death was getting play, too, with the most popular theory being that it was a murder-suicide — that Jean had killed her brother and then herself — although no one seemed to have a theory about how and why the body got into the trunk of a car. Thankfully, my name was not mentioned again, only my car, like it was some sort of stray animal that had wandered into the car wash looking for a good home.

"Who was that guy who yelled out your name earlier?" Mom asked.

"I have no idea, Mom," I lied. I may not lie to Dev or Fehring, but I sure didn't feel bad about lying to my mother. She claims I'm not good at it, but every now and then I sneak one past her, usually for her own good. "Probably some reporter who paid someone to leak my name."

"It was probably those car wash people, Odelia," Mom said. "Maybe you don't tip them enough."

I dropped my head to my chest in defeat. Mom had a remark for everything. "Until this is over, how about you staying put in your complex?" I asked. I wanted to give her a direct order, but that would go over like a fart in church.

"You already told me that, Odelia, when you called earlier. I don't need to be reminded."

"Fehring asked Greg and me to keep a low profile too." Again my words merited a glance from my husband. "Just for a day or two."

"Sure," she said with a sigh. "Besides, I'm still really tired from my trip. I guess old age is catching up to me. That and all the excitement today."

"Are you sure you're okay, Mom?" It wasn't like my mother to be so tired. Even Clark had said something about her being tuckered out from her trip. Greg took his eyes off his book and listened to the conversation more closely. "Maybe you should schedule a doctor's appointment soon for a checkup," I suggested.

"I am overdue," she agreed, "though there's nothing a pill-pusher can do for old age. No late night for me tonight, though. I'm going to go to bed right after this call."

"That's a great idea, Mom. By the way, we heard from Clark. He'll be back in a day or so."

"Yes, I know. He called me right after he called you. He told me to keep my skinny ass at home until he gets here — his exact words. Now is that any way to talk to your mother?"

I laughed. She was fine. "Sweet dreams, Mom."

" 'Night, Grace," Greg called over from his side of the bed.

After I hung up, Greg asked, "Is everything okay with Grace?"

I hemmed and hawed. "She seems okay except that she's more tired than usual." I scooted under the covers and cuddled next to Greg. "Hopefully she'll take my suggestion and go get a checkup."

When I woke in the morning, I was a bit disoriented. This wasn't our bedroom or our furniture. I was alone in a strange bed. Then I remembered we were staying at Dev Frye's house. I settled back into the comfortable bed and listened. Sounds were coming from another part of the house — words being spoken. I concentrated on listening, wondering who might be out there. It was too early for Dev to have returned. A smile spilled across my sleepy face as I realized that there was only one voice — Greg's. He was talking to Muffin, cooing to her, calling her a good girl, a pretty girl, his baby girl. I smiled, happy that we had kept the family together in exile. The smell of coffee also made me smile. Getting up, I made a quick stop in the bathroom, then padded out to the kitchen on bare feet, where I found my hubs wheeled up to the kitchen table, reading the Sunday paper with Muffin on his lap. She was purring like a locomotive while he stroked her with one hand.

"Morning, sleepyhead," Greg said when I came up and gave him a big good morning kiss on the lips.

"What time is it?" I asked, running a hand through my rumpled hair.

"Almost ten."

"Ten?" I was surprised. Unless I was sick or didn't get to bed until the wee hours of the morning, I was not someone who slept in, not even on weekends.

He looked up from the paper. "I don't think Grace was the only one exhausted last night. I haven't been up that long myself. Wainwright woke me so he could go outside. No doggie door here."

"Where is he now?"

With a toss of his head, Greg indicated the partially opened back door. "Wallowing on all that grass, last I looked. I've already fed them both."

"Where'd you get the newspaper?"

"Dev gets home delivery. Fortunately, it was on the front porch. I had Wainwright retrieve it for me."

I shuffled to the counter and the coffee-maker. Next to it was a mug waiting for me. I picked it up and stared at it. "How did you get the mugs down from the cupboards?" I asked, seeing how high Dev's cabinets were compared to ours.

"Where there's morning coffee involved," Greg said with a grin, "there's a will and a way."

I poured myself a cup of coffee. "No, seriously," I said with a laugh. "The coffee can was already on the counter — I noticed it there last night — but not the mugs. What sort of magic did you do? Did you get Wainwright up on the counter to fetch them like he did the paper?" I brought my coffee over to the table and took a chair near Greg.

"I used my brain, sweetheart." He tapped the side of his skull with an index finger. "I found a couple of dirty mugs in the dishwasher and handwashed them. Otherwise, I'd be drinking my coffee directly from the pot."

"My hero." I leaned over and kissed him. "Did you find some breakfast too or will we be fighting the animals for kibble this morning?"

"There's not much in the fridge, I'm afraid. We should have brought a few things with us."

I took a sip of my coffee. "When we run out for breakfast we can pick up a few things, but do you really think we'll be here beyond today?"

He shrugged. "Hard to say, but if we do need to hide out longer, I'll need to decide what I'm going to do about work tomorrow."

"But with the information Elaine gave us about Glick, I'm sure Fehring and Shipman are all over him by now."

"I have no doubt they'll be questioning him," Greg said, his eyes still on the newspaper, "but who knows if they pulled him in yesterday or not." Greg stopped reading and looked at me. "And Glick is probably not our real danger. Whoever killed Zach and his sister is the real threat. And Glick might not be so quick to admit to hiring a killer and giving up the information on them." He shook the paper. "The story about Zach and his sister is all over the news, here and on TV. I'm sure whoever did the killing is watching it carefully to judge their exposure."

I got up from the table abruptly and walked to the back door to think. From there I could see Wainwright sprawled on the grass, flattened against it as if he was trying to hide among the short blades. He must have smelled me because he lifted his noble head in my direction and wagged his tail with enthusiasm. I blew him a kiss and returned to the table.

"I hate sitting around like this," I told Greg. "It makes me even more nervous.

There must be something we can do that won't put us in the path of the killer."

From the bedroom came the sound of a ringing cell phone. "That's mine," I said and headed in that direction to retrieve it. I brought it out to the kitchen and put it on speaker. "It's Dev," I said to Greg, holding the phone between us.

"Just checking on you kids," Dev said. "Everything going okay?"

"Yes," I said. "We're fine, just antsy. Any news from Fehring?"

"She pulled Finch in last night right after I told her about the call you got from Elaine Powers," he told us. "He's probably still in custody." He paused. "But Glick's disappeared, and everyone's looking for him."

Greg and I looked at each other. "So it's looking like Elaine was right about Glick," I said.

"Nothing's confirmed," Dev said, "and Finch has clammed up until his high-priced lawyer gets here, but it's a real good possibility."

"Dev," Greg said, "we were just talking about going out for a quick brunch and a little grocery shopping, if that's okay? No one knows where we are, so a little outing shouldn't hurt."

"Sure, but stay close to my place. Odelia,

you used to live close by, so you know the area."

"There used to be a great little breakfast place on Seventeenth Street, right across from Ralphs," I said. "We could hit both in short order."

"That café is still there," Dev confirmed. "Sorry I don't have more in the house for you guys to eat. I've been kind of winging it until I leave."

"It's okay, Dev," Greg said. "I don't think the killer is going to track us down in an hour or so."

"Just be careful and stay close to your phones. And keep the van out of sight as much as possible. I'll be doing family stuff here most of the day, but Andrea promised to keep me in the loop. She'll probably be calling you too. We're the only ones who know where you are; not even Shipman knows. Andrea let him know that we have you squirreled away, and he's okay with that. Less for him to worry about." Dev paused, then added, "Shipman's not a bad guy, just very intense and ambitious. He hates having civilians in the middle of his investigations even more than we do." I could hear the slight smile behind the words.

"Does Shipman know about Elaine Powers?" I asked.

"Yeah, Andrea passed that along to him. I'm sure Shipman will be talking to you about it at some point, but his first order of business is to find Glick. But trust me, he's not only hell-bent on solving the Finch murders, but now he'll be intent on nailing Powers too. It would be quite a boost to his career for him to do both."

"What about Andrea Fehring?" Greg asked. "Shouldn't she get some of the credit if this gets solved?"

"She'll get some fallout credit," Dev said, "but whenever the feds are involved, they hog most of the accolades. It's always like that. But don't worry, Andrea's cool with it. She just wants to get the murders solved."

We could hear noise in the background on Dev's end, then he said, "Sorry, gotta go. I promised the kids I'd get the bouncy castle up and running. Like I said, stay close to your phones."

After the call, we quickly got cleaned up and went out in search of food. Since we didn't plan on being gone long, we left Wainwright in the gated back yard with his food and water bowl outside. The dog didn't seem to mind. He was still happy playing explorer in the grass.

"Who are you calling?" Greg asked. We

were outside the café waiting for a table. It was crowded but not too bad, especially for a Sunday. The hostess said it would be a ten- to fifteen-minute wait to get a table that would accommodate Greg's wheelchair.

"Mom," I told him, holding the phone up to my ear. "She sounded so tired last night that I want to make sure she's okay this morning."

"Good idea," he agreed. Greg's folks had called him right after the press conference. They'd been upset hearing my name on the TV. Greg had assured them that everything was under control and that I was not a suspect, just the person who had found the body. He left out the part about us meeting with Jean Utley right before her death and Swayze's intrusion, and he certainly didn't mention Elaine. I have complete confidence in the love Greg's parents have for me; they're the best. But I know they'll never get used to their daughter-in-law being a corpse magnet. Unlike my mother, who finds it exciting, they are rightfully horrified.

The phone rang and rang and eventually went to voice mail. I tried again, but still nothing but voice mail. "She's not answering," I told Greg.

"Maybe she went out for a walk around

her complex. Doesn't she do that quite often?"

"Yes. There's a small group of ladies who walk every day around lunchtime, which would be about now. But Mom seldom leaves her phone behind when she goes. She says she needs it in case one of them croaks along the way."

"Your mother is such a little ray of sunshine," Greg said with a smile. "But it's actually a good idea."

"More to the point, my mother is worse than a teenager when it comes to her phone and her iPad."

After a delightful brunch, I tried Mom again. Still it went to voice mail. "I'm getting worried, Greg. Let's go over there."

"It could be dangerous," he said, "or at the very least get Andrea and Dev mad at us." He started up the van.

"Is that a no, we're not going?" I turned in my seat to glare at my husband.

"Of course not, sweetheart," he said with a slight laugh. He pulled out of the parking space and pointed the van toward the exit. "I was just stating the possibilities. Buckle up — we're on our way."

When we reached Mom's retirement community, Greg pushed the code to get us through the gate. The man in the small white guardhouse, a middle-aged rent-a-cop in a gray uniform, smiled at us with recognition and waved as we passed through.

As soon as we parked in front of Mom's place, I hopped out without waiting for Greg and trotted to the door. Thankfully, the distance was a lot less than when I had run after Jean the day before. I mashed my hand over the bell several times, just in case she was home. While I waited for an answer, I leaned far over the partial patio wall and tried to look into the living room. The blinds were drawn closed. My mother always opens her blinds as soon as she's up and dressed. I straightened up and pulled my key ring out of my bag. On it was Mom's key. By the time Greg caught up with me, I was inside, calling, "Mom!"

Although it was a two-bedroom place, Mom's condo wasn't that large. As you walked in, the wall to the right of the front door was the common wall shared with the next townhouse. On it were hung cheerful prints of well-known still-life arrangements, and set against the wall under them was a low bench. To the left was the living room, dining area, and kitchen. Beyond that was a short hallway that branched off to the right toward the small second bedroom and the one bathroom, and to the left to the average-size master bedroom. Midway along the hallway was a closet with folding doors that concealed an apartment-sized washer and dryer and storage for towels and linens.

I dashed across the living room and turned left in the hallway. "Mom!" I called. Her bedroom was empty, and the bed was made. I went the other way. Both the bathroom and extra bedroom were empty. Everything was neat as a pin.

"She's not here," I said to Greg when I returned to the living room.

"No, but her cell phone is." He held up a smartphone that I recognized as my mother's. "It was on the kitchen counter, plugged into the charger," he explained. "That's probably why she didn't take it with her. It was probably low on juice."

My racing heart slowed back to normal. "Maybe she's at the rec room playing cards with friends," I suggested. "You stay here in case she's not and returns. I'll just pop over there."

When I left Mom's, I stopped dead in my tracks on the sidewalk, trying to remember where the recreation room was located. The community had a nice setup, with a large pool, game room, and exercise room located somewhat in the center of the sprawling property, which was honeycombed with sidewalks. An elderly couple strolled by in matching track suits. "Where's the rec room?" I asked them. They pointed across the street to a wide green belt with a sidewalk running down the middle of it. I walked in that direction at a fast clip.

There were three groups of people playing games at card tables in the rec room. One table consisted of two couples playing bridge. At the other, three women played a different card game. It looked like hearts. At the third table, two men played chess. No one was at the pool tables. I glanced through the glass wall that revealed the gym and spotted one man walking on a treadmill while watching a game on the overhead TV.

"Hi," I said, approaching the table of women. "I'm Odelia, Grace Littlejohn's daughter. Have you seen my mother?"

A roly-poly woman with cotton-candy hair answered, "Not today. But most Sundays she's here playing cards with us."

"Maybe she went to church," another woman answered, which caused a ripple of titters. My mother is many things, but a churchgoer is not one of them, and she's quite vocal about her atheist status. The woman making the remark was pale and thin and wore a lovely dress and a string of pearls. Hanging on the back of her chair was a jacket that matched the dress. I remembered meeting her and thought her name was Rose. I also remembered that Mom didn't care for the woman. I'll bet Rose had probably gone to services earlier in the day.

One of the chess players looked up at me. He was a bald African American man with a gray stubbly beard who I'd met several times before. Mom liked him. His name was Art, a widower who I'm pretty sure had his eye on Mom when she had first moved into the complex. I don't think anything romantic came of it, but they did become friends. "I saw Grace driving off with a friend of hers when I was on my way over here," Art told me.

I turned to him with interest and annoyance. Mom had orders not to go anywhere, but my mother's general policy was that orders, like rules, were made to be broken. "Are you sure, Art?"

"Pretty sure. She waved at me as she got into his car."

"His car?" I repeated. "So it was a man?"

He stopped playing and scratched his stubble as he tried to remember. It sounded like fine sandpaper. "More like a kid, really. A red-haired young man, kind of spindly."

Swayze.

Art peered at me with concern over the top of his glasses. "Do you know who that is, Odelia?"

"Yes, I do." I wiped the worry off my face and replaced it with a smile. "Thanks, Art." After I wished them all a good day, I left the rec room and headed down the green-belt toward my mother's place at a jog. With all the jogging I was getting, maybe I should listen to Greg about more cardio or at least start wearing a snugger bra.

When I turned at a bend in the walkway for the home stretch, I saw Greg sitting outside Mom's place waiting for me. He was holding something in his hand and waving it in my direction. Did Mom leave a note? Stupid me. Why didn't we look for one earlier? It would have saved time and my legs.

I kept up my jog until I reached him, then collapsed forward, hands on my knees to steady myself as I gulped air. There was another catch in my side. I half expected Greg to say something about my condition, but he didn't; instead, he shoved the paper in front of my lowered nose.

"Odelia, we have a serious problem."

"Besides me having a heart attack?"

He didn't laugh as I expected. Instead, he

365

shook the paper under my nose again. "Grace has been kidnapped."

I straightened up so fast I nearly fell to the ground in a dizzy lump. "What?" I scooted over to the patio wall and leaned against it for support.

Greg handed me the note. "I found this on the kitchen table, under the phone," he explained. "It was facedown, so I didn't realize it was addressed to you until after you took off."

It was a single piece of paper folded in thirds. On one of the outside folds my name was printed in a juvenile hand that looked familiar. Inside the note was neatly printed in the same manner: *If you want your mother back, stay by her phone. No cops or she's dead.*

"Grace didn't leave her phone behind to charge it," Greg said. "It was left by the kidnappers to communicate with us."

I rubbed a hand over my face and squeaked out between breathes, "Swayze has her."

"Swayze?"

I nodded. "Mom's friend Art saw her get in a car with a young guy that fit John Swayze's description. He said Mom waved at him."

"Was she waving at Art or trying to get

his attention?" Greg asked.

"Good question," I said, finally speaking normally. "But why would Swayze grab Mom? And why in heaven's name would she go off with him after we specifically told her to stay home?"

"Maybe she didn't have a choice." Greg ran a hand through his hair several times, creating haphazard furrows. His jaw was clenched from stress, much like my stomach.

"We need to get her phone." I started to move inside the condo, but Greg stopped me by holding Mom's cell phone up. "Got it." When I took it from him, he added, "I know what the note said, but cops or no cops? It's your call. Swayze is obviously someone other than who he says."

I fell back against the low block wall again in fright. "Oh my gawd, Greg. John Swayze must be the hitman."

I could tell Greg was whirling my comment around in his brain by the way his eyes moved. They almost circled, then darted from one side to the other, as if actually searching for information stored in his gray matter. "I don't know, sweetheart," he finally said. "If he was, why didn't he take you out when he had the chance back at our place? He recorded you. He didn't kill you. And didn't you pat him down, looking for a weapon?"

"I only grabbed his wallet." I shook my head. "I really should have checked for some sort of weapon. It was slipshod of me."

"Not really, sweetheart. You're not a cop. It's not like you called in sick the day they covered pat-downs at paralegal school."

Greg was trying to make me feel a little better, but it wasn't working. John Swayze had my mother, and until he called we wouldn't know why or what he wanted. We were stuck waiting for a call, with no idea of when it would come. I took several breaths of air — not out of exhaustion but to try and center my emotions and thoughts. Like us, Mom lived close to the ocean, and the air was heavy with both salty sea moisture and the dampness of the overhead storm clouds. It hadn't rained yet today, but the threat was there, just as it was in the note.

"Who knows why Swayze did what he did," I finally said. "Maybe he was only scouting for the real killer." I looked down at the note again, studying it closely. "But I think whoever wrote this might also have written the note found on Zach's body."

Greg put on his reading glasses and held out his hand for the kidnapper's note. "Are you sure?" I handed it back to him, and he pored over it like it was a map to buried treasure. "The other note only had two words, as I recall," he said, not looking up.

"No, I'm not absolutely sure, but I think it's a possibility." I took another few breaths. "Both are printed in a similar juvenile hand." I closed my eyes and concentrated. "I really don't recall coming across Swayze before now, so if he did kill Zach and put the body in my trunk, why? What's the connection to me?"

Silence as thick and gummy as oatmeal fell over us while we put our brains through their paces again. After a few moments, I asked, "What do you think we should do, honey?"

"I'm not sure, Odelia." Greg put away his reading glasses. "Other than just wait for whoever has Grace to contact us." He paused. "I don't want to put Grace's life in danger by involving the police, but they need to know that Swayze might be involved."

"I agree." I pushed off from the wall and went inside and grabbed my purse. Greg came in behind me. I pulled out my cell and called Andrea Fehring and put it on speaker so Greg could participate.

"What's up, Odelia?" she answered after

two rings.

"I've been thinking," I began, choosing my words carefully. "I think maybe John Swayze might have had something to do with Zach's death or at least with putting him in my trunk."

"Why do you say that?" she asked.

"Something about the note left with the body has been bothering me since I met Swayze," I continued. "I think I recognized his handwriting."

"And where did you see it?" Fehring asked.

Next to me, Greg mouthed, "Careful."

I hesitated just long enough to swallow. "When I went through his wallet after I bashed his hand. I was looking for ID."

"And he just happened to have a hand-writing sample on him? Maybe he was practicing forgery." Fehring offered up a very terse laugh bordering on a woof. "Give me a break, Odelia. What's really going on?"

"It was sort of a to-do list," I quickly answered. Greg gave me a thumbs up on my speedy creativity. "I remember it having a similar look to the writing on the note left with Zach's body. You know, precise block printing like a kid who never learned cursive."

Now Greg was mouthing, "Don't over-sell."

"Greg and I were talking about it and thought I should tell you. Did you dust the note for fingerprints?"

A big sigh came through the phone. "Of course we did, and we found nothing. Not Swayze's. Not anyone's." A pause. "Look, I'm very busy. We brought in Finch, but Glick's disappeared."

"Yeah," I said, "Dev told us about it. Any breaks?"

"Not yet." There was another pause. "By the way, Odelia, I'm not happy that you didn't tell me about Elaine Powers contacting you yesterday."

Greg mouthed, "Say nothing." It was difficult, but I kept my mouth shut.

"What else are you not telling me?" Fehring prodded.

I took a deep breath. Greg was now silently telling me to tell her about Clark. Instead, I handed him the phone. I was tired of dancing around Fehring's questions and was too worried about Mom to be careful.

"Andrea," Greg began, "Greg here. We also wanted to tell you that Clark has been looking into some background on the Finch family."

There was a long silence on the other end.

"I should be mad, but I'm not," she finally said. "At least he's a trained cop and knows how to be careful. So spill it."

Greg filled her in on what Clark had told us about the Finch family dynamics and the theory that maybe Zach used the kidnapping as an opportunity to hit the road on his own. "He could have even escaped," Greg suggested. "Went into hiding, and maybe the kidnappers found him after all these years. Maybe he was Jean's roommate?"

"No," Fehring said, "we've located the roommate. We got his name from the occupant information on file with the complex's security company. He is an actor who just moved to New York, just as Jean said, and he has long blond hair like on the comb. We also showed a photo of Zach to Jean's neighbors, and none of them recognized him as living there, but one woman who lived in the condo across from Jean did say she saw Zach visiting from time to time."

"So Jean *did* know that her brother was here in SoCal?" I asked, moving back closer to the phone.

"Sure looks that way," Fehring said. "And from fingerprints we took from the body, it looks like he was going by the name of David Moreland. The address on file with the

DMV is a mailbox place, just like with Swayze's. We're trying to get their records now to see what physical address Zach put down. We're also going through all of Jean's contact lists from her phone, computer, and address book to see if she had a physical address for him under that name, but we're coming up with nothing. Whatever Zach was doing to support himself, it was off the grid."

"Off the grid," I echoed. "Maybe that's what got him killed. Maybe Elaine was wrong about recognizing Nathan Glick's voice."

"As much as I don't want to show support for your killer pal," Fehring said, "she stays alive remembering details like that, so I'm not so ready to dismiss Glick just yet, especially since he ran." Another pause. "So are you following orders and staying put?"

"We'd love to go home, Andrea," my hubs said, getting a thumbs up from me on his own quick thinking. He hadn't lied to her but had offered up a comment that could be taken as an affirmative response.

"Not just yet," she told us. "We'll call you as soon as we feel it's safe."

"What about work tomorrow?" Greg asked. "Can I at least go to my shop? I have a business to run."

"Sit tight, Greg," Fehring said. "But it wouldn't hurt to have someone cover for you tomorrow."

"How about my employees — are they safe?" he asked.

"Your business is in Huntington Beach, correct?" she asked.

"Yes, it is."

"I'll make a call to their police chief and see if he will post someone to watch it tomorrow — how's that? I'll see if I can arrange something at Odelia's work, too, just in case."

"We'd feel a lot better about it," Greg told her. "Thanks."

Another cell phone rang. It was Mom's. When I made the call to Fehring, I'd placed it on the counter by my purse. Neither Greg or I made a move to touch it. Instead, we stared at each other with the wide eyes of lemmings who'd just received orders to march off a cliff.

Twenty-Five

"What's that phone?" Fehring asked. "I thought Dev took the phone Powers gave you."

"He did," I said quickly. "That's Greg's phone."

"Yeah. It's my parents," he lied. "I need to take it."

"I'll let you two go, then," Fehring said, "but stay close to both of your phones." She hung up.

Mom's phone rang again, and Greg and I continued to stare at each other, afraid to answer and at the same time afraid not to. Worry for Mom won out, and I grabbed the phone and hit the answer button.

"I see you found the note," said a woman on the other end of the line.

"Yes," I stammered. "We found it." Greg grabbed the phone from me and put it on speaker.

"Who's *we*?" the voice asked. I didn't

recognize it at all but continued to push my memory through its paces.

"My . . . my . . . ," I said, struggling to get the words out.

"It's Greg Stevens, Odelia's husband," Greg said in the phone. "We found the note and Grace's phone. Please don't hurt Grace."

"Wow," said the woman, "a son-in-law worried about his mother-in-law. That's unusual." She laughed, but it wasn't a fun laugh. It was sharp as a knife and edged with cruelty. "Grace will be fine if you follow instructions."

Greg looked at me and silently asked if I knew who the caller was. I shrugged my answer.

"What do you want?" Greg asked the caller.

"Odelia."

"I'm here," I squeaked out, trying to keep my tears at bay. "Please don't hurt Mom."

"No, it's you I want," the woman said.

"Me?" I asked with surprise, staring at the smartphone and wishing it was a visual call. "I don't even know you!" I paused. "Do I?"

"Dumber than a box of rocks," the voice said almost under her breath.

The blood in my veins instantly turned to ice. I shook my head, unsure if I had heard it or not. "Excuse me," I said. "I didn't catch what you said."

"If you don't want to bury your mother, Odelia, then show up at the address I'm going to give you. Show up alone."

"No," Greg said quickly. "I'm coming with her."

"We only have Greg's van," I added quickly. "And I can't drive his van."

"Bring your old man, then," she said with a laugh. "It's added value. But no cops or you will all die. And that is non-negotiable."

She gave us an address. I stopped her so I could grab a pen from a cup of them Mom kept on the counter along with a small notepad. She sighed and waited. When I was ready, she repeated the address and told us we had thirty minutes to get there.

Greg looked at the address. "If we hit traffic, it might take longer than that. Maybe even an hour."

"Then make it forty-five," she said and disconnected.

I stumbled to the sofa and lost it. Burying my face in my hands, I sobbed, my shoulders shaking like I was being electrocuted. And I was — with fear.

Greg rolled over and stopped in front of me. He put a hand on each of my knees and squeezed. "It's going to be okay, sweetheart," he said, trying to reassure me. "We'll get Grace back. You'll see."

I shook my head, still keeping it buried in my hands, which were now sopping wet. He put one hand gently on the top of my head. "Who was that, Odelia?" he asked gently. "You know, don't you?"

Still bent forward, I nodded. "It was Lisa." I raised my tear-soaked face to him and sniffed back mucus. "Elaine's bodyguard."

He took his hands off of me as if he'd touched a hot stove and stared at me. "Are you sure?"

I nodded. "About 90 percent sure. She said I was dumber than a box of rocks just now. She's said that before." I took a deep breath.

Greg ran a hand vigorously through his hair. "So Elaine *is* involved?"

I shrugged as my brain exploded with possibilities. "Either Elaine lied to us about knowing about Zach or Lisa is acting on her own." I stood up and took another deep breath. "But if Lisa is acting on her own, then Mom is as good as dead. She doesn't have the same warped code as Elaine. Lisa has no code. She's a killer through and through."

I grabbed tissues from a box Mom kept on the table between the sofa and her favorite chair and mopped up my face. "Let's get going. We don't have much time, and Mom doesn't have much of a chance of surviving, but she has zero chance if we don't show up. Don't forget to bring Mom's phone."

Greg nodded slowly as he held up the phone as proof he still had it, then turned his wheelchair toward the door while I grabbed my purse.

"What about the police?" Greg asked once we were on the road.

"If we call them and Lisa finds out, Mom is dead. It never dawned on me that Lisa might be acting as a freelance killer. I was thinking that John Swayze was the killer."

"Speaking of which, what do you think his connection is to Elaine and her crew?" he asked.

"I have no idea. As far as I know, Elaine's people are all women." Pieces of information were floating in front of me like helium balloons. I kept trying to catch one or two, but they floated out of my reach. "But if Lisa decided to freelance separately from Elaine, she might not be so choosy." My right knee was bouncing up and down on the floor of the van. "Damn it. If Dev hadn't taken that phone, I could call Elaine and ask her a few questions."

Greg glanced over at me. "You still believe Elaine, don't you?"

"Yes, Greg, I do. I'm not sure why, except that she's had plenty of opportunity to grab Mom and harm us, and she never has. If I'm right and it is Lisa who took Mom, Elaine might not know she's gone off the reservation. And Lisa has always disliked me. Maybe she killed Zach and put him in my car as some sort of sick joke."

"What I still don't understand is if Swayze is working with this Lisa, why didn't he do something when he had you alone?"

"I don't understand that either, Greg."

I pulled out my phone and called Fehring again. This time it went to voice mail after four rings. I hung up and called again. This time she picked up on the third ring. "I'm trying to get in a few hours at home with my family, Odelia, so this had better be good."

"And I'm trying to save my butt," I snapped. Before she could say anything, I ploughed on. "I think Swayze is involved in this in a big way," I told her. "Do you have any information on someone named Lisa who works on Elaine Powers's crew?"

"Not at my fingertips, but I can look it up. Give me a minute, and I'll call you back."

"I don't have a minute. Look for a connection between Swayze and this Lisa — I don't have a last name for her. I think she's broken away from Elaine's group and Swayze is working with her."

"Hold on," Fehring said, "I hear traffic noise. You two are supposed to be at Dev's, not driving around."

"I don't have time to explain. Dev might be able to contact Elaine through the phone he took from me. Have him ask her about it." I ended the call.

A second later my phone rang again. It was Fehring. I ignored it. Shortly after, Greg's phone, which was on the console between us, rang. "Should we get that?" he asked.

"No."

"Maybe we should turn them both off so they can't track us."

I shook my head. "I don't think they can do that as quickly as they do on TV. Besides, maybe being tracked at this point is a good thing."

I looked out the window at the scenery whizzing by as we traveled south on the 405. Greg was heavy on the gas, but this time I wasn't worried. If I could have made the van go faster from my side, I would have. My only worry was that we didn't have time to be stopped by the CHP for speeding.

"Also," I said, amending my last comment, "they'll need to track us to find our bodies."

I felt Greg's eyes on me but couldn't meet them with my own. I couldn't face the fact that not only was I probably going to my own death, but I was taking the man I loved with me.

Twenty-Six

The address Lisa had given us had us going south on the 405, then east on the 133 to where it joined with the 241. Because it was a Sunday and the weather iffy, traffic had been light and we made good time. "Slow down, honey," I said to Greg as I read the directions on the scrap of paper in my hands. "She said to take the first turn on the right. She didn't give it a name, so who knows if it's a real street."

We didn't need to look hard to find it. Shortly after rounding a sharp bend in the road, we spotted John Swayze up ahead waiting for us. When he saw the van, he started directing us to pull in with his bandaged hand like we were parking at a sporting event. All he needed was an orange vest to complete the look — that and to lose the gun he was holding in his uninjured hand.

"Should I hit him with the van?" Greg

asked as we pulled from the street onto a wide paved drive.

"If Mom's life wasn't at stake, I'd say go for it."

As we neared Swayze, he indicated for us to stop. Greg lowered his window. "Pull in behind that building, turn off the engine, and leave the keys in the van," Swayze directed. He took one step forward and glanced behind Greg. "Where's the dog?"

"We left him at home," Greg answered.

"Good," Swayze said, "or else I'd have shot him."

Greg started to make a move, but I put a hand on his arm to calm him down.

"Listen to your wife, hot wheels," Swayze told him.

Hot wheels. That's what my mother often called Greg, especially when she was annoyed with him. I made a silent wish that I'd get to hear her call him that again.

The building in front of us was tall and long and had three very wide, high garage doors running across it. Greg moved the van slowly around the corner of the building and pulled in near a partially open back door with a yellow light burning over the entry. He cut the engine. It looked like the building was a concrete square, with this side as wide as the front with the garage doors. It was only midafternoon, but with the gray skies it felt later. The saffron light cast the only welcoming warmth.

Swayze caught up with us and glanced in at me. "Leave your purse but bring your phones." He grinned, showing crooked bottom teeth. He pointed the gun at Greg, and my heart nearly stopped. "You first. Nice and easy."

Swayze backed up and kept the gun trained on Greg as he slowly opened his door and reached behind his seat to grab his wheelchair. With an ease I'd seen thousands of times, he unfolded it and swung his butt into the seat. Keeping a safe distance from my agile husband, Swayze glanced at me. "Okay, Odelia, now you. Get out and come around the front of the van nice and slow. Pull anything stupid and I'll shoot Greg."

He didn't have to add please for me to do exactly what he asked. Greg had been shot several months before, and I didn't want a repeat of that situation. I eased out of the van, leaving my bag behind as ordered, and made my way around the front of it to stand next to Greg.

Waving the gun in the direction of the yellow light, Swayze indicated for us to head that way ahead of him. Fortunately for

Greg, the parking lot was paved. If he'd gotten hung up on uneven terrain, I wouldn't have trusted Swayze to be understanding. He seemed nervous and unstable, with a thin veneer of false bravado; not exactly the type of person who should be holding a gun. When we reached the door, I opened it wider and held it open for Greg to maneuver the lower edge and enter the building. I followed him in, with Swayze close behind.

Inside, the ceiling of the building was high, with open steel beams. It was an industrial garage of some kind. Whatever was stored behind the three huge rolling doors we saw in the front was behind a wall that ran the length of the building but not all the way to the roof. There was a large door in the wall, but it was closed. The side we were on was much more narrow. It contained an open work area with benches and tools along the walls. Across from us, on the opposite wall, was another garage door, but it was normal size. Next to it was one window covered with dirt, with a jagged chunk of glass missing from one of the lower corners. The concrete floor was stained with oil and grease, and in the center a small beige truck was up on blocks. The overhead lights were on in the place, making it as bright as day inside. I saw no sign of Lisa or my mother.

On the left-hand side, an office had been built with eight-foot walls. The longest section of the office had a glass window that looked out onto the work area, similar to Greg's office. The lights were on inside there also, and it looked cramped and filled with filing cabinets.

"Where's my mother?" I asked Swayze, trying to keep fear out of my voice. Next to me, Greg took my hand and gave it a gentle squeeze. I couldn't tell if he was trying to comfort me or warn me. Maybe it was both.

"Don't worry — you'll see her soon enough," Swayze said. "Though why you want her back is beyond me. She's really annoying."

Before anything more was said, the door to the office opened and out strode Lisa. Camouflage pants and a black long-sleeved tee shirt fit her small, tight frame as if personally tailored for her. On her feet were heavy boots. Her brown hair was cropped, leaving only an inch or two all over her head. In her hand was a gun. She looked like a military action figure come to life or a wood nymph gone bad.

"Odelia Grey," she said with a smirk. "I never thought you'd be useful to me, but here you are." She turned to Greg. "And this must be your husband. I've heard a lot about you from Mother, Greg. It's good to finally meet you, though why a man of your talent is with this loser is beyond me." Greg's hand started to slip from mine as his anger rose. It was my turn to get a good grip and squeeze.

"Where's my mother, Lisa?" I asked. I took several steps forward and Greg rolled alongside me, staying close by my side, until we were just a few feet from Lisa and near the front end of the disabled truck, which faced away from the door.

In response, Lisa stepped back into the office. A few seconds later, she brought out Mom. She was sitting in a rolling office chair and strapped down with duct tape, the same type of silver tape used to bind Zach's body. Lisa gave the chair a big push in my direction. I dropped Greg's hand and met Mom mid-roll, stopping the chair when it reached me. Swayze barked at Greg to stay where he was.

"Mom, are you okay?" I felt tears running down my face as I embraced her.

"I'm so sorry, Odelia," Mom said, her own face streaked with tears. "I should have stayed put like you said, but that creep came to the gate and said Elaine sent him to take me somewhere safe."

Of course, I thought. Mom never would have gone off with a stranger, but Elaine was not a stranger any longer, and Mom trusted her after the meeting we'd had. Elaine had unwittingly led Lisa right to Mom, and Lisa had used Mom's trust to lure her out. But why? The one answer I did have was that I knew for sure that Elaine Powers had nothing to do with our current situation; this was all on Lisa. I kissed Mom's forehead to comfort her.

"Touching," Lisa said with sarcasm as thick as marmalade. "Very touching. Fit for a Hallmark card."

I looked up at Lisa. "You're double-crossing Elaine Powers, aren't you?" I stepped backward toward Greg and the truck, rolling Mom back with me. If we were going to die, we would die together. Swayze moved in closer, keeping watch on us.

Lisa laughed, but it was just a sound. Her lips remained an unemotional flesh-colored slash. Her eyes were dead as dry dirt. "It's called expansion, Odelia. I'm tired of working for someone else. I want to be my own boss." She looked at Greg. "I'm sure you know what I mean, Greg. You have your own business — a thriving one, I'm told."

"You did the hit on Zach Finch and his

sister, didn't you?" I asked, keeping a hand on Mom's shoulder as though she'd disappear if I let go.

"You're half right, Odelia," Lisa said. "I did take the job on the kid, but I didn't do the sister. The job was for both, but the sister was out of town when the hit went down on Zach. The client didn't know that when he set up the time frame. While we waited for her return, the client became difficult. He kept complaining about the way I disposed of Zach's body." She started making yakking signs with the hand not holding the gun. "Bitch. Bitch. Bitch. Bitch. Bitch. You would have thought he was talking to some customer service center in New Delhi about his cable bill. So I told him the girl was out — the job was over. That's something I learned from Elaine: never put up with bullshit from a client. He would have been taken care of last night if the police hadn't pulled him in." She leaned against a workbench.

Color me confused. Fehring had said they'd only brought in Alec Finch and that Glick had disappeared. Had Elaine been wrong? Was it really Alec Finch who had hired the hit on his own children? Or was Lisa making an assumption that the police also had Glick because she couldn't locate him?

"I'm guessing," Lisa continued, "that Zach's good pal Nathan took Jean out himself."

And there it was: the answer. It *was* Glick who had hired the hit.

"I don't know exactly what went down all those years ago," Lisa continued, "but I'll bet she knew too much about it, and once she found out Zach was dead, she would probably go straight to the police and spill her guts. As I said, the original plan was to take them both out on the same day."

"But why involve Odelia?" Greg asked. "You could have made the hit and gone on your merry way. Why turn it into a spectacle?"

For the first time, Lisa's face split into a big smile. "Because after I took the job, I realized I could leverage it against Elaine." She turned from Greg to me. "Elaine needs to retire. She's gone soft — your relationship with her is proof of that. Our crew has dwindled to nearly nothing. When a member wants to leave and start a new life, Elaine is quietly helping her do it, even encouraging it, without the rest of us knowing about it until later. There was a time when Mother was feared all up and down the West Coast.

Now new crews are coming into our territory without fear of retaliation." She pushed off from the bench. "I'm the new Mother. I'm returning the crew to its former respect, with stronger and more dedicated soldiers."

"You mean like dipshit Swayze here?" Greg asked.

In response, Swayze smacked Greg across the back of his head with his gun. Greg let out a sharp cry as his head jerked forward.

"No!" I cried.

Swayze looked at me. "Don't worry — you'll get yours later."

Greg put a hand up to touch his head. When he withdrew it, his fingers were tipped with blood. "I'm okay, sweetheart," he said, looking up at me, his eyes latching onto mine. They were steely and full of determination. I knew that look. He was gathering his strength and controlling it, making it work to his advantage. When the time was right, Greg would strike like a cobra. I only hoped the time was right before we were all dead.

I turned back to Lisa. "If you wanted to grab me, why didn't Swayze do it when he was at my house?"

Lisa's face turned from smug glee to dark and cloudy. "He was supposed to, but he wanted to get a trophy first," she explained.

"He's a collector." She spat the words out. "He decided to film you before he grabbed you."

The hand on Mom's shoulder started shaking at the thought that only Swayze's ego had kept me from being taken from the safety of my home — or worse. Mom leaned her head to the side to touch my hand with it. It was the only part of her body she could move. According to Emma Whitecastle, my father had said that my mother would bring me comfort when I needed it. Was this that comfort? This small, sad gesture, stilted by duct tape? I looked down at my mother, taped up like a leaky pipe, and felt like a failure. I had gotten her dragged into this, and it was my job to get her out of it. I needed to stall for time to think. "What about the note on the body?" I asked. "What was its purpose?"

"The note on the body was my idea," Swayze said with pride. "Just a creative touch. I got a great photo of that too."

Lisa shook her head. "Another one who's dumber than a box of rocks." She shrugged. "But he's family, so what can I do?"

"Family?" I turned to look from Swayze to Lisa. I saw no resemblance.

"First cousins," she explained. "But he's more like a brother since my parents raised him after his mother died and his dad took off. He's been helping me with a few odd jobs since he moved here. He has a real talent for it as long as he doesn't get too *creative.*" She emphasized the last word as she glared at Swayze.

I wondered about Lisa's childhood. What kind of family turns out not one but two psychopaths?

"I still don't understand why you need Odelia," Greg said to Lisa. "Why not just take Elaine out and be done with it?"

Another sick smile raced across Lisa's face. "Where's the poetry in that, Greg?" Lisa took a couple of steps closer and smiled again. "John isn't the only artist in the family."

"I'm sure the police and the feds have gotten Glick to talk by now," Greg said, "and they know it's you and not Elaine who killed Zach." I didn't look at Greg. I didn't want to give away that he was playing Lisa about Glick. I didn't know his plan, but I was along for the ride.

"I doubt that," Lisa said. "You see, when I contacted him, I let him believe I was Mother and that I had reconsidered the job. He thinks he hired her."

"But you do a lot of the killing for her crew," I noted. "It doesn't matter who set the deal up."

"I'm still in the dark about why the body was left in Odelia's car," Mom said.

"Good question, Mom," I said, "unless it was to flush out Elaine all along, like the police first thought."

"Yep," Lisa confirmed. "I needed to get you involved, Odelia. I knew the more the police suspected you, the more likely Elaine would let down her guard to protect you." She paused and shifted her stance. "I'll admit, your mother wasn't part of the plan. But after John screwed up at your house and you hit the road, I had to use your mother to bait you here. Now I'm using you to bait Elaine. Once we're all together, you'll all be out of my hair for good." Lisa gave us another insane smile. "I promise it won't hurt . . . too much."

My mother started crying, and then I heard something dripping. Looking down, I saw that my mother had lost control of her bladder. Urine was running from her chair onto the concrete.

"I'm so sorry, Odelia," Mom said between quiet sobs. "I should have stayed put."

"Is the old lady pissing herself?" Swayze asked with disgust.

"What do you expect?" Mom shot at him through her tears. "I'm old, and I asked to

use the bathroom ages ago. I asked *twice.*"
It was nice to know that even in the face of
death and with wet drawers, Mom was still
a pistol.

"Let's move this along," Lisa said with
annoyance. "Call Elaine and tell her to meet
you here."

"I can't call her," I said. "I don't know
how."

"Don't play any dumber than you already
are, Odelia," Lisa said, her voice getting
edgy. "I know Elaine gave you a burner
phone so you could keep in touch."

"I don't have it," I told her. I showed her
my hand. "This is my personal cell phone.
Swayze said to bring the phone. He didn't
say which one." I wasn't about to tell Lisa
that the police had the burner.

"What about you?" she asked Greg.

"Elaine gave us only one," he answered. "I
brought my own cell with me."

She turned back to me. "Where's your
purse?"

"In the van," I said. "Swayze said to leave
it there."

Lisa rolled her eyes — not at me but at
her cousin. "Go back out and get the
phone," she ordered him. "I can watch
them."

He backed away as if afraid she would

shoot him in the back for his transgressions.

"And shut the damn door this time," Lisa barked. "It's getting cold out."

Once at the door, Swayze made his way out and closed it behind him.

"When he gets back," Lisa explained, "you will call Elaine and let her know where you are. Tell her Zach's killer grabbed you, and you managed to sneak a call." She aimed the gun at my mother. "Make it convincing or else."

Mom shut her eyes tight. "Don't do what she says, Odelia. She's going to kill us all anyway."

"Won't she be looking for you to come here with her?" I asked Lisa.

Lisa shook her head and smiled. "She thinks I'm off running down a lead on Zach's killer, like she told me to do." She paused and listened. "What in the hell is taking that moron so long?"

"It's probably at the bottom of my purse," I offered. "It's a big bag. Greg calls it my luggage."

"Wheel on over to the door," she said to Greg, "and tell the idiot to just bring the whole bag in."

Greg didn't move. Nor did he take his eyes off of Lisa for a second. He was still in his cobra stance. Hot, high tension was coming off of him like a cut electrical wire, but I wasn't sure Lisa could feel it or noticed.

When Greg didn't move, she said, "Never mind." Keeping the gun on us, she side-stepped to the door. As she did, Greg gently nudged me, pushing me toward the nose end of the truck. I immediately understood what he meant. He wanted us to take cover behind the front of the truck. We were just inches from turning the corner, but I wasn't sure we could all make it before Lisa noticed.

Bending down to Mom's ear, I whispered, "Keep your mouth shut no matter what happens." Slowly I wheeled Mom around the end of the bumper, getting her to cover first. She'd buttoned her lip as I had asked.

Lisa was at the door. When she looked back, Greg and I hadn't moved, and the edge of Mom's chair was barely noticeable. "Quit wasting time and bring in the whole damn purse," Lisa yelled at the closed door.

I took the opportunity to edge closer toward the bumper myself. Not that it would do us any good once Lisa returned, but doing something was better than doing nothing. Maybe Greg had a plan to rush them, although I wasn't sure what he could do against two pistols. Hand to hand, he could definitely hold his own.

Greg nudged me again toward cover. "Something's wrong," he whispered.

Then I understood what he meant. Swayze should have been back by now or at least he should have answered Lisa. Somebody outside might have grabbed Swayze and was now waiting for Lisa to show her face. I wasn't sure who it would be, though. We hadn't made the call to Elaine, and the police didn't know where we were. But one thing was for certain: if there was a gun battle, it would come from the direction of the small door with the yellow outside light, and it could happen at any second.

I rounded the corner of the truck myself and saw Mom straining to see over the hood. Her neck was extended so much I thought her head might pop off. Gently I turned Mom and eased her, chair and all, down to the concrete. If I wasn't afraid of the truck falling off its blocks, I would have shoved her under it for safety. She moaned and tried to protest. "Shh," I said and turned her gently on her side so that the chair faced out, giving her at least some protection against flying bullets. Then I hunkered down next to her and poked my own head over the hood to see what was going on. Greg rolled himself behind the truck with us and kept watch.

Preoccupied with trying to decide what to do, Lisa had stopped paying attention to us just long enough for us to take cover. But now she was turned our way, gun aimed, and it was clear what she intended to do. We were now her hostages. Without knowing what was going on outside and what had happened with Swayze, Lisa was hedging her bets. If she needed a hostage, she had three. If she didn't and Swayze was just delayed because he was taking a leak, what was the harm?

With the gun pointed at me, she waved me over. "Come here, Odelia. Make yourself useful." When I hesitated, she aimed the gun at Greg. That changed everything. "I'll shoot him, then your mother. Or you can come here like a good girl. Which will it be?"

I stood up and slowly started for her.

"Take me instead," Greg said to Lisa.

"How gallant of you, Greg, but no," Lisa told him, coming closer and keeping the gun on him. "Odelia would make a much better shield." She waved her free hand at me. "Come on, Odelia. Get that fat ass of yours over here."

Slowly, I made my way toward her. When I was within a couple feet of her, she indicated for me to walk toward the door.

As soon as I got in front of her, she grabbed a fistfull of my hair and poked the gun into my back. Together we shuffled forward. I glanced over my shoulder at Greg. He was slowly wheeling out from behind the truck, anxiously watching, worry etched deep on his face. Lisa jerked my hair to straighten my head forward. I called out in pain.

When we got to the door, she called out again, "John, where are you?" There was no answer. "Whoever is out there," she called from behind me at the door, "I have three hostages, and I won't hesitate to put a bullet in all of them, with Odelia first in line."

Putting me squarely in front of her, Lisa jerked my hair again like I was a disobedient horse she was riding. "Open the door," she told me.

"What?" I asked. Mom wasn't the only one who might experience a bladder issue. Who knew who or what was out there?

"I said, open the door," she repeated. "Turn the knob, then give it a hard kick. It opens out." She pressed the gun deeper into my back.

I reached out and slightly turned the knob, unlatching the door. Using my hair, Lisa guided me back a few steps. "Now," she said in a low, demanding growl like a junkyard dog about to bite.

Balancing on my left leg, I shut my eyes tight, raised my right foot, and kicked the door open, expecting a spray of bullets to hit me full-on. Behind us I heard Greg scream, *"No!"*

Twenty-Seven

Silence. No hail of gunfire. No yelling or shouting, just silence. Lisa still had a grip on my hair and was walking backward, pulling me along with her. I opened my eyes and scooted back, trying to backpedal faster than she was ripping out my hair.

The first thing to come through the door was a surprise. It wasn't the end of a gun, it was a person — Nathan Glick. He was in a dirty dress shirt and trousers, and his arms were secured behind him. His face was battered, and his lips were sealed with tape.

"Let Odelia go," a familiar voice behind Glick called out. "She's not a part of this."

"Part of what?" Lisa said, not loosening her grip on my hair. She backed up as Elaine Powers stepped into the building using Glick as a shield and took several slow steps toward us.

"What's going on?" The question came from my mother. "I can't see a thing." I was glad I'd put her on the ground. The last thing Mom needed was to see her only daughter used as a human shield in a gunfight. She'd already lost one child to violence.

"Shh, Grace," Greg said. He wheeled forward, slowly coming closer. Lisa must have seen him out of the corner of her eye because she shifted us so that her back was against one of the workbenches and she could watch both Greg and Elaine on either side of her.

"I know you used Odelia to get me here to ambush me. John just told me everything about your plans," Elaine said to Lisa, keeping her gun trained on Lisa from behind Glick. "You didn't have to do that, Lisa. You could have come to me and said you wanted to go solo. I would have supported you. I'm tired and sick and getting out of the business."

"Sick?" Lisa asked with surprise. My eyes shot open at the news too.

"Yes," Elaine confirmed. "I have liver cancer, and it's spread. According to the doctor, I only have a few months to live. That's why I've been helping the girls who wanted to leave the crew start over. I would have done the same for you, if you'd asked." Elaine took another step forward. "Let

Odelia go, and I'll turn all the business over to you now. You had to have known that I was grooming you for this."

I felt the grip on my hair loosen and started to get hopeful. Then it tightened again.

"Where's John?" Lisa asked. "Did you kill him?" The gun went from my back to the back of my head, and I thought I would faint.

"He's outside," Elaine answered, "and quite alive."

"I don't believe you," Lisa said with a snarl.

"It's true," Elaine said calmly. "I promised Odelia here that I wouldn't kill him." Without taking her eyes off of Lisa, Elaine asked me, "Didn't I, Odelia?"

I nodded and managed to squeak out a feeble yes.

"I would have walked right into your trap unprepared if not for my gal here," Elaine told Lisa. "But when she told me the creepy guy at the press conference yelling her name was named John Swayze, I knew something was up."

"There's no way you could have connected John to me," Lisa shouted at Elaine. "You didn't know about him."

"You know what your problem is, Lisa,"

Elaine asked with a tired half-smirk, "and always has been? You underestimate people. You always think you're the smartest one in the room, but you're not." Elaine paused, taking a deep breath while her comment hit its mark. "I always run background checks on the people who work for me — *and* their families. And I rerun them every so often. I knew that your parents raised your cousin and that his name was John Swayze, and I knew that John Swayze had moved to California a few years back. When Odelia mentioned his name, I knew you were up to something." Elaine laughed, then winced. "You might not be the smartest person in this room, but you're certainly smarter than your cousin."

Again my hair was jerked, but at least the gun barrel wasn't against my skull. From the corner of my eye, I saw Greg inching forward again. There was only a couple of yards separating all of us but it felt like miles, especially between Greg and me.

"So you did call Elaine and tell her you were coming here?" Lisa asked me. "You knew it was me on the phone? How?"

I nodded slowly. Snot was running from my nose down over my lips. I lifted a hand to wipe it away, but Lisa yanked my hair again. "Don't even think about moving."

Instead, I sniffed and said, "You called me dumber than a box of rocks. Only you call me that. And I knew Elaine would never take Mom." I coughed. "But I never called Elaine. I don't have the phone anymore. It's not in my purse, like I said."

"Then how did you know to come here, Elaine?" Lisa asked. "Even if you did know about John?"

"Call it a hunch," Elaine answered. "That and I slipped a tracker into Odelia's bag when I last saw her at her mother's."

"You what?" asked Greg, inching closer still.

"Oh, please," Elaine said with a smirk. "I knew you two wouldn't stay put, and I wanted to keep an eye on you. She has so much junk in that bag, I knew she wouldn't notice it." She steadied the gun. "Now come on, Lisa, let these good people go, and you and I can iron out our issues in private."

"And what about him?" Lisa asked, indicating Glick. "You should have used John as a shield. I don't care a damn about this loser. I'll shoot through him to get to you."

"I brought him here as evidence," Elaine answered. With her free hand she ripped the tape off of Glick's mouth. He let out a short shriek of pain. "Tell them what you told me," she demanded of Glick. When he didn't respond, Elaine belted the side of his head with the gun, as Swayze had done to Greg. He cried out again. "Tell them who kidnapped Zach Finch," she demanded. "If Odelia and Greg are going to die, they at least should know the truth first."

Through sore, torn lips, Glick said, "We kidnapped him. Zach was in on it."

"Zach set up his own kidnapping?" I asked right before Lisa yanked my hair again. "Ow!"

Glick nodded. "He hated his father." He spat on the ground, and I could see blood in the spittle. "We planned the whole thing. After the game, we dropped Zach at home. Then, later, Ben and I went back and picked him up. He only pretended to go into the house."

"What about Chris Cook?" Greg asked. "He told the police he saw Zach go into the house."

Glick shook his head back and forth slowly. "Zach only acted like he was going in. We used Chris to set that up. He's not that bright, so we didn't trust him to be in on it."

Greg rolled his wheelchair back and forth in a nervous gesture. "So you guys made the ransom call and, after the money was delivered, split it, then Zach took off?"

Glick nodded. "Pretty much, but Zach took most of the money because he needed to lay low and start over. But we did okay with our shares."

"And you've known where Zach's been all this time?"

Glick shook his head again. "Only during the first few years."

"But why kill him now? And why kill Jean?" I asked.

"After a couple of years, Zach was spotted just outside Las Vegas."

"So that sighting of Zach was real?" I asked.

"Yeah, he was living there." Glick cleared his throat. "Then Zach's mom died, and everything changed. I hadn't been at Aztec very long when that happened. Jean met me one night and said she was leaving and meeting up with Zach. She did it without any notice to anyone but me, probably because of Zach."

"Was Jean in on the kidnapping too?" Greg asked.

Glick nodded. "Yeah, from the beginning. Her plan was to work at Aztec after college, get some good experience in the international market, then leave for someplace else. I was surprised when she up and moved so quickly. She claimed it was because Zach was all she had now, and she wanted to be with him. She said he needed her. After she left, they both disappeared, and I never heard from them again."

"So why did you hunt them down in California after all these years?" I asked Glick.

"I didn't; Alec did. He told me he found out Jean was living in LA. I think he hired some PI to find her after he thought he saw her on TV one night. The PI not only found her but discovered that Zach was alive."

"So you tried to hire me to take them out," Elaine stated. "Instead you got her." Elaine indicated Lisa. "Were you afraid the Finch kids would spill their guts to daddy and land you in jail?"

"I didn't hire the hit," Glick quickly said. "I mean, I made the connection and paid the money, but the hit was made on Alec's orders."

My mouth fell open. "Do you expect us to believe that?"

"It's true," Glick said quickly. "I swear. I didn't think either would go to the cops about what we did. After all, both Jean and Zach would be in as much trouble as I would, but when Alec found out both of his kids were living in LA and figured out that it was Zach who had scammed him, he went berserk."

"He never knew you were in on it?" Greg asked.

Another shake of the head from Glick. "No. With Zach gone, Alec approached me and offered to help me out with school and groom me for a place at Aztec, like he would have done for Zach. He may not have been a great father, but Alec really missed Zach. I had the money from the kidnapping but knew that wouldn't last forever, not with college and everything. Alec offered me a great opportunity and future. I didn't want it to go away, so when he said his kids had betrayed him and he wanted them taken out, I made the call to have it done."

"What about Jean?" asked Lisa. "You killed her when I refused, didn't you?"

He nodded. "I snuck into her building and surprised her after you two left." He indicated Greg and me before sniffing back snot. "I didn't mean to kill her, but we started arguing. I told her she needed to leave and disappear again, that Alec knew where she was and wanted her dead, but she refused. She said she was going to stick around to see her father hanged for what he'd done."

"So she didn't know you were the one

who actually contracted for the killing?" I asked.

"No, I told Jean I only knew about it because I overheard Alec make the call." He looked from me to Greg and even at Lisa, looking for understanding. He found none. "I begged her to get somewhere safe, and that's when she dropped a bomb. She said her mother didn't commit suicide, but that Alec had killed her and set it up as suicide. That's why she left so suddenly, because she knew he might come after her too."

"And he did," I said.

"Yeah, now it made sense why Alec was so hell-bent on getting rid of both Zach and Jean." He took a deep breath. "And I also knew that if Jean went to the police about Alec, the truth would come out about my involvement in both the kidnapping and Zach's death, and I'd go to prison." He let out a wet sob. "So I knocked her unconscious, threw her off the balcony, and slipped out the back service gate during all the hysteria."

When Glick was done, a silence fell over the building broken only by the sound of heavy rain hitting the roof high above us. When it had started raining hard was anyone's guess. We'd been too wrapped up in Glick's confession to pay attention.

"Very pretty story," Lisa said. "Are you done?"

Glick, contrite and miserable, nodded. Before his chin came down a second time, a shot rang out from just behind me, and through my heart-stopping fright I saw Glick go limp and fall to the floor.

TWENTY-EIGHT

I was shaking like Jell-O and would have fallen to the floor myself had Lisa not still had a tight grip on my hair. My legs were rubbery. Puking was imminent. Across from me Nathan Glick lay sprawled with empty, open eyes. Behind him Elaine stood, feet apart, her gun held in both hands, trained on me and Lisa.

"Let her go, Lisa," Elaine said. "You want me. No one else needs to be involved."

"Yes," I heard Greg plead in a choked voice. "Please let Odelia go." Somewhere in my muddled mind, I heard my mother weeping.

Maybe they held out hope, but I didn't. I was almost certain that Lisa would never let us go — any of us. She didn't have a shred of decency in her black heart.

My stomach gurgled and I fought back a couple of belches. My fear was not mixing well with brunch. Staring at a dead man wasn't helping either. "I'm going to be sick," I said to no one in particular.

In response, Lisa tightened her grip on my hair. "Nice try," she said.

I was trying — trying my best to hold it back and get a grip — but it was no use. Out it came: a fountain of eggs, Canadian bacon, hollandaise sauce, home fries, and coffee. With Lisa's grip so tight on my hair, my efforts to bend over were fruitless, and it bubbled out and down the front of my sweater. I started coughing on my own vomit.

"Damn it, Odelia," snapped Lisa. She jumped back, releasing her hold on me. I fell to my knees and vomited again just as the warehouse erupted in a short explosion of gunfire.

My first thought was that I was dead. I was blanketed in silence as thick and fluffy as a cloud. Then I smelled the gunpowder. The silence seemed fitting; the acrid odor of gunpowder did not. Then the silence was broken by screams and shouts forcing their way through my blocked ears.

I opened my eyes to see Greg sailing in my direction. "Odelia," he kept saying over and over, but I saw the words more than heard them. "Odelia," he shouted again once he was in front of me. "Are you okay?"

This time I heard him, not clearly, but better. The gunfire must have partially deafened me.

I reached out a hand toward my husband, and that's when I realized that at some point I had gone from my knees to flat on the floor. Greg helped me get back to my knees. Before I could lift myself onto my feet, he enveloped me in his arms. Still on my knees, I laid my head in his lap, grateful we were both alive.

"Odelia!" The cry penetrated both my ears and my heart. It was Mom. Struggling to my feet, I shuffled as fast as I could to where I'd stashed her behind the truck. I uprighted her and held her tight for several seconds. "I'm okay, Mom," I cooed as I worked on her bindings. "See? Filthy and stinky but okay."

"Oh, Odelia!" was all she said over and over.

Someone rushed into the building while I finished loosening Mom's hands and feet. I looked over the hood of the truck to see Dev come in with his gun ready.

"Odelia," I heard Greg call to me. "Come here, quick."

"Mom, stay here." She started to protest, but I cut her off. "You're safe. Just stay here in this chair and rest until you feel strong enough to walk."

"You're not leaving me here," she insisted. She got up from the chair but was wobbly on her feet. I started to argue, but one look at her frightened face and I knew there was no way she was leaving my side. Taking her arm, together we made our way across to Greg.

As we passed Lisa's body, I looked down. She was on her back, bullet holes in her chest. One shoulder was torn open, the flesh ragged under the torn fabric. Her arms and legs were spread out as if she were making a snow angel on the dirty concrete. Her eyes were open, looking up, counting the steel beams in the ceiling above. Next to her was a pool of my vomit. Mom shivered and let out a choked whimper. "That could have been you."

It could have been all of us. I turned away from Lisa. I knew I should feel something, but I didn't. It's hard to mourn a rabid dog intent on destroying the people you love.

Greg had wheeled over to Elaine, who was propped up against the wall by the door. Her eyes were open, but unlike Lisa's they were focused. Dev was standing in the open doorway talking to someone on his phone, giving directions. It was still raining steadily outside. I turned Mom over to Greg. As she leaned against his wheelchair, he wrapped an arm tight around her waist to support her.

I stepped over the body of Nathan Glick and knelt down on the floor next to Elaine. Her breathing was labored, but she smiled at me. There was a bullet hole in her upper right chest, just below her shoulder. Her left arm was draped around her middle. I touched it and she winced. "I took at least one in the gut," she explained, "before Dev nailed Lisa."

I looked up at Dev, but he was still on the phone getting help. I turned to Greg for answers. "Dev shot Lisa from behind," he said. "He was watching everything through that broken back window."

"I called him," Elaine said in a labored voice, "on the burner phone when I was following you here." She tried to grin but it turned into a grimace of pain. "He picked a damn good time to start trusting me."

After a few seconds, Elaine said to me, "Hold me, Dottie."

I paused, looking down at the filthy gunk on the front of my sweater.

"I don't think she'll mind, Odelia," Greg said gently, noticing my hesitation.

I sat on the floor and gently tilted her forward, slipping slightly behind her so that she was cradled against me and not the cold wall. She gritted her teeth to hold back her moans as she was moved. I put my arms around her and held tight.

"That's so nice," she said once she was settled and closed her eyes.

"Help's on the way, Elaine," Greg said softly to her.

"No," she said hoarsely, opening her eyes. "I don't want help. I'd rather die here than in a hospital." She moved her right arm, groaning as she did. She inched it along until her fingers touched the hand I had gently laid back on her left one. Blood was seeping from her torso, staining her clothing and mine. The sleeves of my sweater were soaking it up like a sponge. Elaine looked up at me and another small smile came to her lips. "Here I won't die alone." She closed her eyes, nestled against me, and let out a soft sigh.

I pressed my cheek against Elaine's forehead. It was cool and clammy. Elaine opened her eyes again and whispered something I didn't quite get. I leaned my head closer to her face, and she repeated the words. Slipping a hand into the pocket of her light jacket, I pulled out a phone that seemed to be recording. I held it up toward Dev. "It's Glick's confession," I told him.

Dev nodded and took the phone from me.

I tightened my arms around Elaine and pressed my lips against her forehead. A few seconds later, I felt her body go limp in my arms.

"Is she dead?" Mom asked softly. I looked at my mother but couldn't speak. She and Greg were holding each other. Mom was nearly sobbing, and Greg's eyes were wet.

Dev leaned down and placed two fingers against Elaine's throat, just under her jaw. After a few seconds, he nodded.

TWENTY-NINE

Elaine's funeral had been depressing, not just because she was dead but because she really was alone in the world. Lisa's family had taken possession of her body, but no one had done the same for Elaine. She had arranged everything ahead of time through her attorney, who had contacted the police about the body when he heard the news. Fehring had contacted me about the interment time, knowing I might be interested. Elaine had quite a bit of money saved, which she had left to charities that help women and children. Her body was laid to rest in a cemetery in Pomona under a headstone that also bore the name Dorothy Powers — her sister; the one and only true Dottie. Elaine's name had already been engraved, and all that was left to do was to insert the year.

There was no real service. A chaplain associated with the cemetery came at our request and said a few basic words over the casket before it was lowered into the ground. Greg and I attended the burial, and so did Mom, Clark, and Dev. Even Seth and Zee came out to support me. The only flowers were from Greg and me and my mother. It felt oddly like I was burying a favorite aunt. After, we all went to a nice restaurant and had some lunch, even though no one was particularly hungry. Andrea Fehring joined us there.

"So what's the final scoop on Zach's kidnapping?" I asked Fehring.

"Alec Finch isn't saying a word about his wife's death except to insist that it was a suicide," she said. "And he's lawyered up to his eyebrows with high-powered legal muscle. But the more we dig, the more Glick's confession is sounding like the real deal."

"What about Swayze?" Greg asked. "What's happening with him?"

"He's pretty squirrely," Fehring told us. "A real psycho. He'll heal from the knife to the gut Powers gave him, but I doubt he'll ever see freedom again. He's definitely a collector. We found enough photos on his home computer to link him and his cousin to several unsolved murders. We also linked some of them to Gloria Connors."

"What?" I nearly choked on my iced tea

when she said the bit about the newscaster. "*She* was involved in the killings?"

"We don't know exactly what Connors's connection to them is yet, only that she seemed to have the scoop on the stories before any of the other media. She's claiming the stories were fed to her by Swayze, but that's it. Meanwhile, she's been suspended from her job until the investigation is over."

"Did you ever uncover anything more on Zach's whereabouts all these years?" Zee asked.

Fehring nodded. "He was living in Venice as David Moreland." She took a drink of iced tea and shook her head. "Here was a kid who could have gone down all the wrong paths after running away, but instead he got his GED and put himself through college. He was working as an independent contractor in the computer industry."

"I wonder," I said, "if keeping ties with his sister over the years kept him grounded."

"Could have," admitted Dev. "He had cash, and he wasn't totally alone in the world. It probably kept him off the streets." A silence hung over the table as we considered Dev's words.

"So you're staying around a little bit longer?" I asked Dev.

"Just a few weeks, until all the hubbub about the shooting is laid to rest," Dev answered. "I'll be staying at my daughter's since my place has been rented." He chuckled. "It figures," he said with a short, sad laugh. "I'm days from retirement, and I go and shoot someone."

Lisa had been shot several times by both Elaine and Dev, but it was only Lisa's gun that had taken out Elaine. According to Greg, after Lisa released her grip on me and I fell forward to be sick, Elaine and Lisa had exchanged fire. From his perch at the window Dev shot Lisa, nailing her in the shoulder, which gave Elaine time to take aim and put a few bullets in Lisa's chest.

THIRTY

"I see you couldn't stay out of trouble while I was gone." Steele was lazing in the visitor's chair across from my desk. He looked relaxed and happy. On the desk in front of him was a wrapped gift and a box of Swiss chocolates. He'd returned to work the day before, but I had taken the day off to attend Elaine's funeral.

"What can I say, Steele? Without you around, my life goes to hell in a handbasket." My words were delivered without their usual bite, and he sensed my funk.

"I'm sorry about Elaine Powers," he said, leaning forward. "I know in a weird way the two of you had become close. Do you need more time off?"

Had marriage scrambled his brain to the point where he'd become a sensitive human being? "You're offering me more time off?" I asked with surprise.

"I'm making the gesture, Grey. I didn't

say I *wanted* you to take it."

There he was, the Mike Steele I knew and loved. He and I looked at each other across my desk, and soon I felt the trickle of a genuine smile return to my face. "I'm good, Steele. Really."

He smiled back. "Glad to hear it. When we heard the news, Michelle almost lost her mind with worry, what with the FBI, bodies in trunks, hitwomen, and kidnappings. But I explained to her that that's a slow week for you."

My smiled widened. "It's good to have you back, Steele."

He leaned back again in the chair. "Now be a good girl and open your present. I have to get back to work."

I unwrapped the gift and found a beautiful wooden cuckoo clock inside. I started laughing. "Are you trying to tell me something, Steele?"

He grinned. "If the cuckoo fits, wear it." He leaned forward and pointed at something. "See that label? That means it's a Lötscher clock. They make the only genuine Swiss cuckoo clocks in the world." He pointed at the front. "And those two goats move. I named them Greg and Odelia." Steele got up and started for my door.

"Greg's going to love this," I said. "Thank

you very much, Steele. Tell Michelle thank you also." I started tearing up.

"What's with the waterworks, Grey? Would you have preferred Hansel and Gretel on the front? Or how about a hunk of Swiss cheese marching back and forth to music?"

I shook my head. "I'm just so happy and grateful to have such loving friends and family." I got up and went to Steele, giving him a good solid hug.

"Shame on you, Grey, making a pass at a married man."

I broke off the hug and looked up at him. "Ass," I snapped, but I said it with a smile.

Steele laughed and gave me his own hug. "I'm glad you didn't get yourself killed . . . again." He pulled away. "Now get to work before you make *me* cuckoo."

After putting the clock back in its box, I opened the chocolates and popped one into my mouth. It was heaven. I was about to have another when my cell phone rang. The display said it was Emma Whitecastle. I was surprised. I must have come up in the world for her to unblock her phone for a call to me.

"Hello," I answered. "Emma?"

"Hi, Odelia," she said. "I hope I'm not reaching you at a bad time."

"Not at all." I sat down at my desk. "My

mother loved the signed photo, by the way. Thanks."

"You're welcome." She paused. "I've been watching the news for the past several days. Are you okay?"

"I'm fine," I said a little too quickly, then amended it with, "Still a little shaken up, but better. Thanks for asking."

"Your mother was right, Odelia, we are alike in that we both get into serious scrapes. If you ever want to talk about it — you know, for support or an understanding ear — please call me. We can get together for lunch or something."

I sat up straight. It was a very generous offer coming from a famous and busy person. "Thank you, Emma. Sometimes I do feel rather alone and confused about all this."

She laughed. "Me too." She paused. "There's actually another reason for my call."

"My father again?"

"No, not this time, but a spirit has come to me determined to send you a message."

I didn't know what to think. My earlier experience with Emma Whitecastle had been both disturbing and interesting, but I still wasn't onboard with all the ghost stuff. "Okay," I said with caution.

"Remember when I was at your house and called you Dottie?" she asked.

"I do, and I should have told you then that the name Dottie did mean something to me. I'm sorry. I was just surprised."

"Well, Dottie is back and has a message for you."

"You mean the spirit of Elaine Powers is giving you a message for me, don't you? Elaine — the woman who was just killed — always called me Dottie."

"Mmm, no; it isn't her. For the past few days, the spirit of a woman named Dottie has been bugging me to contact you."

I sat up straight, my eyes fixed on the colorful print hung on the wall across from my desk. "And?"

"She says thank you."

I shook my head a little, wondering if I'd heard correctly. "She asked you to tell me thank you? That's it?"

On the other end of the phone, Emma conferred with someone, but I didn't hear the other person's remarks, only Emma's. Then Emma said to me, "Dottie says to tell you thank you for everything you did for her sister."

"Anything else?" My head was starting to swell like it had been clubbed.

"No, that was it," Emma said. "She's gone

now. Spirits generally do that. Once they get their message across, they disappear as quickly as they show up."

After the call with Emma, I sat in my office staring at the print on the wall again, this time for several minutes. I wasn't studying it but going over the conversation with Emma several times in my head until my office phone rang. It was Steele. I answered it on autopilot. "Yeah, Steele?"

"Come in here, Grey, I have some questions on one of those companies you organized."

"Be right there," I said and disconnected the call.

I didn't get right up and obediently hustle into Steele's office. Instead, I continued staring at the print until it morphed into a picture of the gravestone at the Pomona Cemetery. Two names. Two graves. Sisters, tragically torn apart, now united forever. Picking up another Swiss chocolate, I held it aloft as if making a toast. "To you, Dottie and Elaine. May you both finally rest in peace." I popped the chocolate into my mouth and closed my eyes, letting the rich goodness slowly melt in tribute.

ACKNOWLEDGMENTS

Always and forever, thank you to my agent, Whitney Lee; my editors at Midnight Ink, Terri Bischoff and Rebecca Zins; and everyone else at Midnight Ink/Llewellyn Worldwide who has a hand in each of my books.

ABOUT THE AUTHOR

Like the character Odelia Grey, **Sue Ann Jaffarian** is a middle-aged, plus-size paralegal. In addition to the Odelia Grey mystery series, she is the author of the paranormal Ghost of Granny Apples mystery series and the Madison Rose Vampire mystery series. Sue Ann is also nationally sought after as a motivational and humorous speaker. She lives and works in Los Angeles, California.

Other titles in the Odelia Grey series include *Too Big to Miss* (2006), *The Curse of the Holy Pail* (2007), *Thugs and Kisses* (2008), *Booby Trap* (2009), *Corpse on the Cob* (2010), *Twice As Dead* (2011), *Hide & Snoop* (2012), *Secondhand Stiff* (2013), and *Hell on Wheels* (2014).

Visit Sue Ann on the Internet at
WWW.SUEANNJAFFARIAN.COM
and
WWW.SUEANNJAFFARIAN.BLOGSPOT.COM

The employees of Thorndike Press hope you have enjoyed this Large Print book. All our Thorndike, Wheeler, and Kennebec Large Print titles are designed for easy reading, and all our books are made to last. Other Thorndike Press Large Print books are available at your library, through selected bookstores, or directly from us.

For information about titles, please call:
  (800) 223-1244

or visit our Web site at:
  http://gale.cengage.com/thorndike

To share your comments, please write:
Publisher
Thorndike Press
10 Water St., Suite 310
Waterville, ME 04901